VIPER

NAGA BRIDES #1

NAOMI LUCAS

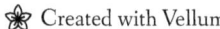 Created with Vellum

To LY, Tiffany Freund, and Mandy. My three fabulous editors. I couldn't do this job without you.

BLURB

Long have we been alone.

Without brides, without females to warm us during the long nights. Without sweet mates.

But we see them, from afar, brides that could be ours. Kept away from us by walls and weapons. Females we long for greatly.

Obsessively.

Human females.

And the one with red hair? I want her. I saw her first. I will fight for the death for her.

She is MINE.

So, we'll come together and make an exchange with their men that will benefit us all.

After that?

To the winner goes the spoils...

Let the hunt begin.

But the red-headed female is mine.

—-

One day I'm a confidant for our leader, and the next I'm escorted out of the settlement by armed guards. Before me now lies the vast and dangerous wilderness of Earth, ravaged by aliens that long ago vanished.

They left their devastation—and their technology—behind.

My leader wants that technology. He'll do anything to get it, even trading me to those who have it.

Serpent men. Nagas. Half-men, half-snake beast aliens rule these lands—misbegotten monsters warped by something we don't yet understand.

They want me.

Especially the ruby red demon that stares at me with such an intensity my soul quakes.

But I refuse to be any man's broodmare, especially an alien's.

If he wants me so badly, he'll have to catch me first.

Unfortunately, that was the whole point after all…

NAGA NAMES

Vruksha— Viper
Azsote— Boomslang
Zhallaix— Death Adder
Syasku— Cottonmouth
Jyarka— Diamondback
Zaku— King Cobra
Vagan— Blue Coral
Krellix— Copperhead
Lukys— Black Mamba
Xenos— Sidewinder

ONE
THE PACT

Vruksha

"Our truce ends after they release the females," I growl, peering at the males around me. The King Cobra's mane flutters, the Boomslang nods. Others react; some don't respond at all. I take their silence as agreement.

We're the strongest of our kind. The oldest. The deadliest. We saw the humans' ship breach our sky and land within our forest.

We're also competitors. The fact that we've all come together for this—*for them*—is a miracle. It shows how much we want *them*, how desperate we are to have *them,* and that we would risk our lives to make a deal with *their* keepers.

Their puny males.

Males who do not deserve the warmth of a female. They don't realize how lucky they are to have females, so we will take their females and covet them, mate them, make them queens to the lands we rule. As is how it should be.

There are many wrongs that need to be righted, and many mistakes in our past that need to be fixed.

My fingers tighten around my spear as I scrutinize the nagas gathered today, sizing them up. Some of us won't survive.

Humans are different from us, at least from what I've seen, and it's more than the way they look.

We thought them long gone. A species that had been eradicated when we were born on this Earth. Neither I nor the other naga males around me have ever seen a living one, not once, until recently.

They flew down from the sky in a large metal machine. Machines like the ones here, but not overgrown with weeds, roots, and vines. Not ruined the way Earth was ruined.

No, this machine—this ship of theirs—came to us clean of the forest and landed outside the old ruins of a civilization long gone, deep in the mountains. Other smaller machines came out with weapons and cleared the ruins. They erected a barrier and cut down the trees.

The humans restored the ruins into what it once was: a military facility.

Meanwhile, I watched the robots from afar, from the shadows of the trees, and soon found other nagas watching them too. We didn't know why they were here, or what they wanted, but we are determined to keep our secrets...secret.

At first, there were only machines. We didn't realize there were humans on the ship. The robots poured from their vessel in droves, destroying the terrain we once knew. A growl tears from my throat at the thought. The robots left us alone, though, having one singular purpose, a purpose we nagas did not know until several weeks after their landing.

They were making the facility ready for human inhabitants.

Thinking back on that day quickens my heart.

Her red hair. My fingers twitch. I can imagine the softness of it running between my fingers. I've never seen such a shade of red as my tail...

Zaku, the King Cobra, went to the humans when we realized they had females among them. He made our presence known. He wanted to meet them, court them, mate with one... We were stronger, larger than their males, and thought that because of it, they should be ours.

I did too.

Perhaps we could offer our help in return? Who knows?

Zaku came back enraged. The humans turned their weapons on him, refusing his request. They told him this land was theirs, as it has always been, and as long as he abided by that, they would not kill us.

Hah. I would like to see them try.

I'd wipe the humans from these lands but they have females...and for that reason, they remain alive.

I want my red-headed beauty.

I'll have to fight for her, kill for her. And I'm willing to do more than that, but I do not want her hurt. And fighting? I've seen enough death to know accidents happen. They have machines, and not all machines can be trusted.

It wasn't that long ago. Days, maybe? Seems like an eternity. The other nagas came together after word spread of what happened to Zaku. It wasn't hard to win me over. I would do anything for *her.*

When I first saw her, everything changed.

Gone was the bloodlust, the anger. Real lust took its place. Red hot desire, with a wild mane of red hair to match. Transfixed, I stared that first day as she descended from the ramp, realizing something more miraculous than machines had fallen from the heavens. She looked around with wonder and curiosity.

She had gazed at the sky and the clouds above. She had touched the grass at her feet. Her tongue poked out to swipe at her lips.

Her eyes had found mine, even as I hid beyond her barrier, in the shadows of the forest. From that moment, she was mine.

A human female, wondrous in her rarity, who with one look ruined me.

My female.

The way her eyes widened. The way her lips parted...

The fear on her face hadn't bothered me at all.

She was mine. I expected her to face her fear and come to me then, but instead, she turned away and rushed into the shadows of the facility, leaving me bereft, lusty, and angry.

She had looked at me, though, had met my gaze. She saw me, and that was all that mattered. Now I know I am in her head. She will always remember the first time she saw me. For I am a strong male, a vicious one, and refused to be forgotten.

It would be dangerous to forget me.

My anger returned after I lost sight of her, and my agitation at these human interlopers built. My need for this female stole my mind. Reclaiming the facility and this land meant nothing if I couldn't have her. I wanted both but only cared about the latter.

I saw her first.

She saw me first.

She was in *my* head. No other naga's head mattered

unless they were hanging from a rope off my belt or lobbed off and impaled on my spear, decorating the entrance to my den.

Except whispers of human females spread through the forest—the mountains—the other nagas had similar thoughts. My female wasn't the only one, and nagas from far afield, males I have not seen in years, returned to see them, to steal them, to mate with them, and hoard them away in our respective nests.

The heat overcame us all like a storm. To conquer. These females came from the skies to be ours. We became very aware of our diminishing numbers, and with the threat of invaders from the skies on our minds...our biology altered against us, clouding our minds.

I started giving off a strange scent.

I wasn't the only one who changed, nor the only one desperate to nest. A piece within us unlocked, and it can't be undone. Some nagas feared the change and fled, hoping the change would reverse.

Less to die by my hands. I hiss out a breath of air.

Azsote, a Boomslang, snaps his tail. "And if they don't release them?"

"We invade with our weapons and strike them down. They need to know this land is not theirs, not without a price," Zaku snarls. Some of the other males snarl with him. The King Cobra is out for blood, one way or another. A king, even though Zaku wasn't one, doesn't like being told what to do.

Zaku's only king in name, and he holds no more sway or dominion than the rest of us.

"They will pay for it with females," I say.

Azsote snaps his tail again. "Yesss."

"They want our technology, our land... We will give them a little for a lot more," Zaku agrees.

I eye the facility far, far in the distance, through the trees and across the shattered landscape, hoping to see her. A splash of red among the green. But she's nowhere to be found from our vantage point way up on the cliffs.

I haven't seen her in many days. Venom leaks from my fangs. I need to see her soon or I may do something crazed, like storm the humans' barrier and take on their robots for just a glimpse.

She is the same color as me. I never thought such a female existed besides my sisters. One with Viper in her blood.

My hands tremble with the need to comb my fingers through her hair. My nose itches to burrow into her neck and languish in its warmth.

"We give them nothing, and they won't be the wiser," I hiss, "while they give usss everything in return."

The other males beat their chests and hoot in agreement. The coming hunt excites us. I feel it in my veins, the way my blood pumps heavy. I slam my fist against my chest and hoot with them.

"How many females are there?" Vagan asks when we settle. "Not enough, last I checked." His blue scales and long, slender body are like mine, except he is blue where I am red. Vagan is of the Blue Coral clan, a ruler of the dangerous waterways. He may be brightly colored like me, but to face him near water was certain death.

Of all the nagas gathered, Vagan is the one I watch the most. Him and the Death Adder.

Except Zhallaix, the Death Adder, is not here. He would rather kill us than work with us. An enemy to us all. He has no honor, nor allegiance. Ruthless and wild, he is probably fucking a mossy rock and spitting venom some-where off in the hills. I have not seen Zhallaix since the ship first appeared.

"I have only seen three," Zaku answers. The King Cobra is fearsome, but I do not watch him like Vagan and some of the others. One bite and the Cobra could take out any one of us. I do not watch him because he has some honor in his cold veins.

Honor I do not know if I have. Zaku isn't just honor-able, he's pompous and hard-headed. He's rash. Everything is beneath him, and it shows in his inability to help anyone but himself, even in this. If Zaku could steal a female human for himself, he wouldn't have gathered us. Some-times I think he's not honorable at all, just overzealous.

I keep an eye on him anyway. If Zaku doesn't win one of the females today, he's going to destroy the world. Or die trying.

As for everyone else? They watch me.

I tighten my grip on my spear, meeting their eyes.

"Three? Three is not enough!" Vagan shouts. "There are at least seven of us here, and more yet in these woods. How will three brides appease us all?"

"They won't," I say. "We will fight for them when they are handed over."

Some growl, some hiss in agreement. We size each other up, considering who we could off now before the humans arrive.

The Boomslang with the shimmery green scales slips to the ledge, his voice lowering. "Why not fight now? Until there are only three of us left?" Azsote suggests, waving his hand.

"Why not let the females choose who they want to mate with?" another offers. I look at the naga and bare my fangs. It's the Copperhead. He is a quiet one. I'm surprised to hear him speak at all.

"No," I snap.

"That won't work," Zaku says at the same time.

"We will not honor their choices," I add. If my female chooses another over me, I would kill him and take her.

I am not honorable, after all.

The Copperhead nods. He knows what I say is true. The females can't have the luxury to choose, not now that their very presence has created a strange fervor.

Our members have filled up with unspent spill, causing pressure, bringing us pain. When I first saw my human, my shaft flooded with seed, seed that has been dormant for years, and I have had to milk my shaft nightly to relieve the pressure.

If I'm suffering, the other nagas are too.

"Three females is a problem," says Zaku. "But I have an idea. If we fight for mating rights to them, there is a chance they will run while we battle. It is paramount that the females do not come to any harm. Especially by us or our ways. They may be all there is, and we can't lose them. We must keep them safe."

We mumble in agreement. I love the red of my female's hair, although it is the only red I wish to see upon her. I do not want to witness her blood outside her moon cycle. If she is bloody, she is hurt, and that means I have failed...

Zaku continues, "If they run, the animals could kill them, the pigsss. They could get hurt—"

"So what's your suggestion?" Vagan interrupts.

"I suggest we spread out when the human males hand them over. So we do not fight. I suggest they run, we follow, and we hunt them down. Whoever catches the females first wins nesting rights to them."

Silence hangs over us as we ponder Zaku's words. It is a good suggestion, not the greatest. My redhead is already mine. But the other male nagas will want proof, and a hunt —because I know I will catch her—is a good way to prove it.

"I like this idea," the Boomslang speaks up first.

"Of course you do," Vagan snaps. "You are a hunter of the forest."

Azsote shrugs. "I am. That does not change that this is a good suggestion."

"And what about me? What about Syasku? We fare best in the water. A hunt over land cripples us."

Nobody cares about Vagan or Syasku. I don't say this aloud. My thoughts are strong enough. "There is water nearby, a lot of water. If the females head for it, then you have an advantage."

"And if they don't?"

I turn back to the facility, not caring enough to answer.

"I will accept a hunt," says Syasku of the Cottonmouth clan. *Good.* If the other water naga accepts a hunt, then Vagan has no grounds to argue it.

Vagan scowls.

"It is settled then," Zaku declares. "We will hunt for nesting rights to the females."

Another wave of shouts soars the air. I lift my spear and release a bolt of electricity to the sky. I like this. I will win. I have destiny on my side. Vicious, red destiny.

The other males pound their chests, and some release their well-hung and hard members from their scales. Tails coil and thump the ground. For a frenzied moment, excitement and real camaraderie return to us. It is a rare thing. We are deadly as a group.

We are deadly alone, but together... The world would tremble with fear.

The excitement does not last. I turn back once again to see if my bride is outside, if she's being gathered with the other females to be handed over.

And for a second, I see her. My heart stops.

She's being led to one of the flying transport machines. Another female is fighting, kicking, and screaming behind her. She's lifted off the ground and hauled to the machine.

My female goes calmly.

She knows her fate. Knows who awaits her

Me.

Venom fills my mouth. My heart revs back up.

The others have gone silent, and I know they are watching as well.

"She is the one I want," Azsote rumbles. My eyes flick to the Boomslang watching my female, and I slam my spear into his side.

I attack him, striking out with my tail, knocking him over. He evades my speartip, rolling away before I can plunge it into his gut.

"She is mine!" I roar, fury surging through me. "Mine!"

How dare he want her. How dare he even look at her! Azsote strikes back, hitting me with his fist, slicing me with his claws across my bicep. The sting of pain erupts. I barely notice, needing to see his blood splattered across the ground.

Hands grab us, pulling us apart.

"Enough!" Zaku shouts.

Fighting his hold, I spit venom in Azsote's direction. He pushes his capturer away and shrieks a battle cry. Furious, only his blood on the ground and his spine in my hand will appease me now.

"I sssaid enough! They're coming! Do not let them see us fighting." Zaku shoves me away, getting between us.

Growling, I rise to fight the King Cobra as well, but he's facing the horizon.

Behind him, the humans' transport vehicle is heading our way. It glides soundlessly through the air.

All thoughts of Azsote and the others fall from my mind. My female is heading for me.

In mere moments, I will see her up close for the first time. My body tenses to not only fight, it wants to rut as well. It wants both, simultaneously, right now.

"Present the technology," Zaku orders.

Vagan hands Zaku a small metal box. A data collection. An ancient thing left here by aliens. Both this technology and humans once shaped this world, but for countless years, both have been ours. Times have changed and now the technology is wanted by these humans that have returned from the sky.

I don't care about the technology. I have my den, my weapon, and enough resources to last me into old age. These trinkets that we are giving the humans are nothing compared to what we keep hidden.

The transport flies past us to land on the clearing behind. Some of the males scatter, readying themselves for the coming hunt.

When the transport opens, the only ones left are me, Zaku, and Vagan.

I will not lose this chance to finally see my female up close.

My fangs drip. A male dressed in a powersuit steps out.

My spine stiffens when another man follows after.

Where are you, little female?

I clench my hands.

Then I see her, and my mind blanks.

TWO
THROWN TO THE SNAKES

Gemma

"DAISY, CALM DOWN," Peter says.

Daisy sniffles louder. "Fuck you."

"Crying isn't going to change anything. You're acting like a damn fool."

I glower at Peter, sitting across from us in the skiff, and tighten my arm around Daisy. "Can you blame her? You're throwing us to the wolves."

"Earth doesn't have wolves anymore."

"Fuck you." I agree wholeheartedly with Daisy here. "You said it would never come to this."

"No, *you'll* be the one fucking an alien snake. Not me. High and mighty Gemma Hurst, fallen from grace. You knew this course of action was in the cards the moment the locals offered a trade. What's at stake is too important..."

"It's only been weeks! We've barely begun our search—"

"Central Command does not want to wait."

I hold Daisy against me as I glare at Peter. I can't believe what a prick he's become. I've worked with the guy for nearly two years, and I've never seen him be so cruel, especially to someone under his command.

Peter pointedly looks at the screen in his hand.

He can't even meet my eyes. He knows what he's doing isn't right. Maybe he thinks if I hate him, it'll be easier for both of us. It's not.

I get it.

I get it—and I hate that I do. Central Command is breathing fire down our necks, demanding a solution to *their war problem* and to bring them that solution fast, now that Earth is safe to travel to. Peter's feeling the heat. It's his neck on the line if he doesn't give Central Command what they want.

It's my neck too, and Daisy's. Except we're not as high-ranking as Peter. We don't get what he gets. We're expendable. At least more so than Peter.

What he's doing still isn't right, but I get it, in a deranged, depressing, horrendous way. Depressing because I can almost forgive him for this. He's desperate, and desperate people do shitty things.

Daisy trembles and any chance of forgiving Peter flies out the window.

"What about you, Collins?" I cut my eyes to Peter's second-in-command. Collins is gazing out the window, unable to look at me or Daisy, just like Peter. He doesn't even try. His face blank, unreadable. He's shut down.

None of the ranking crewmen can meet my eyes.

Because it's us that's making this sacrifice. It's the women who are being made to give up their lives to save the team, and we haven't even been on Earth a month...

"What about me?" Collins mumbles, avoiding my gaze.

"Don't you feel bad for doing this to me and Daisy? When it could be Shelby sitting here with us?"

Shelby is Collins' girlfriend, and she was spared because of it.

Apparently, Shelby's pregnant. That fact came out last night when Peter gathered the three of us women and locked us in a room together. Collins fought for her, sparing her. We can't risk a child—especially when that child could become a soldier one day.

Lucky lady. Shelby gets to stay. Hopefully, she'll reach Central Command and tell them what's happening down here on Earth.

Collins shrugs, doesn't answer.

Of course he doesn't. He saved the only one of us he cares about. He's not going to go to bat for anyone else, not with what's at stake.

Because we've been sent to Earth for one thing and one thing only: alien technology.

It's the only thing that can save us in the war against the Ketts, a species of blob-like aliens that are highly intelligent, extremely adaptable, and fully capable of consuming all organic matter in their path. They're always hungry, and humans make a great meal. Our bullets pierce their flesh except they leave no mark. Our lasers sear their gelatinous bodies but then are absorbed. We can't fight them with hand or fist, or weapons of old like swords and daggers. We can't even crush them...

They just reform.

We're losing the war.

The Ketts are growing, breeding, expanding at an exponential rate, hunting humans down like cattle because we pose the only threat to their existence.

It's only a matter of time before we find a way to hurt them.

Humans have a way of prevailing.

Which leads to me and Daisy being sacrificed. Whether the locals want to eat us, experiment with us, or something far worse... I don't know. And I refuse to find out —the same goes for Daisy.

She's a petty officer, whereas I'm Chief Communications Officer of our ship's bridge crew. *The Dreadnaut* is now outside the moon's orbit, hiding on the dark side so we don't alert the Ketts to our plans on Earth.

Until now, Earth has been a dead zone. A place to avoid at all costs. Occasionally humans ignored space law and visited the human mecca, though most never returned. The lucky few who did morphed into something... not human.

Alien technology did that, and a whole lot more. Long ago, back before I was born or humans even knew the Ketts existed, a species called Lurkawathians descended to Earth and made a pact with mankind.

For a while, their arrival had been good for humanity. Mankind established its first space port and got to study the Lurkawathians—dubbed Lurkers. We learned about the universe and reaped the benefits of their advanced technology.

They helped us develop as a cosmic society and introduced us to intergalactic travel. They cured our diseases and traded us resources that were in short supply.

In return, the Lurkers set up their own port on Earth and were allowed to study us.

Through all of this advancement, they kept their technology secret. The Lurkers gave us just as much as they needed for us to comply with them and no more. They took us into space but never helped us expand or allowed us a foothold elsewhere. They discouraged it. They resented us for trying.

According to my history discs, we were their special pets and they wanted to keep us that way.

As for my ancestors and the rest of humanity... Well, we don't like being told no.

I stare at Peter head-on. "Once Central Command finds out about what's happening, you're going to lose your title, your ranks, be stripped of your credentials. You won't even have the certificates to work as maintenance staff."

His brow furrows before smoothing. "You don't understand the pressure we're under, Gemma. The pressure I'm under."

"Try to make me understand. For all our sakes, try." I know he's taking heat...

But how much heat?

He shakes his head and looks out the window. Daisy wipes the snot from her nose and does the same.

I take a deep, unsettling breath.

Humans expanded anyway, despite the Lurkers' limitations. Relations with them soured. Sanctions, taxes, killings. In the end, the Lurkers, realizing that we couldn't be controlled, offered us a Trojan Horse of a deal. They offered to return Earth to its ancient glory. To purify our oceans, to give us back our forests, and to clean our skies.

The government accepted this 'gift,' not realizing that to do so meant our destruction.

The Lurkers unleashed devastation into the environment that manipulated and changed everything it came into contact with. Everything died. Everything.

Those humans out in space were the only survivors, watching as our blue and green world turned brown.

Afterward, the Lurkers left, never to be seen again. That was nearly fifteen hundred years ago.

Lurker technology remains on Earth though, and now that Earth is safe to travel to again, it's ours for the taking.

There's just one problem: finding it.

"Peter, please," I urge, trying hard to remain strong, when inside I'm panicking. My pulse drums in my ear. Peter ignores my plea. He ignores me completely.

The Dreadnaut and Peter's team—us—aren't the first to land on Earth in the last century, and we won't be the last. Though we're the first team to land near the old Lurker and human military base.

According to records, that's what the facility was, the same one now growing small in the distance behind me. We'd just begun to explore what was left of the ruins when a whole other problem presented itself.

A shiver of fear skitters up my back.

The locals.

THREE
SERPENT MEN

Gemma

MY GUT HOLLOWS OUT, and I swallow down the bile creeping out my throat.

A shiver courses through me, and try as I might to hide it, Daisy looks up at me. Our eyes meet for a moment, and she hugs me back. I take the comfort she offers.

All we have is each other.

Before yesterday, we had never spoken. Today, we're sisters.

I'm trying to be strong, but it's hard. I'm scared. I know what's awaiting us when Peter and Collins drop us off. I know what—who—will be there.

Him.

The red-scaled creature hiding in the forests beyond the facility. I saw him the first day I arrived. The facility had been deemed safe and clear, Peter and his guards inspected the place thoroughly enough, and the rest of the crew was given allowance to leave our transport ship.

I hadn't even stepped off the ship's ramp when I spotted him. He hid in the shadows of the trees just beyond our jurisdiction.

His dark eyes took hold of mine, and I knew it was a *him*, his large physique unmistakable. I've seen many alien worlds and have even encountered a Kett blob. Despite this, I've never met a being like the one in the woods. Like him.

Earth wasn't supposed to have sentient life on it. Or human life for that matter, but I can't deny what I saw.

A half-human, half-serpent male staring at me.

My skin prickles with the memory.

He had been large and ruby red, a red that I've never seen on another creature. He was a jewel, a bizarre, glistening beacon among the green of the forest, and I was shocked to discover later that I was the only one who saw him.

Because he was huge! With discerning human features and a male's chest, a man's musculature. Though I couldn't see all of him, I now know he has a tail because soon after I saw him, another one of the local aliens approached our compound to talk, causing a riot.

And the serpentine male who dared enter the compound had the largest, longest tail I'd ever laid my eyes on. Unlike the scary red demon from the trees, the one that visited the facility had been yellow with dark brown and black stripes. He had an enormous cowl.

I bite my tongue.

We'd trespassed on their land, and now they want reparations. Reparations or death.

The striped alien had the technology we came here for.

He knew where it was.

And he knew how to use it. Or so he threatened. It was enough to catch Peter's ear.

Right now, lost Lurker technology is the single most sought-after thing on this side of the universe.

Who cares if Daisy and I are the price for it? She's quiet under my arm now, and I hope she hasn't gone into shock.

Have I?

I glance out the window of the skiff as we descend. We've flown to a plateau with a clearing. The skiff lands soundlessly, and I immediately search for the locals.

Swallowing against the lump of fear in my throat, I see the red one, and my heart plunges to my stomach. Staring at me and only me, his eyes blacken out the color of him, stealing my awareness momentarily.

How can he see me? The glass is shielded.

His eyes are darker than I remember, black as the abyss and framed by deep shades of red. Above was a smattering of short black hair. Holding a spear, he rises on his tail as my eyes trail down his body, strutting like he knows I'm looking at him...

He can't see me through the glass, can he?

I barely notice the two males beside him. I don't want to see them. I have enough nightmare fodder clogging up my mind already. One is the male who threatened us, his giant build and strange cowl unmistakable, and the other is a deep, sapphire blue—with a startling orange face that practically glows amongst the hue of his indigo scales.

The door to the skiff opens, and Peter grabs my arm, dragging me out. Daisy's hauled out next with a cry. I tear my eyes away from the group.

I don't quite know what will happen next, but I know I don't want the red one to catch me... Not him. When I run, taking the chance I can reach the transport ship, I don't want any of them to catch me, and that's especially true for the red one.

He eyes me like I'm already his.

He eyes only me. His gaze has not gone to Daisy or Peter or Collins, not once.

My throat tightens.

He's been haunting me. He's done terrible things to me in my sleep. He's made me scream, beg, and run as if my life depends on it. The only reason I'm not running now is that I don't want Peter to shoot me in the back. Because he will.

Daisy wipes her nose on the back of her hand and straightens. I'm proud of her. I wish I could be proud of myself.

I'm scared, a lot more scared than I'd care to admit.

"You still have the knife Shelby gave you?" I whisper.

Daisy nods. "Yeah."

"Good." If my voice trembles, she doesn't acknowledge it.

Collins glances over, and I go quiet until he turns back to the aliens. He's speaking to them. I don't listen, scanning our surroundings instead.

The plateau we're on is high up on a mountain, but there are possible trails along the ledges for a quick descent down from it. If Daisy and I ran for one of the ledges, they would return us to the facility the quickest, though we would be exposed for the entire climb down. Not only that, below is a river that we'd also need to cross. If we managed to make it there, we'd have the cover of the forest on the other side. There would only be one path from that direction—and every alien would know it because the forest lies in a gorge and on every side? Mountains.

Mountains and forest as far as the eye could see.

The cliffs stop Daisy and I from making a quick getaway back to the facility, but ahead and on either side of us, beyond the clearing, are ledges and the forest. We'll have to detour, find a different route, if we want to escape this fate.

We'll need the cover of the trees for any hope of that.

"We'll stick together," I tell Daisy. "We can get out of this."

"How?"

"The first chance we get, we run, we fight," I lower my voice. "Once we're in the trees, the ones to our left, we can hide. We'll make our way back to the facility from there."

"Pointless," she breathes. "Peter and Collins and the others will just give us back."

"Not if we get to Shelby first. Not if we sneak onto the transport ship and send a comm to *The Dreadnaut*. They don't know what's happening down here."

Daisy stops. "They don't know?"

"No." I can see the spark of hope that ignites in her at my words. It buoys my own hope. "We just have to make it there. That's all we have to do."

"Okay."

Peter and Collins turn our way, and I shut my mouth. They grab Daisy and me, forcing us over to where the aliens await.

We've been stripped of everything except for the clothes on our backs—Peter didn't allow us to pack, or bring our com-ware. Our knives were smuggled to us by Shelby this morning, slipped into the shower units we were allowed to use one last time before being forced into the skiff.

The big one with the cowl holds a metal box in his hands. He scowls when his gaze roves over me. He hesitates when he sees Daisy. His eyes harden, and his hold on the box strains. "You," he hisses.

Daisy cowers.

"Where isss the third female?" the male suddenly barks, jerking his head up. His cowl flutters.

Collins stiffens. "She is not for you."

"We were promised three females," another male says, the deep blue and black scaled one with a burst of bright orange coloring over his face. "Give us the third or we take our secrets to the grave."

"She is not for you," Collins snaps. "She is pregnant with my child, and we're soon to be married."

The blue one coils his tail. "Do you think I care? We still want her. She is oursss."

The red male comes forward. "The third female can remain with you. We will take these two."

I don't want to look at him. I don't. I try hard not to, but my eyes slide to him anyway. Our gazes meet, and my limbs lock up tight.

Sharp, exotic features fill my vision, thick arching brows and lean muscles covered in ridges and scales. Not several yards from where I'm standing, waiting for him to come forward and chain me, I'm transfixed. I couldn't run if I wanted to. And I want to.

I want to run far, far away.

He's beautiful, a deadly beauty meant for one thing: to lure idiotic prey like me.

Standing beside the other two, he's the tallest. His tail lifting him high off the ground. He may not be packed with muscles like the male with a cowl, but he's built. I don't think my little knife is going to help me.

"Just two?" the blue one balks. "Two to fight over? Do you know how many of us are waiting in the trees? Three was not enough! It will be a bloodbath!"

"Enough, Vagan!" the yellow and black one says. "We

will not take a gestating female from her mate. The females are not to come to any harm, and that goes for the one out of our reach." He glares at the men. "For now."

Collins shakes despite his best attempts to hide it.

Vagan snarls but doesn't argue further.

"So we still have a deal?" Peter asks.

I hate him.

"We have a deal."

"Hand over the box, and we'll leave you to it."

I hate Peter even more—if that's possible. I want to wring my hands around his neck and squeeze.

The black and brown alien thrusts the box at Peter. "Take it then and leave."

In a blur, the next few minutes rush by. Daisy loses it when Peter and Collins enter the skiff, refusing to listen to her pleas. I stand stunned, fearful to move, wanting more than anything to grab my knife and fight. It's not until the skiff takes off and a tense silence returns that I acknowledge the three very big, very scary males staring at Daisy and me.

Their eyes feast on our flesh. Their stances are rigid and ready.

My chest constricts, and I turn my head away.

I shuffle to Daisy's side and help her stand, grabbing onto her tightly, locking my fingers.

"We need to be brave," I whisper, clutching her. "It's up to us now."

It's up to me. I outrank Daisy by a lot. She'll look to me for guidance.

I swallow my fear and stare back at the males.

"W-What now?" I ask, squeezing Daisy's hand.

"Now," the red one smiles wickedly, addressing me, and only me, "we hunt."

FOUR
SOFT FLESH

Gemma

I DRAG DAISY BEHIND ME, rushing through the forest. The trees are thick, the bushes so full my clothes tear, caught and ripping on branches at every turn. My skin opens up as sharp twigs abrade my flesh.

I don't know if we've been running for hours or minutes.

I don't see the forest or anything in it. I see him. His intense, serpentine eyes and sharp lips. I see the blue male's hard, bright orange cock, too long to fit in any human female without terrible discomfort. It was in that moment that I knew Daisy and I were to be nothing except slaves, or worse to this strange species. They don't want to eat us, or experiment on us... They want to use us.

A twig slices my cheek and I flinch, stumbling over my feet. Daisy catches me, and we surge forward.

Fuck reasoning with them.

Another large branch slaps me in the face, and I fall

back stunned. Daisy tugs on my arm and forces me to keep going. "Don't stop! We can't stop!"

I love her more than anything at that moment. Shaking the pain away, I rush after her. I'd kill for her.

I hear hissing behind me.

"Daisy," I gasp. "They're catching up!"

"Don't stop!" she cries.

The hissing grows louder, and with it, the clash of males fighting. Their animalistic roars fill me with fear.

Spotting a ledge up ahead, we head straight for it. Daisy hits it hard, letting me go and pulling herself atop first. I catch her foot and push her the rest of the way up. When it's my turn, I jump and haul my body up, thinking Daisy will grab my hand and help me. When she doesn't, I claw the rest of the way over the rocks.

Rising to my feet, I search for her.

"Daisy?" I gasp between breaths.

No answer.

"Daisy!" I shout.

A shrill scream answers ahead of me.

"Daisy," I whisper, yanking my knife out from under the lip of my pants, where it's strapped to my leg. "Daisy!" I scream, hoping she'll respond. "I'm coming!"

She doesn't scream again. I call her name a dozen more times, receiving no answer. I don't stop shouting, even when I know she must be gone. I eye my surroundings wildly, hoping for signs of passage or tracks. A few minutes pass, my mania gaining momentum.

She's been caught.

And calling for her will bring the aliens down on me.

"Fuck," I breathe, coming to a stop. I try to stabilize, resting my hand on the trunk of a nearby tree wrenching my eyes shut. "Fuck, fuck, fuck." I've lost her.

Hitting the tree several times with my fists, I calm a fraction.

I can't stay here.

Looking around, there's forest on every side. I don't know what to do without Daisy. We never even had the chance to discuss what to do if we got separated. I can't even see the sky. I have no idea where I am or what direction I should run.

Tears bud in my eyes.

I won't be a broodmare.

I won't.

Shaking, I lift my knife and point it at my chest. I tremble, gripping the knife's shaft with sweaty palms.

I press the tip into me and grit my teeth. My hand shakes. "Do it," I whisper. "You can do it."

Something hits my hand, and the knife goes flying.

My eyes snap up to find the red male before me. "You will not leave me so soon, female," he growls. "Not now that you're finally mine."

I stagger backward.

His words are thick, accented, primal, but clearly in the common tongue. I fall back, hitting the tree behind me. I curl my hands protectively over my chest as the male slides my way. He's holding a spear in one hand. I vaguely remember seeing it on the cliff.

One long red tail dances behind him. A tentacle covered in ruby scales. I think I see blood splattered across them...

"I'm not yours. I'll never be yours," I rasp between breaths.

His brow cocks. "Oh, but you are. You just didn't know it until you met me."

He reaches for me. Covetous eyes lean closer.

I push as far back into the tree trunk as I can go. "I haven't met you."

"Consider this that time. We've now met."

His hand is about to be on me, and I turn my head to the side. Will it be cold or warm? Will it hurt? Will he rip my clothes off and take me? Or will he touch me softly?

I don't get the chance to find out. My vision blurs, and I'm yanked off the ground.

Air rushes over my skin. A roar explodes in my ears, below me. Gasping, I find it's not one hand on me, but two. They grip me tightly under my armpits, and I'm flying through the air.

Not the air... I'm bouncing through the canopy of the trees.

The red male is a spec on the forest floor as I'm jerked from one large branch to the next. Sparks of light shoot at us, coming from the end of his weapon. My belly curls and I taste bile.

"Azsote!" His terrible shout shakes the leaves. "You will die!" he screams. "I will see your blood seep into the dirt and your body rot! I will see the maggots feast on your entrails!"

My breath *wooshes* from my mouth. Leaves rush past me in a blur. It takes a stunned second before I'm struggling in this new male's grip.

"Stop," the one holding me orders, slinging from one tree to the next. "Or you will fall!"

I struggle harder, and when the male shuffles me under the crook of his arm, I kick and scream, clawing his scales wherever I can reach. I don't care if I hurt him. I want him to let go of me.

He grunts and curses things I don't understand, trying to get me to stop. I'd rather fall than have my choices taken away from me. The blur and the jerking, the pinching of my flesh weaken my attack. I flinch, hair blowing in my eyes.

"Female, you will fall!" He pulls me forward, twists me around until I'm face to face with a bright green male with black eyes. He squeezes me against his chest, and I draw back to pummel him with my fists.

"Let me go!" I shout.

"You are sssafe with me! I won't hurt you."

I don't want to hear it. "Then let me go!"

"Never."

"Azsote!" I hear the boom of the red male's furor. A voice filled with so much rage; it goes straight to the marrow of my bones. I finally still.

The green male stiffens as well, lips twisting into a snarl. There are small, shiny scales on the sides of his face, and they move with the wrinkling of his skin. I focus on them to stop my sudden dizziness.

I open my mouth to scream, and he spins me around and covers my lips. "Quiet," he demands. "Or *he* will hear you."

My nostrils flare.

Good.

Let the red one come and start a fight. It'll give me another chance to run for it.

I cock my head and bite the green male's hand as hard as I can. Blood gushes into my mouth as my teeth pierce his flesh. He shouts and jerks away.

I scream at the top of my lungs.

The male jerks me hard as I thrash. "I don't want to hurt you," he yells.

"You already have!"

A day ago, I was a respected member of the military. I

was at the top of my field: Communications Director on the bridge of *The Dreadnaut*. A coveted position I worked hard to earn. I'd spent years working as a lackey, slowly rising in the ranks, taking classes, taking every training offered to expand my resume.

It was hard, grueling work. I sacrificed relationships, leaving my family to improve my chances of being bridge crew.

I earned my spot at the top and I intend to keep it.

It's mine.

I hadn't sacrificed my youth just to be used as a human sacrifice for Peter. I'm not just some piece of meat to be handed off.

I buck wildly. I see a flash of red coming straight for us through the trees, and it's enough for him to loosen his grip.

"No!" he shouts. But it's too late, I'm slipping down his sleek, scaled body. His hands grab the cloth of my shirt, ripping it as I continue to fall. "Vruksha! Catch her," he bellows. "Now!"

The air breezes over my skin as I'm freed from his grip. Yes! I wrench my eyes closed for the painful impact I know is coming. Whether it's branches or the hard ground, it'll hurt like hell—if it doesn't kill me.

Two large arms clamp under me, startling my whole body. They wrap around me protectively, holding me close into a steely chest of rippling muscle. I feel it under my cheek as I'm pressed into it.

It frightens me.

I still wait for an impact that's been denied me.

"You have tried to take her and have lost. Leave now or die," the male holding me says. "She fell, almost died in your grasp, within minutes of you having her. You do not deserve a female."

A hiss fills my ears.

"Ssshe is a fighter."

"All females are until they're nested."

Another hiss. "And you think you deserve that honor for catching her?"

"I have caught her twice and will catch her a third time if you try to take her again. Let us battle and be done with it!"

I pry open my eyes. The red male holds me close as the green one, Azsote, the red one calls him, is several yards away. His eyes meet mine. I can't help shying away from the fury—the anguish—in them.

I don't think I can escape him again. I see it. He won't make the mistake of letting me fall a second time.

"Do not be afraid of me," Azsote says, softening his demeanor. Maybe he sees my terror.

The red male clutches me closer. "Do not speak to her! Leave now or die."

Azsote juts his chin. "Why not let her decide?"

My eyes widen. *Choice?* Will they give me a choice? There's hope in that. That means they can be reasoned with.

"No."

"Let me choose!" I gasp, finally unlocking my joints to jerk in his arms. "Please?"

He tenses and looks down at me. There's doubt—and something else—is in his gaze.

They're smart, these aliens. Smarter than they have any right to be. They look like us, kind of. They speak the common tongue, even though they have a thick accent. What else can they do? What do they know?

A plan forms in my mind. I'll go with one, learn what I can, find the alien technology, and steal it. I'll bring it back to the facility and save Daisy in the process. And when I'm back with my people, I'll contact *The Dreadnaut* and tell them about Peter's and Collins' treachery.

Some of my fear vanishes as the plan becomes clear. I just need to keep my legs closed in the process. I just need to survive until I have the chance to see it through.

"Let me choose," I whisper again as the black eyes of the red male bore into me. He has scales on his face like the other, but he also has ridges on the sides of his jaw. Those ridges run down his shoulders too.

"You are mine," he warns. "You've been mine since you walked off your ship."

He remembers.

"Let her choose, Vruksha, and no blood will need to be spread. If she chooses you, I will leave you be, and if she chooses me...you slither away and take your chance with winning the other human female."

His *name is Vruksha.*

"Her name is Daisy," I say, still thinking of my plan.

"Daisy," Azsote corrects. "What a strange name."

He doesn't ask me for mine.

A branch snaps in the distance, followed by several others. A rustle of leaves, a scattering of stones. The males straighten. Tension fills the space.

Others are coming.

Azsote's voice lowers, hurried. "More are coming, Vruksha. We can fight, allow them to gain on us, and battle the others. Or we can let her choose and be gone before they arrive."

The red male—Vruksha, I now know for sure—continues to watch me. Hard. I wiggle in his hold because it's all I can do. I no longer have a knife to plunge into his heart. His dark eyes slide from my face and over my body, lingering on my ripped shirt. I reach over and pull it taut to hide my skin.

I don't like his eyes on me. I don't want to know what's happening behind them.

"Fine," he says. "Choose me, like you know you should."

"Let me down first," I urge.

"No."

"Let her down," Azsote rumbles.

"Never," Vruksha growls.

The rustling of leaves grows nearer.

"We don't have much time!"

More males don't sound ideal to me. The two I'm already facing are enough to contend with. I squirm even more, hoping for an escape.

"She's going to choose me, so why would I release her?" he snarls.

Fuck him. "I choose Azsote," I announce, finding my voice surprisingly level for my circumstance.

Vruksha's fingers wrench on my skin. His lips pull back to reveal two curved fangs.

"Give her to me," Azsote says, smiling, inching closer to us.

Vruksha doesn't look away from me. Is that betrayal etched in his features? My gut churns. I strain away from him.

Azsote is the better choice. He's more willing to compromise. He'll be easier to manipulate, I think this despite the sinking feeling in my belly. I'm good at judging people... *people,* not half-human, half-snake aliens.

"Azsote, is it?" Vruksha says, his voice so low it gives me pause. "He is who you want?"

I flinch.

"I want to go home," I manage. "I don't want any of you."

"She's made her choice! Hand her over and leave," Azsote snaps.

Vruksha tears his eyes from mine. His muscles bulge.

Azsote, noticing, bares his fangs in response. Their stances shift, tails sweeping forward with sharp tips. Vruksha hauls his spear in front of me, shielding me in, loosening his grip on me as he does so.

"Then we fight," Azsote mutters, slinking back.

Vruksha raises his weapon and swings it in an arc. The tip glows yellow and sizzles. It slices through the branches above, sending them crashing to the ground.

Azsote shouts, clearly offended by Vruksha's change to the battlefield.

Vruksha takes off, carrying me into the forest. He holds his spear out with his free hand to slice through branches and trees, clearing our route. I struggle to get free of his hold, and glimpsing the forest behind us, he leaves a wake of falling branches and trees.

I stare at the carnage.

Azsote's rage can be heard throughout it all, over the snaps and cracks and crashes.

Having a choice in the matter? Too good to be true... I press my hands into my eyes, stopping my tears from flowing, grasping for the modicum of calm I had reclaimed.

A short time later, Vruksha pulls his spear in, and the light from it diminishes. It's just a primitive wooden stick again. We're still slipping through the forest at breakneck speeds, and I can't get a great look at the weapon.

All I know is that I want it.

Destruction follows us for a time, and so do Azsote's yells.

When we outrun his shouts, Vruksha only speeds up more. The blur of trees makes me light-headed, and a little looney. The sunlight above dims, hailing night. I'm still not calm, but I manage to keep my tears in.

There's a strange, intoxicating scent that keeps stealing my attention. Turning my face into Vruksha's chest, it floods my nose.

Exhaustion hits me while breathing his scent in. There's no escape, not right now. Not at night. Not in the dark. Especially weaponless and in a strange land. All my years of training can't help me here.

I feel useless, and suddenly, exhausted because of it. I settle in Vruksha's arms and close my eyes. Tears bead them.

I don't want to escape, not anymore. Not while it's dark.

I will tomorrow.

I can't give up.

FIVE
MISCOMMUNICATION

Vruksha

My FEMALE SLUMPS against my chest as we flee to my den. It's not close by, a day's travel from where the human base is located. I can get there if I journey overnight.

Though I contemplate turning back to collect Azsote's head, I keep moving forward. My honor and pride mean nothing to me right now, not while I have my female in my arms.

She has been sliced up by the whips of sticks and leaves. I smell the tiny dabs of blood on her scrapes.

She is not supposed to bleed, ever, unless it's her moon cycle. I am not equipped to see my female bleed in any other way. Returning to face Azsote is out of the question. I cannot risk more blood.

There are predators and darkness to deal with. Blood-lust is on my mind despite her wounds, and I hope we encounter bears, or better yet, the forest's monsters. My female chose another—Azsote, of all nagas. He is a contender like any one of us, though he is not as vicious or as fearsome as me. Instead, he is cunning and quiet.

But Azsote? A growl tears from my throat. *She chose him?* My bloodlust stems from needing to wipe his existence from this world.

I am lucky to have my spear. A weapon like mine is rare, and it gave me the upper hand against the Boomslang. Azsote could have camouflaged himself within the trees and struck a deadly blow without it.

My eyes flick up.

Azsote could be hiding in the branches above, quietly trailing me. I can't lose my head in memories and fantasies. He is a dangerous foe from the shadows, a sneaky snake. His coloring is meant for such an advantage. One bite from him will put me to sleep and upend the contents of my stomach. I'll be knocked out for hours.

My female will be taken from me. I can't let that happen.

The mere thought of it fills me with tension.

She sighs, settling further into my arms.

Heavy, triumphant warmth invades my chest.

I have never felt this sensation before, this madness that rises when I think of this female. It makes me want to turn back all over again and bash Azsote's head in for touching her, cut off his tail, and slice off his scaly hide. I would carry the Boomslang's skull with me always, as a lesson for any male who thinks about stealing my female.

And then I would burn his hide on a pyre until his scales shrivel and become ash, making my female watch.

He touched her and nearly stole her away.

I clutch her closer.

He may have even succeeded if she hadn't called out for me.

It had to be for *me*.

Oh, yes.

Her call was for me.

Still, this sensation in my chest pulsates. I want to kill, to claim, to mark my territory with the heads of the offenders and show off my beautiful prize for all to see.

Jealousy...

The word whispers through my head. *So this is what it's like to be jealous...*

It's not a feeling I enjoy. It's madness and frustration balled up in one. I'm already frustrated. I don't need to lose my mind in the process.

Not when my world is nearly perfect, and the future is bright. Why can't I shake it?

I take a short rest and glance down at my female to make sure she is okay.

Her eyes are closed and her breaths are light. *She slumbers.* Her face is cast in shadows, her nose pressed to my chest, her arms limp.

Tightness strangles my heart, squeezing to the point I'm nearly suffocated. She is everything I have wanted, everything I have fought for this long life of mine. And she is so small, with no scales, fangs, claws, or tail to defend herself with. I am already crazed with paranoia that I may lose her.

And it's getting worse, having almost lost her to another. On the first day.

She chose him.

My fingers curl.

It doesn't matter. She doesn't get a choice. She never had a choice.

Once she's within my den, she'll know she belongs to me and only me. I will care for her like a pet, and treat her like a female, a precious rarity. I will show her we are meant for each other. That I am a male, a warrior, and a master, and she is a woman. I will fill her with my spill and mark her with my fangs. She'll never look at another male again. Human, naga, or otherwise.

And if she does? It will be with revulsion.

The image alleviates some of my jealousy. I tug her sleeping frame closer to my chest, careful not to bruise her skin.

I have a female. A female!

My arms tighten even further. If she bruises, I will kiss them better.

If I have it my way, she'll never see another male again. She will see me and only me from this night forth. Her mind will be consumed with me; I will make it so. She will want nothing more than to sing my name, licking the excess spill off my scales.

I harden thinking about what's to come.

She'll apologize for her choice with her tongue, I decide. My jealousy vanishes entirely knowing how much she'll need to use it to be forgiven.

My eyes trail over her scaleless face, cementing it in my head. I had taken her in when she stepped off the small ship back on the plateau. Seeing her this close is different... I want to study her, but the forest isn't safe. It's quiet now, although it might not stay that way, and even the quiet brings monsters. With her in my arms, we are an easy target for any hungry beast.

I search for a safe place with enough moonlight to see her.

Spying a clearing to my left, I head in that direction. I come upon a rusty metal structure from the old world and test it with my tail. The structure is overgrown with plants. It holds when I thump it. When I move closer, I recognize it as one of those vehicles humans used to travel by. A car, a large one.

Outside the mountains, there are thousands of them scattered across the wastes.

I carefully set my female on the forest floor and search for the door, finding it quickly. I use my spear to cut through the stems, removing the vines keeping the vehicle closed. Once gone, I tug the handle.

The door comes off with a crunch.

My female moans.

I stop, waiting to see if she wakes up. Thankfully, she doesn't. I turn back to the vehicle, setting the broken, now crumbling door aside, and gently lift my female into my arms, slithering into the space, leaving the majority of my tail outside.

It's dirty and broken inside, and the seats are not comfortable. But the frame remains sound and the over-growth on the sides makes it relatively private. There's a hole in the roof, and I push the vines aside to allow in moonlight. My sweet burden twists in my arms. I pause. She eventually settles back into sleep.

She's fascinating.

I've seen many human females, though I thought they no longer existed. I've grown up with their unused tech-nology hidden all around me. It's everywhere if one looks hard enough. Even now, I see an orb on the seat next to me and pick it up, dusting it off. All orbs are connected like all the technology is.

There's a relay near the plateau that feeds power to the

tech that remains, and though I have never seen it, I know it's there, hidden.

It belongs to Zaku.

The orbs I have collected are within my den, and I've watched videos through them, whatever I ask them to play me. And human females are often on them. These fake humans have kept me company since my father slipped into the forest, never to return.

To my dismay, the screens only show me things of the past and what can be immediately viewed in the present. They only work if they've been in the sunlight to charge, then they last for hours.

My father once told me that he, my sisters, and I were the only Vipers in the world, and though as a youngling, I didn't believe him nor understand him, I do now. I have never seen another like me. Not on an orb, not on a screen either.

Females of my kind... were not common. My mother was the only female Viper until she laid her litter, bringing me and my sisters into the world. And like all naga women back then who conceived a litter, she died giving birth to it.

Inhaling, I curl my arms around my female, trying to make her comfortable. I lean us back against the vehicle's interior frame.

If she is comfortable, she will sleep longer, and I will get more time to enjoy her.

I reach for her hair and twirl it with my fingers. It had been pulled back earlier though it's now tangled around her shoulders. I wish I could see the redness of it, but the moonlight and shadows bleed out the color. It's wispy and soft like gently flowing water.

The moonlight shines down on her face, stealing my attention from the feel of her strands, and my gaze shifts down. She wears blue-colored clothes that match. Using my free hand, I tug at the cloth, confused as to why anyone would wear so much at once. It is the hot season, and I can't stand any barrier on my skin in this heat.

Humans on the screens often wore clothes unless they were bathing—or mating. Since my female is sleeping, I let her keep them on. It can get chilly at night.

I notice a tag on her chest, and my fingers pinch it. Plastic? Something is written on it, and I spin it around to read what it says.

Gemma Hurst.

Bridge Officer and Communications Director.

She communicates with others? She is specialized in this?

I'm intrigued. How can someone specialize in communication? If her world is anything like the one I've seen on screens, then I can venture a guess...

I've seen a lot of miscommunication.

I release her tag, and it rights itself on her shirt. Sliding my upper tail under her legs, I bring her closer, reveling in the sensation of her against me.

Her body weighs little, though I felt the strain of her muscles pushing at me as I carried her earlier. She is strong despite her size, too strong. She fought me and Azsote and nearly got herself killed in the process. A rumbling leaves my throat. If she had died, I would have sought retribution. I would've attacked the facility where the other humans are and destroyed them.

I still might.

I would kill Zaku too, for spurring such a plan that resulted in her death. I despise the King Cobra as much as I am thankful he got the human females out of the facility for us.

Because otherwise, I would be gathering my weapons and infiltrating the base.

Hearing a soft moan, my eyes snap to Gemma's mouth. She sucks in and groans, shuddering once all over. It happens again with the next breath. Fear strikes me from the rasping sounds, and I shake her.

"Human? What's wrong? Wake up!"

The rasping turns into another moan as she startles and opens her eyes. She catches sight of me and—

I slam my palm over her mouth, muffling her scream.

She's tearing at me the next moment, and our limbs hit and knock the rusted walls around us. Some of it gives way. Dirt and dust cloud the air and falls upon us.

"Stop!" I snap. "You will alert otherss to our location."

"Let me go," she cries when I lower my hand from her mouth. "I won't be your plaything!"

I catch her fist before she slams it into my face and hold it tight, trapping her other arm next. She struggles until her burst of energy leaves her. I watch it happen, and the clarity of her situation returning to her eyes.

She's panting and stiff—fear and confusion etched across her face—when I loosen my hold. When she doesn't start hitting me, yelling, or trying to get away, I slowly relax. She doesn't, I notice. I miss her pliant body lying against me.

How fleeting it was.

She's watching me with fear and defiance, her confusion diminishing. She tries to curl her limbs into herself and make herself small. The space we're in doesn't allow it. No matter where she moves, my tail is pressed up against her, holding her open for my secret perusal.

If only she were naked...

I would like bare flesh on my scales.

I can't believe she's here.

She glares at me when she's done searching for a way to escape from my limbs.

"I won't let you go," I say.

"I know that now." Still, she scoots her feet closer, her knees to her chest. "I've forgotten..."

"Forgotten what?"

"That I don't want to escape."

I go still. Has she...? Has she accepted me? Chosen me? I can hardly believe it after she tore into me, but perhaps I scared her. Maybe she believes I deserve it. She did wake up in a new place and in the dark. "You will not fight me?"

"I didn't say that."

My eyes narrow. "Then you have not accepted what's between usss."

"There's nothing between us. I don't even know you. I don't know what you plan on doing to me..." she trails off.

So she doesn't know. Her males have kept her in the dark.

I puff out my chest. "I will give you shelter, food, clothing, and a place to nest," I announce. "A home where the monsters of this world cannot reach you or our future brood. I will provide everything you need and protect you."

"Monsters?" Her eyes shift to the darkness outside our small shelter, straining her neck. "Brood?"

I slip my claws along the column of her throat. "Do not be afraid. They cannot get to you now that you are with me."

She tears off my hand and shakes her head, grabbing it, burying her face in her hands. A dry sob escapes, and it hollows out my gut. I reach for her, but she shies away from my touch.

"I won't let them hurt you," I tell her, softening my voice.

She cries harder, shaking and rubbing her eyes. It re-emphasizes how tiny she is compared to me. She was the tallest human on the plateau, taller than even the human men. Yet, next to me, she is small. She is not safe in this world of mine, and she doesn't belong. She belongs in the sky, among the stars, where all hope and dreams thrive.

Unfortunately, she's here now, and I won't let her go. She will get used to it. I will help her.

I will be her protector. I will teach her the ways of this land. It will be difficult because she is unhappy. I will have to make her happy first.

She cries for a time, and I sway part of my tail to pet her in comfort. Her sniffles are the only noise breaking the quiet night. I wait, knowing she needs this. She cannot accept the future if she does not grieve the past.

An hour passes before her tears dry.

When she wipes her nose on her sleeve and looks at me, I know she's done.

"I vow it," I tell her. "Nothing will hurt you as long as you are with me."

For I am strong and vicious, and a master against anything that might lurk in these woods. She will come to see this soon.

"It's not that." Her voice hitches. "I had a life, a job, ambition—and then some fuckers took that all away from me like I don't matter, like I'm just a bargaining chip. And for what? Technology that may or may not help us with the Ketts? For something we may have discovered ourselves in due time?" Her voice gains steam. "Fuck them. Fuck Peter, fuck all of them. And to think I was friends with Peter? I thought he was a good boss, a good man—"

I grunt. If I see this Peter again, I will stab him with my spear.

"—and he does the worst, most cowardly thing a man in his position could do, forcing others to make all the sacrifices. I hate him. I hate all of them."

"You're better off with me, sssafer with me." *Yesss,* I coo, petting her hair.

"Am I, though?" Her voice lowers, her fury vanishing. "Are you going to rape me?" she whispers, hugging her arms tighter.

Rape? She thinks I would rape her? "I will have you," I growl. "I will have you in *every* way. But I will not rape you. I will never do that."

She looks away. "Then you will never have me."

My anger ignites. "You deny us? Still? I have caught you. You belong to me now! You ran and I caught you, my bride. Baring yourself to me and giving yourself over to my protection is all that is left!" I want to grab her, pull her to me, and shake her with sense. "It is what I have won! What I am owed!"

Her face shudders in shadows. "I owe you nothing. I didn't choose you."

I slam my hand against the side of the shelter. It goes through the metal with a pop, sending the metal around it crumbling down. How dare she? How dare she deny me? She thinks she can have my protection for nothing in return? She thinks her actions will not have consequences?

"Mates rut," I snarl, jerking my hand back. Her eyes widen. "They fuck," I say again, feeling my member pulse under my scales, using the ancient slang from the videos. "You understand this."

"Vruksha is it?" Her voice is hesitant, low. I nod. "Just

because you say we're mates doesn't mean it's true. Let me go, and you will never have to see me again."

"Never."

"I will never *fuck* you. We are not even the same species."

"You will."

"Humans don't have mates!" her voice gains steam.

"They do now."

My agitation cannot be controlled. Finding the handle of an old door behind me, I jerk it open, snapping the vines on the other side. I slide through the shelter and out, uncaring of my female within, and grab my spear. If I stay, I will hurt her. I will bring the shelter down upon us both and bury us within it.

I am a Pit Viper. A dangerous foe. A red devil. She should be begging for my protection and all I have to give her. If I were taken to the stars and placed in her world, I would seek a master—a mate—for guidance so I may rule my enemies, but she doesn't even look at me as her savior—she doesn't want me at all!

I am trying to understand her... I can't.

"Vruksha," she says softly.

My scales straighten and stretch.

I can't look at her without mounting frustration. Instead, I swing my tail and lash the plants around me to shreds, expelling my fury like she just expelled her tears.

Tears. I spit.

I pivot to her. "You will come to realize your situation and the generosity I provide. I will let you fight it now because I do not think I can take you gently in my current state. But you will join with me. You will come to understand that Earth, this Earth, is nothing what it used to be, and that ssstarts with me."

I slip into the shadows of the forest nearby before she can respond. Her wary eyes find mine in the darkness.

If she does not want me, then she will have to watch me in my madness. She will witness what she does to me by her mere presence alone. She will see what she is missing, and I will show her that coming to me is the only way. Because the only protectors of this world are brutal and territorial, and I am kind in comparison to them.

My kindness has limits. Limits—that I have a feeling—she will test repeatedly.

For some reason... I am looking forward to it.

"What is your name?" I command from my place in the trees. I know it, but I want to hear her say it. I want to hear it aloud. I want to see if she'll listen and give me what I want. It would go a long way in soothing my agitation.

A prize, I convince myself, calming. *Her name is a boon.*

A gift.

She doesn't answer me at first, and despite what she said earlier, I assume she is considering running now that I have allowed space between us.

"Gemma," she says after a minute, loud enough for me to hear.

"Gemma," I repeat, my voice raspy. "This is what you do to me."

I slide out from the shadows and into a beam of moonlight. The scales at my groin pull back. With my spear gripped in my free hand, the other cups my hefty member, revealing it to her. It's heavy, engorged with seed, and painful; it's what she's done to me.

It's what I suffer for her. Weeks of torment, weeks of flooding torture as seed continuously fills me, swelling my hide to the brink. Females do not suffer in the ways that males do, so we make them suffer by stoking their arousal, only to deny them. I have seen it.

Her gaze slides down to my middle, where my pelvis becomes my tail—where my shaft usually hides beneath. Except it's not hiding now, and her lips part as she takes it in.

"I am in pain," I hiss. "So much pain. For you."

SIX

A GAMBLE OF WANT

Gemma

I can't help staring.

An alien male is pumping his cock mere yards from where I'm sitting. Heat surges to my face. Uncivilized, quick to anger, but intelligent, Vruksha's nothing like the serpentine beast I believed he was.

And yet, he very much still is.

I catch a glimpse of his tongue when he hisses low and deep.

There's a small fork in it, and it vibrates on every S sound.

His intelligence and uncanny knowledge of my culture confounds me. It doesn't make sense. I don't care, not really, the nonsensicalness of it. Aliens are never what they seem upon first contact. I knew these locals spoke the common tongue, how could they not, having bartered for me? He can be reasoned with, and that is all that matters.

His hips snap forward.

I grip the vines inside my shelter as he releases his cock to my full view.

Dark red scales glisten in the moonlight, gleaming across his frame. Large arms, abs, and sharp muscles make up this strange, angry male before me. I barely take in his strangeness or otherworldly beauty because of the dick being presented to me.

It's a different color than the rest of him, darker, tumescent, and bulky. The shadows cast upon it hint of ridges and a large thickness in the middle of his length. He's long, longer than any human male should ever be, but only truly engorged at the center. Despite its shape, Vruksha's cock is ramrod straight and pointing up, bouncing a little when his tail shifts. The eye of its tip glistens with cum.

A drop slips out and falls to the forest floor.

I press my thighs together, nervous that his cum would somehow find its way between us, and if I don't stop it now, Vruksha's threats will come true. I don't want them to be true. I need to hold onto hope for as long as I can, and fight. Stay vigilant.

I can't help shivering, my flesh prickling. A man has never presented his dick to me before. I lean back into my shelter as my muscles tighten, because I'm watching closely all the same.

Because despite everything, he's physically alluring, and his smell is intoxicating. Sniffing, I can almost scent him.

I sniff again to make sure. His smell...is...really nice. Really, really nice.

He grabs his member, squeezing the thickness in the middle. His palm presses into it, and his fingers wrap tightly, massaging it. His gaze hoods, staring at me.

Staring at me and touching himself. Heat rises to my cheeks.

"Ssso much pain," he groans, rolling his S. The hiss rumbles through the air and tickles my ears.

Shock hits. I know what this is because I'm not averting my eyes and throwing things at him. My breaths shallow and as much as I don't want to, I stare. Hard.

I want to be that person who's righteous and virtuous, but I'm not. I never have been. Seeking spirituality and God is for those who don't have the kind of job I do. There's nothing virtuous or spiritual working on the bridge of *The Dreadnaut*.

He's an intelligent, sentient alien... My original, brief assumption of him is now mired in confusion.

Vruksha loosens his grip on his knot and pumps his length instead. His tapering tip, where his cum drips, is pointed and slightly curved, and could be a weapon in itself.

"Gemma," he rasps my name, and my skin rises even more. "Gemma," he mutters again when he slides his hand back down.

My heart riots. I turn away, but the motion is harder than I expected.

"Gemma, Gemma, Gemma," he continues. What he's doing goes against human decency, except he doesn't know or even care. "Gemma." He says my name with each thrust of his hand, his hips. "*Gemma.*"

I listen, his pace increasing. I steal another glance, practically mesmerized from the mantra of my name.

Primitive darkness glints his black eyes, bursting with fervor. His angular face tilts downward, arching, ribbed brows lower to show menace or... or want? I don't know, and I tremble. He looks at me like he really is in pain, and that the only thing in all the world that could relieve him is *me*.

I face him and the virility he's displaying. As I swallow, I find that my throat is tight. My mouth is dry, like I had been gaping.

His arm jerks, tempo building. The sounds of my name become nothing more than a guttural, animalistic gasp on his lips. The rasps he releases roughens.

He's showing me what he intends to do with me, and what's in store if I can't find my way home. Will it be bad? I hug my legs to my chest, making sure my ripped shirt covers me entirely.

Will it be...okay?

"Gemma!" he shouts my name one final time, bowing over as his hips thrust outward. His tail slams against the ground. The leaves above shake, some fall.

I jump, startling as he crumples onto the forest floor, thrusting still. I'm still watching this male jacking off, and I lean out to see if he's okay.

Something wraps around my ankle. "What are you doing?!" I shout as he drags me out of the shelter and toward his pumping hips.

I kick once, trying to dislodge his tail, but he lifts and grabs me, pulling me under his large body.

He pushes his hips between my legs, spreading them. I press my hands to his chest. His cock slaps against my stomach. I suck in.

It's hot and wet.

He pins me with his eyes as my clothes dampen with his cum.

"Do you sssee now what you do to me? What I need from you, Gemma?"

I swallow, holding still.

All I can think about is that my legs are open and his body is between them. I try not to press them closed, clenching, straining, uncertain.

"Why me?" I gasp, pushing at his chest.

"Because, my sweet little human, you are mine." His eyes twinkle. His tongue comes out and slides up my cheek.

My whole body shivers.

"And soon, you'll be licking me like how I'm licking you."

I gasp and the delicious scent of his smell invades me fully. I gasp again, sucking it in, needing more. Greedy little human that I am.

His mouth moves over my ear and I turn away, and then it's upon my throat. It's warm and wet and demanding. I hate that I clench again, that I grit my teeth because it tickles.

This isn't happening, I tell myself. Darkness or not, protection or not. Heat running through my veins or not. *I need...fresh air.*

His lips caress my throat. They're warm, soft...

I have a plan. He's just a means to an end.

Daisy.

The second Daisy comes rushing back to my head, I push at Vruksha, fighting to get out from under him. "Stop!" I yell, breaking through my shock, and the cage of his scent. He rises, and I scoot back until I'm pressed up against the shelter.

Darkness clouds his eyes. The twinkle, gone.

How could I forget about Daisy? I have no idea what happened to her or where she is. What she must be going through... If it's anything like this?

I pray she's okay.

Vruksha pushes his cock into the confines of his tail, the

bulge in the middle of it now gone, and it disappears behind a slit of scales. I finally manage to turn away, shame rising to my cheeks. I rub the feel of him off my neck.

"Now that you know what you are in for, I suggest you get some sleep," he says. "Tomorrow, we will reach my den, and you will become mine. Sleep is of the essence."

I hear him slip away and I close my eyes.

I'll never be yours, I vow. Never. My time on this planet will be short.

I'll never become an animal like you.

Yet that heat... It remains. And his smell?

I shudder.

SEVEN
THE AIRFIELD

Gemma

I BARELY SLEPT, and I feel it. The little I got the night before hasn't helped at all. And I'm hungry. As dawn breaks through the trees, my stomach grumbles. I push onward.

My feet drag through the damp overgrowth.

I can't stop thinking about what happened between Vruksha and me last night. He came back to me when the Earth's sunlight broke through the trees, telling me it was time to move on. I thought he would regale me on his *need* again, instead, he handed me a cupped leaf full of water and helped me out of the shelter, asking if I was...okay.

Am I?

I told him I was. Should I have said otherwise?

The amazing scent coming off of him had disappeared during the night.

"How much farther?" I ask, hating that it's me breaking the silence. Again.

We haven't spoken more than a few words since we left the largely-broken shelter hours ago. When he tried to lift me in his arms and carry me after I finished the water he offered. I held him off. It made him furious.

I might be tired, but I've been carried enough by these aliens to last me a lifetime.

Besides, I don't trust him to not bring me up into the trees. Glancing up, I study the branches. They do not look like they could hold my weight, let alone the weight of a male like Vruksha.

A sigh escapes my lips. I rub my eyes with the back of my hand, wishing I hadn't lost my hair tie in the fight yesterday.

Massaging my neck, I still feel Vruksha's tongue. It's elsewhere too, or at least I'm imagining it elsewhere. Warm, wet, and mobile. Ticklish at the fork. It's a sensation hard to describe. I shake my head. His tongue tickles.

A blush rises to my cheeks.

If I were to be asked if these Earth aliens were voyeurs yesterday, I would've gifted a response of utter confusion. Today, I just want to laugh. Laughing is easy. The incredulous giggle tickling the back of my throat is all that keeps me walking forward, the only thing stopping my thoughts from drifting to darker subjects.

If I'm laughing then I'm not screaming or crying.

Vruksha threatened me with all of himself, showed me what he had to offer. No human man would've considered doing the same. They're all words, easy flirtations, and gifts. There's protocol in wooing a lover within the field—on a spaceship—and jacking off in front of them isn't part of it.

Perhaps it should be.

I've been asked out on dates and have gone out for a drink with men in the past. Sometimes I even enjoyed the flirty messages sent back and forth. Never has a man showed me his skill and stamina, or what he has hanging between his legs before a physical agreement, a contract.

Contracts are important legal documents, ensuring both parties are entering a physical relationship willingly. Oftentimes a relationship officer oversees them. Having a contract in place protects both parties. It protects the babies born between such unions too.

I can't get the scene of Vruksha thrusting out of my head.

My face scrunches.

"Through the trees," he answers, not even glancing at me. He's focused on the forest around us, checking the sky and trees constantly. I'm glad he is. At least one of us is. I hear animals but do not want to meet them. I'm not an idiot. If I do choose to run again, I know I'll have to contend with these *'monsters'* Vruksha mentioned. If I run, it would be away from the one being who keeps me safe from them.

I eye his spear.

I want it.

I'm going to need it when the time comes. Bringing back a weapon like his—obviously Lurker-made—would be leverage.

"How can you tell where we are?" I ask, wanting to learn about the world I'm facing. Something hoots in the branches above, and I flinch.

"The land is flattening."

"Oh." Has it been? I hadn't noticed. All there's been is trees, trees, and more trees. And the occasional oddly-shaped structure overgrown with vines and leaves. It's not like the trees are strange to me. Most habitable planets I've seen or visited have trees like the ones on Earth.

"We are close, very close," he adds. Vruksha cants his

head in my direction except he doesn't say anything more. He's been quiet since his show last night, and though it didn't bother me at first, it is beginning to now. Questions, so many questions are at the tip of my tongue, waiting to be asked, needing answers.

I want to ask so many things and each time I'm about to, I look at the alien who's captured me, his tail, muscles, and blatant, in-your-face strength and then intimidation thwarts me.

Nighttime didn't do Vruksha justice. The moonlight on his scales was beautiful, though it's nothing like seeing him in full light, in full view. I've gotten to watch him for hours, he's the only thing I've watched for hours. And my observations prove that this male is nothing like the men I grew up with. Vruksha intimidates me. Not even the captain of *The Dreadnaut* intimidates me. This half-man, half-serpent does what the most powerful man on my ship can't.

All my questions die on my tongue.

Vruksha is built, lean and long, and his tail seems to go on forever, flicking, wrapping, and testing the forest. He uses it like a third arm, a third leg, whichever he needs at the moment, and it's mesmerizing. I recall the sensation of his tail on my skin, his scales, sleek and soft although hard when pressed against. They're armor, and considering all the scratches on my arms, I envy him for that. My fingers twitch, hungry to explore his scales more thoroughly. To discover how strong they really are.

Can they be pierced with a blade? A bullet?

His scales shift as well, rising from his skin ever so slightly when a strange noise comes from the forest. Among them are ridges. Ridges that appear as inflexible as his scales.

And *oh*, is this male flexible.

Like an acrobat, Vruksha uses the world around him as a playing field. Using his tail and hands, he swings up into trees, slipping up to the very tops to peer out over the landscape at a moment's notice.

Yesterday, he carried me like I weighed nothing, and he carried me for *hours*.

It was probably easy too, I grump. With the length and size of his tail, that alone probably weighs three times what I do, if not more. He'd have to be mighty to climb with that weight hanging off him.

I'm not heavy, although I am tall, and I do have some curves. My weight should have hindered him somewhat. Recalling back, I don't think it did.

"We're here," Vruksha says, pulling me from my thoughts.

I see nothing but more trees around us.

I hug my middle. "Here? Please don't tell me you live in a treehouse."

"Treehouse? No, human, I don't reside in such an easily accessible place. I am not Azsote." Vruksha swings his spear out and moves the heavy branches in front of him. There's a clearing on the other side, a field almost. He moves aside and nods for me to pass through.

I hug myself tighter and walk past him, trying to avoid touching him. His tailtip brushes my leg.

A shiver goes through me, and I quiet it as fast as it rises.

Sunlight hits me, and the clearing widens as I move forward. Vruksha follows behind. He doesn't stop me, so I keep going until there's a field of intermittent trees extending beyond my sight. There are no bushes here, nor overgrowth.

It's like an orchard, but not entirely, instead there's just dirt and long fields of grass between the trees, and old, dead leaves covering the ground. And the ground? It's mostly level.

"What is this place?" I ask.

He slides past me and deeper into the field, toward a worn path on the ground where he's clearly moved many times.

"I think this used to be an airfield."

"An airfield? Like a landing port?"

"A landing area for planesss."

"You mean ships," I correct.

He shakes his head. "Planes. This was built for planes."

No one uses the term plane anymore. To know that at one point, humans were all stuck on Earth, without any access to space, unsettles me. The lack of freedom would have driven me mad. Where would someone go to get away from another? At least in space, the possibilities are endless. I could lose Vruksha easily if I had access to my tech.

I follow him deeper into the field. "How can you be so sure?"

"The robots have told me."

I still. My eyes snap to him. "Robots? What robots?"

"The ones still living and maintaining Earth."

"They're still here? They work?" How can that be? It's been... ages. "That's impossible."

Vruksha turns his head. "They are still here. They never left like humans did."

"Humans didn't leave. They were killed off. The only ones who survived are the ones who weren't on Earth when the Lurkers committed genocide."

"I survived," he grunts. "Yesss... the Lurkers."

"Were you alive when the Lurkers destroyed us?" I snap, knowing it was impossible. There are long-living beings in the universe, and none of them can survive for fifteen hundred years. At least none that humans have encountered thus far.

"No. I came after, when the plants and the trees returned to the world, according to my father. No naga remembers a time before that, before this world grew again," his voice lowers.

"Half this planet is still growing," I say. "Entire continents of this world remain without life. Only this mountain range has truly become acceptable. It's why I'm here, why any of us can be here."

"Ah yes, the dust wastes."

My eyes shoot to him. "You've seen them?" From my readings, the nearest wastes were a little more than a hundred miles from the facility, in every direction. It's as if the facility was the epicenter of this dead world's regrowth. It's why our team chose it as our base.

"I have seen them." He gives me an unreadable expression. "You may know more about this world than me, but you do not know this forest. This was once a place called an airport, and it is where I have made my den. A home I am eager to show you."

"But there are robots?" I'm still hung up on this. There'd been no working technology in the facility. In fact, the base had been practically stripped clean.

Which now I find odd...

"Come. I'll show you."

Vruksha glides to a half-bent tree that has a single large boulder beside it covered in moss. When I get closer, I realize it isn't a rock at all. It's a pile of... *something*. He swipes some of the moss off, and straight, angular edges reveal themselves. Man-made edges.

I move closer. "What is it?"

"What's left of a plane."

"Planes aren't robots," I mumble. I reach out and touch it, brushing off more of the moss. So much of it is bent and broken, and there's even some rust. I step back to get a better look. "This can't be a plane," I say. "It's not big enough."

"It's all that's left."

I stare at it, my belly churning, not liking his explanation. All that's left? I look around, trying to see what this place was like at one point. I can't imagine it. The past eludes me. I can only see a strange orchard with a strange growth pattern.

"There is more," he tells me when I finish circling the structure.

"There is?"

"Oh yes."

"Show me."

His eyes glint and something wicked darkens them for a second. He pivots away, and I chase after him to catch up.

EIGHT

A DEEP, DARK HOLE

Gemma

WE DON'T GO FAR.

Vruksha stabs his spear into the ground and reaches down when he comes to a random clearing. Turning, I can see the plane in the distance. He grabs something with both his hands and yanks. A thick metal hatch pops up from the ground, displacing a pile of leaves. Leaning forward, there are stairs on the other side of the hatch that leads down into a hole.

I jerk back. "I'm not going in there."

He reclaims his spear. "Yes, you are."

"Hell no, I'm not."

"My den is within. It is safe. The safest place in the world for you."

"I don't care. There's no way in hell—"

Vruksha grabs me, rounding his free arm around my back and tugging me to his chest. I squirm and fight, but he's too strong. He hauls me against him and carries me into the dark.

The walls close in.

"Let me go!" I shriek, kicking and batting at his chest. "Let me go!" He ignores me and shuts the hatch with his tail, closing off the remaining light. I'm blinded by darkness, and my fear returns tenfold. I got too cozy with curiosity. "Vruksha," I gasp, hoping that saying his name will help me. "Please!"

Then my world lights up, and the cold pathway reveals the walls on either side of us. There are small hanging glass orbs attached to them, and some glow, though most flicker weakly. He's taking me downstairs, down, down deep. The light grows brighter and brighter the deeper we get.

I'm still battling to get out of his hold when he comes to a stop at the bottom of the stairs where a long room reveals itself with dim lights and weak colors.

I spin away from Vruksha when he sets me down. I brandish my hand to keep him at bay. "Take me back out," I gasp, barely paying any mind to the colorful things around me. "I want out."

People go into holes to be forgotten about, or worse, to die.

"Soon, human. When you calm again. When it is safe."

"I am calm!"

"When you submit to me then," he says, his voice lowering. He sets his spear against the wall next to the stairs.

I swallow and back up another step. "So that's your plan? Keep me captive until I do what you say?"

"I will keep you captive regardless of whether you listen to me or not. I cannot let you roam the forest when there are predators, and there are always predators. Ruthless, bloodthirsty creatures who would like nothing more than to feast on your flesh."

My stomach sinks. "I refuse."

He slips toward me, and I back up even more. He continues until I fall upon a barrier and something crashes to the ground. It's not big. Regardless, I grab it and hold it in front of me as a shield. "Stay away!"

"Human," he hisses, rearing up and forcing me to strain my neck, to cower. "I will never stay away from you. If I did, you could be hurt, or stolen away."

"I can't stay here," I whisper.

"You are afraid?" He puts his hands on the wall on either side of me. "Why are you afraid this time, little female?"

"I'm..."

"You're?"

"I don't like being trapped," I breathe, pressing hard against the wall at my back.

Vruksha lowers his face to mine. "Then don't think of this as being trapped. Think of this place as a shield." He glances at the thing in my hands. "A better one than that," he mutters, taking it from me, whatever it is, and sets it aside.

My arms curl around my chest again. "I can't be in a hole, I can't. I know we don't know each other, but you seem... reasonable. Is there someplace else you can take me?"

I stop before I say Azsote's treehouse.

Vruksha's face snaps back before mine, and I startle with a hitch.

"This isn't a hole. It's a bunker. And if you take a

minute to look around, you'll find it is not all that disagree-able," he growls.

He sounds unhappy.

Have I insulted him? I chew on my lip. Does it matter if I have?

Yes. Yes, it does, Gemma. You're now stuck in a hole with him. Don't insult those you're stuck in a hole with.

Even spaceships have port windows to help with claustrophobia. They have giant gardens with wild animals, and lagoons to swim. The nicer colony ships do at least. Those meant for higher castes of people.

Somehow, I know this place has neither gardens nor lagoons.

I'm not happy. I still haven't accepted my fate. There are correspondences I need to address, meetings I've made with my subordinates, and I have a checkup with the ship's physician in five cycles. Time is money, and lives, or so the higher ups say.

And there's this male here who unnerves me, a male who pulls out his cock and touches it in front of me.

No, I haven't accepted my fate yet.

I sure hope I'm not here long enough to do so.

"Are you calm now?" he asks, his head swaying side to side, his hot breath heating both of my cheeks.

But a hole? I can't do a hole. "No," I say, turning my face as Vruksha's sways. "I'd rather take my chances above ground."

He leans back, and my lungs open for air.

"Orb, initiate," he barks, looking to the left. My eyes follow to see what it is as I dash under his arms and move away from the wall.

A buzzing fills my ears, followed by a dry, mechanical

voice. "What can I help you with today?" the orb says. A small, round ball drifts into the air. Lights come off it in flickers, like it's dying. Like the lights on the walls.

I've seen something like it before. We have similar speakers on the ship, although there they are integrated into the structure and appear more as holograms.

I think I remember seeing one of the other nagas on the plateau with one.

The old humans of Earth were highly advanced, this I know. And with the Lurkawathians guiding them, they had access to things far beyond anything we can currently create. Still... it unsettles me, seeing these relics of the past. I'm beginning to wonder if I'll know Lurker technology when I see it or if it's only old human tech that's left.

"Tell me what predators are nearby," Vruksha demands of the orb.

The lights on it twinkle once. "Scanning now," it says.

Vruksha turns to me. "This is why I can't let you leave." He reaches out and twirls a strand of my hair. I swat his hand away.

He plays with my hair a lot.

Vruksha recaptures my hair with his other hand. His eyes soften as he stares at the strands between his fingers, and this time, I don't swat him away. It's no use. He's going to touch me if he wants to. My scalp tingles as his fingers move and goosebumps rise on my arms. He's being gentle.

I hold still, waiting to see what he does.

His eyes lift from my hair and find mine.

Staring intensely, he brings my hair to his nose and breathes in. His eyes roll back and close as he groans.

My heart quickens, mystified. He hums next, like breathing in the scent of my hair is not enough for him, he tangles his hand into more of my strands and burrows his face into it, rubbing his cheek, his nose, against them. His groaning turns into a rumble, matching the thrum of my heart.

And then his tailtip curls around my ankle and wanders up my pants.

Startling, I dodge away and out of his hold.

He growls when I do, "Why? You are mine." He turns to face me.

I search for an escape but the space we're in is long and narrow. "No."

He stalks towards me and I'm back against another wall.

No. Not even if you look at me with softness, not even if you vow to keep me safe on this strange planet. I can't let his gentleness seduce me, nor his clarity, or his knowledge of my language. I won't be manipulated.

I've spent my entire life mastering a skill set to become an asset to my people. I clawed up the ranks and worked my way into a higher caste. Giving that all up for him and what he offers? I'll never do that. I can't let my blood, sweat, and tears go to waste.

His arms come back up to trap me again.

"Scanning complete," the orb announces. It couldn't be at a better moment. I turn my face away when Vruksha tries to lock me with his intensely hungry eyes. His muscles bunch, showing veins and tendons outlined where the scales are a little thinner. His strength is always on display.

I wish I could do the same.

I'm trying to be strong, except inside, I'm nothing but a little, lost girl, still wishing my parents were living on the same ship as me and wondering why it was so easy for them to give me away.

Depressing feelings rise, and I force them away before they take over.

"To the north lies several packs of wild pigs and a bear," the orb says as I ignore Vruksha's staring. "East is another, larger pack of pigs, heading south."

"Pigs aren't predators—" I whisper. I don't know what bears are.

The orb brightens, and a screen materializes in the air. I blink as it catches my attention, breaking the spell of Vruksha's gaze. We both face the screen. Whatever it's showing us is hazy, fuzzy, and dirty. Through the messy streaming, shapes emerge.

"There are three more bears west, following a herd of deer, and south lies two snakes," the orb finishes.

I take in the sudden imagery, hoping to get a clear view of what it's trying to show. I want to see these predators, what I might be up against when I make my way back home.

I need it to distract me from the way Vruksha is making me feel. I shiver.

Giant shapes appear. They are large, furry creatures standing on all fours. They must be these bears, since I know what pigs and snakes are. They don't look frightening to me, although their size gives me pause.

"Show the snakes," Vruksha demands.

The airy screen blurs, shuts off momentarily, then returns with a crackle. At first, all I see are trees. Nothing but thick branches, bushy leaves on some, while others have pine needles and cone-shaped baubles hanging from them. The same trees I've been seeing for weeks now.

"I don't see a snake," I say.

"Wait for it," Vruksha tells me.

Something emerges. It's slight at first, perhaps an

appendage? Whatever it is, it coils around a branch slowly. Covered in scales of black and grey, it gets bigger and bigger. It reminds me of Vruksha's tail. Another one of his kind?

The tail slips out of sight, and I search for where it went.

One of the branches shakes and flings, and something large drops to the forest floor.

"A snake?" I gasp.

The rest of a serpentine tail comes into full view, and so does the male the tail is attached to. My gut twists.

"Death Adder," Vruksha murmurs. "Zhallaix."

The image wavers, but the male before me scares me to my bones.

He isn't beautiful like Vruksha, or even the green one, Azsote. He's large, scarred, and crooked, with stripes of thick black scales from chest to tailtip. His muscles are meaty and ripped, his hair is tied to the top of his head, and he wears garish white trinkets which are attached to his hair, arms, and waist.

Bones?

He's wearing them as trophies...

There's a scar trailing from one of his eyes and into his mouth, making it appear like he's scowling. There are more scars. Some of them are deep, as though there are chunks of his flesh missing.

His dark eyes whip in my direction.

My back straightens. I know it's not possible—I think—but the male is glaring directly at me.

His tail strikes out, and the image disappears. I stare at the air, waiting for the picture to return.

It doesn't.

"That's not a snake," I whisper.

"No, that's a Death Adder," Vruksha mentions that name again. I'm not a fan that *Death* is in this male's name. "One who will break you and use you, if he were to get his hands on you. Zhallaix, he's called. He's made his den in another bunker on the other side of the airfield."

I swallow. "Will he come here?"

"No."

I blow out a breath. "Are you sure?"

"He will lay traps and wait for us to come to him. Zhallaix does not hunt."

That's not better. That sounds worse. Much worse.

"Why is he called Death Adder? What's a Death Adder?"

"Zhallaix is gifted with exceedingly powerful venom. He is a rabid male who once tried to rule us with his power. We have all fought him at one point to keep our territory. He has survived us all. I don't believe anything can kill him. Especially not a small human female."

I tighten my arms over my chest. "How do you know he'll hurt me?"

My plan to run wavers.

Vruksha snarls. "You underestimate me if you think us understanding each other means we are not savage creatures. I have fought him and nearly died on several occasions, and I am sure we will fight again, he and I. He will hurt you because he does not use nor trust the mechanical beings of this world. He destroys all technology he finds. Death Adders are rapists, of his kind and technology, and the reason why there are no more females. He is a menace. A blight."

I don't understand half the things Vruksha says, but his

mention of the females of his species stops me. My eyes shift to him. "Where are your females?"

"Gone."

My lips flatten. "Dead?" I ask warily.

He shakes his head in answer. "No. Show the other snake," Vruksha barks at the orb.

The orb glitters with lights again. "The other snake is no longer in range."

Suddenly exhausted, I turn away from both Vruksha and the orb to take a look at my surroundings. *Vruksha's den*. The hole I'm trapped in. He's right, I concede. Just because Vruksha isn't forcing me to mate with him doesn't mean one of these other males wouldn't.

For now, I won't fight him to leave. I want to live, because I know I can survive this.

I can survive him. *Maybe not the other...*

I try to forget Zhallaix. He's another problem I don't need, same with the bears. Getting Vruksha's spear is a requirement now—if I want to survive the trek back to the facility too. I won't take my chances on luck. Luck is for the wishful, for the unplanned. I'd rather plan.

Silence descends between us while I glance about, feeling the burn of Vruksha's eyes on my skin.

His bunker is long. It spans far out in front of me. It comes to an abrupt stop at the end, where there's a door. The ceiling is curved like a half-dome with ribbing, and between the cement ribs are lights—or what could've been lights long ago. None of them are on. And though there's light throughout, the longer I stare, the more it seems to dim to a comforting multi-colored warmth.

The main chamber is crammed with so much stuff it eclipses a lot of my view. There's no straight path from the stairway to the very back, and most of the stuff between me and the end, I know nothing about.

Wait, could it be?

I step deeper into the space as the thing I used as a shield catches my attention. It's a metal box with openings on one side, partially covered in dingy scuffs.

"What is that?"

It's not Vruksha who answers me though. It's the orb. "A toaster."

"Toaster?"

"A machine to heat and crisp bread."

"Oh..." That makes sense... The mention of bread makes my stomach grumble. "And that?" I ask, pointing to a contraption of bent and rounded metal pieces connected together.

"Parts of a bike." This time, it's Vruksha who responds. "Orb, off," he adds with a snap.

The orb's lights fade and it settles on a silver disk on a ledge beside the stairs.

Vruksha catches my eyes again as he slides forward, making me back up so I won't accidentally touch him. He scowls when I do. "Follow me."

His mood has only soured. For a moment, I stare after him and his winding ruby tail that remarkably avoids brushing against anything.

Master of his domain, Vruksha has skills I envy. In my job, knowledge is power. If I'm not constantly learning and honing the skills I've already acquired, I could lose my position to someone who has.

And then I feel it, the exit at my back, unblocked and beckoning. His spear is right there, waiting for me to grab it and flee. The realization strikes me like a heady force that steals my breath. Vruksha left the path open, and if I wanted to, I could make a run for it. I could turn and sprint up the steps and hope to the stars I get the hatch open in time before he catches me. I could use his spear on *him*.

I may never get another chance. A better time to make a run for it.

I follow Vruksha deeper into his den.

NINE
TO TRUST A HUMAN

Vruksha

I REPLACE the battery to my generator as I wait for the food to warm. My den is powered by a giant generator that I found long ago, locked away. I've come to understand it was once used for the airport. It doesn't fit in the main space where Gemma awaits. It's in a separate room off to the side.

It took me months to pry the door open. The claw marks on the metal is evidence of this.

The generator takes up the entire smaller room, giving off heat, giving off rich *power*. I used to stare at it, wondering how such a large, metal machine was made. It used to excite me, knowing it was mine, and no other naga knew I possessed anything like it.

Like Gemma.

Now such power doesn't help my mood.

After I led Gemma into my den yesterday, intending to take her to my nest, she could barely pick up her feet halfway through. She yelped when I carried her to a pile of cleaned pelts and encouraged her to rest. Except she would not do so with me so close... I was forced to move away so she would be comfortable enough to slumber.

She continues to deny us.

I see it in her eyes, etched on her face, and in the way she looks around as if searching for something to help her escape. Her cunning is easy to see because it's what I would do...if I were trapped with a being I didn't want to be trapped with.

I hiss.

Haven't I told her that she is safe with me? It is the world outside that is dangerous.

Gemma is not like the human females the screens have shown me time and time again. The broadcasts are from those final days before humans and all life was wiped from the face of Earth. Those females held their mates, their children; they fought for them, and their survival. They reported with fear as sickness took hold of them, they followed orders given to them, and they accepted their fates.

Gemma is not accepting hers.

I stuff the dead battery into a side pocket on the wall for it to charge. If I have learned anything living among the unliving relics of the past, it's that they would die if you let them, but if you don't, they continue to do their job. And this generator... it needed a lot of handling for it to continue.

Unlike many of my other treasures.

Treasures I have gathered, maintained and learned. Each piece I have found or fought for, collected from ruins across the land. Some are from my father and others were stolen.

My hoard comforts me and shows my wealth amongst the nagas. It also bestows security. *She does not care.* She would rather take her chances in the wilds. She'd rather sleep in crumbling structures, with little coverage from the elements and lurking predators.

She'd rather face all of that rather than being protected! She is not keen on being one of my treasures. I am trying to understand her...

It is not easy.

Gemma is nothing like the females desperately searching for security and safety on the videos. They screamed for it, they begged. I have heard those screams and begs so many times, I made certain if I ever met one, I would be able to provide them what they so desperately sought.

Safety and security I have spent years achieving. Years guarding, years perfecting. All in a terrible, primal need to strengthen my domain and keep others away. For what reason before? For me, for ghosts on screens, believing a female would never actually grace this space, but from the moment I first saw Gemma, my den has become something else entirely.

A nest. For her. For us.

Since then, if I wasn't watching for her, desperate for a glimpse of her while I scouted the facility, I was preparing for her.

Leaving the generator room behind, I find Gemma staring at the food on the burner, holding her ripped shirt and jacket closed.

I long for a peek at her flesh, if only because she's adamantly hiding it from me. I want it more with every breath. I sniff the air for blood just in case she might be hiding a wound. I have done so many times already, except

I can't help the doubt that niggles me when she hides each time I near.

The food cooking on the burner though? It reeks of bear droppings.

My female seems to like the smell. Her nostrils twitch as I study her. Military rations, packaged and sourced many years ago, I brought them to my den in case of an emergency. And today? I have no interest in going out on a hunt for fresh meat. It's been nearly a week since I've returned to my den, not since Zaku approached the humans.

There is no fresh meat because of him.

Gemma's eyes find mine, and her back straightens.

I try not to scowl.

Why does she remain tense around me?

"I will not hurt you," I snap, and she flinches, her eyes going back to the food. I slide to the burner and roll the food over with my tailtip.

"Don't! You'll burn yourself," she gasps.

It's the first thing she's said to me today.

I pick up the food and set it down. "I feel nothing except warmth through my scales." Does she know nothing about this place and my kind? Wouldn't she have the same technology as I? Do I have to teach her the ways of this world, and the ways of *her* people too?

She shivers and leans closer to the burner. I leave to find a plate, bringing it back.

"I don't understand how it's working," she mumbles, still staring at the burner.

"Batteries. Power?" I pick up the ration and put it on the plate for her.

I may not burn easily, but she does. Humans—as far as I know—don't have scales.

"Batteries die, erode, and power needs electricity. Both are things that Earth should no longer have." She shakes her head.

I turn off the burner. She blinks, rubs her eyes.

Lost in thought, my female is. *Lost in thoughts that are not of me.*

"Earth has both. Though you need to know where to look for them," I explain. I like hearing her speak, the sound of her voice. It's not often I hear anything more than the buzzing of my machines or the hum of my heart, the orb, or screens in my den. A real human voice, with real inflection, is strange and exciting. "Everything living died, not the things made by the living," I add.

"But preserved without upkeep? For so long?" She pokes her ration. Steam wafts from the perfectly formed rectangular shape. "Human tech and Lurker tech?" She blows on her food.

A growl sounds from her belly when she does.

I settle across from her and watch. It will be interesting seeing her eat.

She visibly shrinks from my gaze when she realizes I'm staring.

I keep my scowl off my face. The tension between us bothers me. She is afraid of me.

"Both, perhaps," I answer.

"You don't know?"

"I never cared to find out what was made by who, only how the things worked and how they could be useful to me." My gaze shifts to the many objects around my den. "The rest has never mattered."

"And you? Where did you come from?"

"Me?"

Her face turns to my tail, to its long length, until she's facing me head-on again. "You are not human," she clears her throat, "Not entirely. Nor are you a Lurker or—or a Kett, or any other sentient species in the universe I know of, and I know all of them. Where did you come from, why are you here, and how do you know the common tongue?"

"You know little," I say.

Her brow furrows. "I assure you I know plenty."

"Yet you don't know what's around you, or the home you originated from, and your men are struggling to navigate both. That is clear. Even from the forest, that was clear."

"How would you know that? We've only just arrived."

"They would have never given you to us if they did."

A pink glow rises to her cheeks that compliments her hair. I ache to sink my fingers into those strands again and bury my face in her tangles. They would be beautiful spread across my nest. They would also be beautiful wrapped around my member, soaked in my spill.

"We can't *find* the technology. Using it isn't the problem."

"It will be. Eat," I demand. The steam rising from her ration has diminished greatly in the last few minutes.

She opens her mouth then closes it when a soft rumble from her belly sounds the space again. She gently picks up the ration and nibbles the side of it. Her eyes go distant as she chews.

I lean forward. She only has blunt teeth, no fangs. I'm amazed that her teeth are sharp enough to tear into the ration. My fingers twitch to pry open her lips and see.

Her throat bobs, and she lifts the ration to peer at it. "Interesting," she says. She takes another bite, this one bigger, more assured. I don't know how she does it. I've eaten these rations twice before when I could not rise after a terrible wound, and I had to force them down my starving throat.

I still don't know what was worse, the gash to my lower tail tendon or the taste of the ration.

On her third bite, I ask, "Interesting?"

"It tastes like chocolate. Really weak chocolate."

"I cannot stand the smell or taste."

"Chocolate is a delicacy for humans. It only grows on Colony 6." She finishes the ration, and her eyes meet mine. She flinches like she always does when she notices me watching her and wipes the back of her hand across her mouth. "We'll figure out how to use the technology once we find it. We have experts," she says, returning to the previous subject now that the food was gone. "People who have spent their entire lives studying Lurkawathians and their technology."

She licks her lips and my blood races. Her lips seem soft and sweet. The need to ravish them claws at me. To do more than that feasts on my instincts. Even if she tastes like rancid chocolate...

This is a dance I do not know.

I thought I knew how mating would work, and this is not what I imagined. It's confusing. After fantasizing about having her in my nest and taking my member inside her, the fact that I'm desperate for just a touch of her eyes eats up my insides.

She is repulsed—frightened—when I mention joining with her though.

She chose Azsote.

I do not understand why. I want to convince her that

she should have chosen me all along, that I am worthy of her, but she wants to talk about other things.

Unimportant things. Things that simultaneously alarm me and bring back the curiosity of my youth. Questions I wish to not dwell on any longer...

I'm afraid that if I force her to confront her fate, she will only choose another male. Again. I will answer the questions she asks because I want her voice in my ears, but there are things on Earth that she does not need to worry about.

The Lurker tech being one of them.

That is why I can't let her leave my den, not anytime soon, and it has little to do with the bears, pigs, and the Death Adder nearby. Although the pigs worry me.

I don't know what pigs she has up in the stars, but the pigs here on Earth... They are intelligent, ferocious, and cruel. They will eat anything and chase prey for miles. They travel in large packs and are incredibly resilient. The best a hunter like I can do is kill one to distract the rest, because they will stop to eat their fellow rather than come after me.

Unfortunately, pig meat is the tastiest meat, which means I will be facing them again soon to procure some so I may hear Gemma moan.

I will feed my female the best food there is, and chocolate rations that must be a thousand years old are not the best.

She wipes her hands on her pants and stands. She peers at the stuff around us now that she's awake and fed, rising on her tiptoes to eye the items further down the bunker. My nest is in the back, hidden, and I wonder if she's looking for it.

I tense, my member pressing against my scales. I hope she is searching for it.

My nest. Where my scent covers every inch, where she will soon bask naked for me to gaze upon, getting my scent all over her. Where I will hold her down and claim her body. Where I can tie her up in my tail...

The mating act between humans is... feverish. I have studied what the screens have shown me thoroughly.

"Do you have any Lurker tech here?" she asks.

My hands' clench. She is not searching for my nest at all.

"Yesss."

"Can I..." She meets my eyes. "Can I see it?"

I sit back, mulling her question.

"No."

"No?" A wrinkle forms between her eyes.

"You and your people are here for their technology. You've made that abundantly clear." It's powerful and hard to find because the other nagas and I keep it hidden, although I know where there are caches of it, caches others are not aware of. "I want something in exchange," I decide on the spot.

She regards me warily. "Exchange?"

I nod, rising. Her eyes flip to my tail, which slides to coil around her. She pulls her limbs in. "I want to see you in exchange." I indicate her body. Perhaps she is hiding a wound that I cannot smell?

This is a fair exchange, but the way the blood rushes from her face tells me otherwise. She grabs hold of her torn clothes and bunches them in her small hands.

I will not relent.

"You want to see me?" she whispers.

She knows what I mean.

"As badly as you want to see this alien technology. And much more so."

"That's unfair!"

"Why?" I cock my head. "You have seen all of me. It is only fair I get to see you."

"You showed me your cock of your own volition, not because I asked," her voice quickens. "That's completely different."

"You are a communicator, aren't you?"

Confusion flushes her face. "Yes..."

"Then you know what making a deal is, and how deals benefit both parties? I will show you what you want if you do the same for me."

The blush returns to her cheeks. "My body is not part of any deal, especially one made between males who think they're unbeholden to anyone else."

Her words anger me. I keep it locked away. "There are no other males here, only me, Gemma. Only me. Only ever me. If your human males hadn't discarded you, I planned to steal you anyway. I was readying to do just that before Zaku approached the facility. Your body and who it belongs to will never be questioned again. It is mine by right."

"No, Vruksha, it's mine."

I slip my tailtip closer to her feet, and she doesn't seem to notice. "And the Lurker tech you so desperately want is *mine*."

She crosses her arms, pulling them to her chest. Another shield, one she uses often against me, though a weak one at that. It makes her chest rise, emphasizing her curves, and I like her curves.

We stare at each other for a time, and I can see thoughts running behind her eyes.

An hour passes in silence, neither of us backing down. She is considering the arrangement.

My pelvic region tightens, the scales around the sheath of my member itching to release it.

When I think she's about to give in and accept this perfect exchange, she rises, turns her back on me, and steps over my tail. I watch as she finds a corner between some of my treasures and curls up on the ground, facing the wall. Her stiff shoulders rise and fall for a while, and when they ease, the tension brought on by our exchange leaves her.

The little human has shut me out.

Again.

Impatience and curiosity settle within me.

Hours go by as I watch her sleep—or try to sleep— adjusting and tossing, again and again. At one point, I bring a large bear pelt from my nest and wrap it around her, and watch as she snuggles into it with a sigh, loving the way her red hair gathers amongst the fur. I debate picking her up and carrying her to my nest where I know it's most comfortable.

I wanted to the night before, but whenever I approached, she shrank from my touch.

My exhaustion builds as the day comes to an end. Still, I wait, keeping her trapped, unable to leave my post.

I want her answer. I have all the time in the world.

I know she's thinking about my proposal between her dreams.

That is why she tosses and turns. I grin.

How badly does she want what I have? What only I can give her? The warmth and protection I can offer? I only ask for one thing: her submission—for her to choose *me*.

When I finally manage to tear my eyes from her body, I leave my bunker to check the position of the sun, finding the world has returned to dusk. Our third day together is coming to an end—and I still have not claimed my mate.

I snarl at the rising moon and head back down.
She's sitting up, waiting for me as I descend the stairs.
She's decided.
My blood races through my veins.

TEN

PAST THE POINT OF NO RETURN

Gemma

I HATE HIM.

I repeat it again and again in my head as I try to sleep. Why can't I believe it?

I'm beginning to trust him. Giggles linger in the back of my throat at the absurdity. He hasn't hurt me or forced himself on me, he's fed me and given me a warm place to sleep, and now I have this pelt wrapped around my body... the largest, softest blanket I have ever experienced.

There's no reason not to trust him, right?

Soft fur tickles my cheek, and denying my comfort—the most comfort I've felt in days—is utterly useless. Vruksha scares me. There's no *denying* that. There's a glint of something dark in his black eyes... that I can't get past. But he hasn't used his strength against me, and that's saying something.

Human men love having power and rank for the very reason I'm beginning to trust Vruksha. If the wrong man had what Vruksha had *and* a woman at their mercy, they would take advantage, exploit the situation. I know because it's happened to me.

I've worked for many captains, and some of them were only captains for the power they can wield having that position. Fortunately, I'm not particularly beautiful, and so their attention never remained on me for long.

I can't shake the nervousness, that it's all a trap, and that once I begin to give in, Vruksha will do the same. Because there's literally nothing in this world stopping him from doing whatever he wants to me.

He wants to see me naked. Is it because he wants to know our differences? His eyes say otherwise...

I shiver.

Has anyone seen me naked? I tug the pelt against my mouth. I don't think anyone has. I've been with men before, though not so vulnerably. I could never risk being vulnerable when there was no telling if the men I let into my bed might someday be my subordinate, or worse, a future boss on the ship I made my home. Sex was about relief, and nudity didn't play into that. Not for me, at least.

I never knew if someone would record me or take a picture to use against me later. Staying as clothed as possible was prudent. Especially in my position of authority.

But Vruksha wants me naked. He wants to see what he thinks he owns. I scrunch my face. My back tingles, knowing he hasn't moved and is still watching me.

I wish he'd go away. I can't rest knowing he's right there, waiting for my answer. I also know I can't stay like this forever. I can't sleep forever.

Do it. Let him see you.

Get it over with.

He's going to see you eventually. You can't stay in dirty clothes forever either. And though Vruksha has allowed me to use the bathroom in private so far on our trek, I don't know if that will change going forward.

It might take weeks for me to escape this hole.

I hear him move, and then I hear him leave. I sit up, twisting to see where he's going. His tail slips out of view as he ascends the dark stairway. I relax, pulling the pelt over my shoulders. I didn't know how much tension was in my muscles with him so near.

I still feel his tongue on my cheek from days ago.

Warmth tickles my belly.

But naked?

Maybe letting him see me won't be so bad. Perhaps he'll find me disgusting, we are different after all. I don't have a tail, scales, or fangs like he does. Once he sees me naked, he might come to his senses, realizing fully that I'm not of his species and he doesn't really want me.

My heart twists at the thought, making me frown. I force it away. I don't want him to want me.

I nod, knowing it won't convince me even when I do.

Though, if he wants me, that gives me power...

And if he doesn't want me? I pull my pelt closer. If he doesn't want me and I can't make it back to the facility, what happens then?

For some reason, that question scares me just as much as everything else right now.

I'll have to figure out a way to survive on my own, and without catching the attention of other, more terrifying naga males who may not be like Vruksha at all. Like the black striped one from the orb's screen... or the one with a hood—Zaku, I believe—from the plateau.

My eyes glaze over as I stare at the stairway, realizing

I'm waiting for Vruksha's return. He took his spear, which means I could be waiting a while.

My fingers go to the buttons of my jacket, tugging at them.

He's not going to show me the technology without me in return. I need the technology for leverage when I get back to *The Dreadnaut*. I need him to want me too... if my original plan fails.

I'm going to give him what he wants.

I suck in my stomach when the thought solidifies.

Seeing me naked isn't that much to give... He could have asked for much more, and he still might, if I keep denying him, and asking questions he clearly doesn't like answering. If I don't give him something, he might make me pay for every inch of his hospitality going forward.

I hear a noise and my heart ramps.

He's back sooner than I thought he'd be.

I sit up straighter when he appears, when he finds me and his eyes smolder.

He's beautiful. I can't get past it. All ruby and ribbed, so sleek with the way he moves. His prowess intrigues me. It's evident in everything he does. He knows how to survive. Men like that are incredibly rare above. They know how to manipulate, weasel, belittle, but truly survive? Unless they were trained as combat soldiers, they're just weak bodies, and weak minds under their suits.

I feel... lucky to have been chosen by Vruksha. Appreciative now that I've had food, warmth, and sleep. From what I thought my circumstances would be days ago, this isn't nearly as bad.

Truthfully, I thought I'd be dead by now, or broken and wishing for death.

Though there are still pieces of Vruksha that force me

to temper the pull he has over me, refusing to accept that I even feel a pull at all. Like his fangs. Sometimes I think I see them drip with something, and I know that something isn't saliva...

Or the blatant lust in his eyes.

His delectable smell. My nose wiggles.

Has he ever been with a woman before? Before they all vanished? *Why* did they vanish?

He's staring at me again like he's waiting for an answer.

My hands shake when I manage to say, "You only want to see, right? Nothing more?"

His nostrils flare, his eyes dipping to my body hidden behind fur. "I want to spend my spill inside you." His voice is dark, gruff. "I will accept seeing you tonight. I would like to make sure you are not hurt."

Hurt? I shake my head. His words make me shudder. They also warm my cheeks. I've imagined what it would feel like with him inside me... How could I not?

Gooseflesh rises on my arms.

"Okay," I say.

I release my grip on the pelt and let it fall. My hands move to the buttons of my jacket again. Better get this over with before I think about it anymore.

"Wait," he jerks forward.

My fingers pause.

Vruksha stalks closer, and I stiffen. He stops several feet away, coiling his large tail under him. "I want you to stand."

Stand? "You'll show me the Lurker tech if I do?" I need to make sure.

"Yesss," he hisses long and low. "Little human, I'll show you whatever you want. I will give you this world if I could."

His voice is eager.

I rise to my feet, praying for calm. My fingers find my ripped jacket again. This time, when I unclasp the buttons, he doesn't stop me. His eyes are glued to me instead.

If I didn't know I was in a hole, on Earth, all alone with a strange male, I would think I was on a stage about to strip for all the rowdy men on *The Dreadnaut*. There were sex workers who did that very thing.

But it's just me and him—and the flimsy trust we've built. Too soon, I've reached the last button. I grab the lapels of my uniform jacket and tug it off, letting it fall to the floor.

Next, I reach for the clasp of my pants, loosening them. Vruksha hasn't moved, hasn't breathed. Heat flushes my cheeks knowing how intensely he's watching me.

I push down my pants to gather around my boots.

My belly swarms with nectarflies as his eyes roam over my bare legs. I kick off my boots, toeing the pants out from under me.

"No scales, not a single one," he murmurs. "How can you survive without basic protection?"

I don't answer. I can't answer.

I bring my now trembling fingers to the bottom of my top, clasping it. Before I can change my mind, I lift the fabric over my head and drop it onto the ground where my pants and jacket lie.

The scales on Vruksha's tail shift, straightening outward. His eyes sear my naked flesh, flashing over my body like lightning. I place my palms flush to my stomach, waiting for his response.

"I'm not young," I whisper, unsure why. "Not the type of woman most men want anymore." I hurriedly add, "I'm not old either." I've seen thirty-three standardized years, and where most women my age have already had children and are raising a family, I chose a career in a higher caste instead.

He may not know that. My body isn't perfect and sweet like it once was. I stay fit because my job demands it, though if I had it my way, I'd never leave my rooms on *The Dreadnaut*, reading and drawing all day, every day instead.

Those simple desires are denied me. Sometimes I wonder if I've made the right choices... I mentally shake the thoughts away. Having water rations and food is more important than books and free time.

"The rest," he demands when I pause. "I want to see everything. I want to check you for wounds." His forked tongue lashes out and steals all my thoughts momentarily.

You can do this, Gemma. He won't slip his tongue between your thighs when you're not looking.

Or will he?

He won't, I tell myself. I have not been able to wash since the day I was bartered away. I've never gone more than a day without being sanitized and scrubbed. Three days of being unclean? My nose wrinkles. Yesterday's morning dew is all I've had to scrub my skin since being here. Once he sees my scrapes and bruises, he won't want to look upon me further...

His eyes catch mine. "I want all of you," he says, gentler this time, as if he read my thoughts. "I am glad you are not hurt. I want to see what is mine."

Bringing my hands to my bra, to the clasp in the front, I unhook it. I let the bra fall down my arms, using one of them up to hide my breasts. My heart is racing. His hands fist at his sides.

"Drop your arm," he orders.

Anger rises, but I do what he says, letting my arms fall.

Air brushes my nipples, my exposed skin, making my shivers worse.

I pray he's not a liar.

Because if he is, there's nothing except the thin fabric of underwear, now several days worn, stopping him from taking me. I feel so unclean that no man or woman on *The Dreadnaut* would even get close to me right now.

Vruksha is not a man—or a woman—he's a primitive alien. What I might think is dirty, might be clean to him.

His member emerges from his scales, thick and throbbing. I take a step back.

"Don't," he rasps, shifting forward.

"You promise you wouldn't touch me." I shrink further as he nears to a hairsbreadth from me.

"And I won't—I will look my fill, see our differences, and show you how it makes me feel, unless you do not want the same allowance when it comes to your tech?"

My cheeks burn. I can't muster any words.

It's not fair.

"Now, the rest."

His body heat blankets over my skin. He's that close. This fierce, alien male. If I trip, I'd land on him, in his arms. If I stumble, it would be into him. If I breathe too hard, we'd touch. And if we did... I don't know what would happen. I focus on the bulge of his biceps, on the scars there I missed before.

The way his tail has curled back around me when I wasn't paying attention. He still isn't touching me but...

The hardness of his member, clearly deciding it *does* want me.

The wildness in his gaze.

I stick my fingers under the band of my underwear and slide them down my legs, almost taunting. When they're with the pile of the rest of my clothes, I straighten to my full height and lift my chin.

"There," I snap. "There's nothing between us anymore. We've seen each other."

I don't know if it's because I'm hyper-aware of the difference in power between us or because I hate him that I'm angry all of a sudden. It's definitely not the tickling, knotting, increasing heat dancing within me. The excitement of the risk I'm taking. His wickedness.

Vruksha's throat bobs. "You are…" he trails off.

"I'm?" I snap again.

"Fantastical."

My mouth drops at his odd choice of word. *Fantastical? A fantasy?* I've never been anything close to that to anyone in my life. No man, human or otherwise, has ever approached me like Vruksha, like he may die if he doesn't have me. But fantastical? No. I'm diligent, disciplined, and loyal. A perfect fit for the position I've earned. Not fantastical…

Fantastical people become stars and models. They are beings everyone in the universe envies. They are a caste all their own. They get to paint and draw pictures all day. They get to read and write their own novels during war.

No one envies me, no one wants my job with the stress of humanity's doom on their shoulders.

My eyes hood and I reach up to wipe them, finding my lashes wet.

I quickly rub them dry before Vruksha sees. I blink several times, clearing them, keeping my face downcast. I don't want to be here, where he can see me vulnerable. I want to hide in the big, fluffy pelt at my feet and vanish. And it's not my nudity that I don't want him to see. I don't want him to see my tears, not again.

He might not think I'm fantastical anymore if he does.

"Gemma," he begins. "You are a dream."

I stop him before he can say anymore. I step into him and hide.

He stills, and his member presses between our bodies, hot against my belly. He's warm, and here I can hide against him and pretend things were different.

His arms don't go around me, and that's okay. I don't need him to hold me; I just need him to hide me, at least for a little while. I lift my arms and curl them around his back, resting easier into him. His scales are velvety under my skin, under my fingertips, and I pet the ones on his back that I can reach.

"Thank you," I tell him, knowing he won't understand. How could he?

His arms go around me, pressing me into him. It's awkward and I don't mind.

I don't even mind the pulsing of his cock sandwiched between us. Somehow, I trust him.

"For what?" he rasps, clearly confused with what I'm doing. Clearly wary... of *me*.

I smile. Good.

"The compliment," I whisper.

We stand like this for a time, and I take in his scent. It's musky and raw, and something I can't place, but it warms me. It's not strong right now. It's not muddying my mind. It's perfect. It makes my skin prickle sometimes. It reminds me of this planet and all its mysteries. It suits him, I decide. I breathe him in, nearly shuddering when I do.

It's not a bad scent.

His cock remains hard, and as the minutes tick by, I grow increasingly aware of it. I can't hide against him forever. My tears dry up, and I swallow.

He's growing less wary of my reaction. If I want to attack him, I should do it now…

His hands slide down my back, pressing me harder into him, into *it*. A rumbling, breathy noise comes from his throat, and I can't help going rigid in his embrace. More of his scent floods my nose, making me warmer… everywhere.

I jerk away.

His nails scrape across my skin as I do, and he hisses, "Why?"

"I can't," I gasp, covering my body.

That hint of darkness glints in his eyes, and my throat closes up. He stalks forward, gliding, and I back up until I'm pressed into some sort of metal crate.

"You have been playing games with me," he growls. "I will be your fool no more." He pulls my arms from my body.

ELEVEN
NO PLACE LEFT TO HIDE

Vruksha

Her fingers tickle my back.

Chosen.

She wants me.

She comes to me bare and presses her warm body to mine, and even pets my scales. Her breath fans my chest. Her cheek rests upon me. The soft touch of her fingers on my scales steals my mind.

Gemma has come to me.

Why? She has fought me thus far, so why now?

Regardless, I hold back a roar of triumph. I want to rush to the surface, shouting to all the other males who did not claim a mate, that she is mine.

Chosen.

I wrap my arms around her small, trembling frame.

I will treasure you. I will shield you.

A groan of pleasure rumbles through me with her body tight against mine. A groan of worry joins it, knowing how delicate she truly is and how the only way I can keep her is if I protect her with everything I have. I vow it too. I will die for her. After spending so many countless moments alone, this is worth dying for. I'll never be alone again.

I squeeze her in my arms

She tears out of my hold.

She slips from my hands and gifts me a look of stunned surprise.

"I can't!" she cries.

I blink back my shock, and my frustration rises as she flees from me. My fingers twitch with loss. Does she think I'm a fool? Does she think she can tease me with what I want most and then take it away? My gaze sharpens.

Or is this a mating dance?

I move forward to reclaim her, to end this contradiction once and for all. "I am done with your gamesss," I hiss.

Her eyes widen, and they glisten like they've been wet. I trail her face. Her cheeks are ruddy, and her hair is a mess tumbling down her shoulders and over her pale, scaleless body.

She covers her breasts and mound with her arms and hands. "I'm not playing games."

I realize... *She came to me when I told her what she was, what I see her as...* I swallow my frustration, trying to understand.

"Why did you embrace me?"

She shakes her head.

"Why?" I demand.

Her eyes shift elsewhere, her body pushes back onto the metal crate she's nearly perched on. She doesn't want to answer me. *Gemma Hurst, the Communications Director...*

Humans do not communicate at all!

"Why?" I ask, louder this time.

"I—wanted to hide," she answers. Her gaze has landed on my tail and she's staring hard at it.

"Hide? What do you need to hide from?"

"Everything."

Cocking my head, I study her. She looms with uncertainty, her skin rising with prickles as my eyes caress her naked curves. Her thick, shoulder-length red waves have gone limp, but her hair retains its gleam. I have an urge to pull it back and have her face clear before me. I don't want her to hide. She should never have to hide, not while she's with me. My voice lowers, softens. "Hide from everything? Why would you need to do that?"

Is she in some sort of danger?

Her arms tighten across her chest. Tearing them off her body and tying them behind her back so she may never cover herself from me again would be a service to us both.

"You wouldn't understand."

"You can hide here. With me. No one can find you here, and if they do, I will kill them. You have nothing to fear."

Her eyes meet mine. Her lips tremble.

Oh, how I want her lips to tremble upon mine.

I shift closer, and she doesn't startle away. "You may hide as long as you want, but never from me. I will give you what you need." My desire for her makes me her begging slave.

A glittering tear beads on the corner of her eye. This time when she nods, I accept it. I want to know why it's there, why she's suddenly changed, except I don't ask. I curl my finger and bring it slowly to her face instead. She stiffens but doesn't move as I catch her tear, softly wiping the skin under her eye and taking the tear away.

I lick it from my finger.

I watch her while I do it. Dewy lips parted and eyes wide as black stones—filled with confusion—fill my vision. I savor the salty taste of her. She tastes like fresh prey, the sun on my scales. She tastes how I would imagine the blood rushing through my veins during an exciting hunt would.

"You're not like any man I have ever known," she breathes.

"Do not speak of other males," I growl as a fresh wave of jealousy invades. "I cannot bear it. I will not have it." No new tears form on her lashes. No more salt. I settle back to enjoy her nudity once more. "Drop your arms, Gemma. No more hiding. There is no reason to anymore. Your clothes offered little protection. Your hands and arms, less."

She hesitates, and I wait for her to decide. Slowly, she lowers her arms again. My scales flutter down my back. My mate, naked, for me and only for me. Only ever for me. How I've imagined this countless times, in many ways, but none of it was as delicious as the real thing.

Gemma will always be naked in my mind, with nothing except her red hair to cover her.

Her breasts are shapely, and the rosy tips are pointed, readied to be teased. The way they appear on her chest makes me hungry to take them in my hands and explore. Seeing her breasts reminds me of my young self, viewing a naked female on a screen for the first time.

A strand of her hair slips to fall upon her chest, and my muscles tense.

"Vruksha?" she says my name in question. I check her lashes and see no new tears.

"Yes?"

"Have you ever been with a woman before?"

My head cants. "Woman? Females are gone." I thought I told her this.

"Why? Where are they?"

It is not a subject I want to speak of. "They die during birth. Long ago, those who were left fled together from these lands, never to return. That is all I know."

"Oh."

I slip my gaze back to her body, lower this time, dropping down until I'm eye level with her sex—the enticing mound between her thighs. A mound with no hair. I see the peak of her little, swollen nub. She clamps her legs together.

"Open them," I demand.

"You can—"

"Open them. Do not make me ask again."

"I need to wash!"

I shoot her a look of uncaring frustration, and her mouth closes tight. She scents of heaven and rain to me.

For a short time, all I hear are her breaths. "You won't touch?"

This time, it's me who shakes my head. "I won't, unless you're hurt."

She inhales and shifts her feet apart. It's not enough to sate my curiosity. "Where's your hair?"

"I... don't have hair there. Not anymore." Her voice is no louder than a whisper.

I hum, staring at the milky gift. My prize.

"Can I close them now?"

"I want more."

"More?" she squeaks. It's a funny sound coming from her throat. My eyes snap up, and she's staring at me dumbfounded.

"More. I demand to see it."

Her cheeks redden feverishly. "I can't."

"Yes. You can."

"No one's ever—"

"I will, now," I snap. "I will see it, and all of you, now."

Her chest rises and falls, and she's hidden her breasts behind her arms again. She'll lower them when I demand it, I am sure of this now.

But I grow impatient at her continued hesitation.

"Gemma," I rasp, "Let me see what I have won. You are a prize, one I will die for, die to keep, and I will see what I have won." If she backs out now, I don't know what I'll do.

A terrible tension is filling my loins. It's the same tension that filled me the first day I saw her. Then, it nearly destroyed me, weeks later, I have conquered it. Though the continuous creation of spill is burdensome.

Her feminine heat is so close, it's upon my face, where I am as a servant before her. Her scent, purely female, is in my nostrils. My member is engorged, swollen with spill and dripping.

She shudders at my words, like they tickle her, and her legs twitch. To my surprise, she drops her arms to grip the edge of the crate, hauling herself to sit up upon it. I rise as she does, and she deliberately spreads her legs. Choosing to show me what I want to see so badly. She leans back.

At once, I'm at the crux of her thighs, staring at her center with a strangled growl.

Luscious nether lips meet my gaze. Pink and succulent and precious. They cling together with glistening arousal, obscuring my view of her center. Her female button is on display, framed by two indents of flesh. It's tiny and perfect, and my mouth waters to press it, to get a reaction from her.

What would she do if I touched her and did just that?

I close my eyes and groan.

Her legs slam closed, but her knees catch on my arms. In a flash, I'm pressing them open with my hands, flush and spread against the edge of the crate.

Gemma jumps, struggles and I hold her still. Her hands grip my hands, tugging. "You said—"

I squeeze her thighs. "You touched me first, twice. It goes two ways, little mate."

Her nostrils flare, and her hands go white where they're gripping mine. She shakes under my grip. I dive back down between her legs, uncaring.

Her folds are open now, and they are slick.

The little hole that'll take my member is sweetly on display. It's tight and closed. Primitive, hungering need slams into me.

She's so tense I can see her quiver as I stare at it.

"Mine," I breathe.

To be this close to my mate and not have her?

It's heaven and torture all at once.

I do not envy the naga males who did not capture a female. I do not envy them at all. Because if they knew what they were missing...

Paranoia hits me as hard as my mating fever. If the other males had an inkling of what they were missing, they would never stop coming after us. My tongue slides over my fangs.

I need to claim her, mark her. My eyes dilate.

She gasps. "Your smell... it's doing something to me."

Tearing my gaze from her sex, I meet her hooded eyes. I don't know what she's talking about. As I keep them, I slide my hands up her thighs.

Her brow furrows. She is so tense, holding herself prone, she refuses to accept the blatant arousal gathering between her thighs.

She also doesn't stop me.

I continue sliding my hands until they're right at the

dent of her thighs. Gemma still grips my hands under hers and with an inhale, she releases them.

Triumph.

My member rises, and my tail coils onto the crate, enclosing her in my circle.

Triumph. *Yes.*

"Yes, female," I whisper. "Let me in."

She closes her eyes and leans back on her hands.

With a growl of elation, my fingers inch between her thighs, diving in as I snap forward and suck her tiny button between my lips.

TWELVE
STRETCHED AND

Gemma

I GASP, bending back. He said he wouldn't touch!

I don't stop him as he penetrates me, as he pushes his face between my legs and sucks my clit between his lips. Sensation zips up my spine, pleasurable warmth joins it. It feels good. There's no pawing, no rough handling, it's just... nice.

Vruksha's touch banishes all my worries.

Somehow... a part of me doesn't want to stop him. I inhale deeply, taking in the musk wafting off of him. Dizzying, I feel my body... warm.

A niggling thought scratches the back of my mind far too quickly and I grasp onto the pleasure he's giving me. How does he know we can even have sex together? I don't want to think about it. His rough mouth sups at my bud, and the question vanishes. Gasping again, he rolls and hooks his finger inside me, touching my special spot. That elusive spot...

"Rough and wet, like I knew it would be," he says, mouthing my clit.

My nerves vibrate.

He pushes a second finger into me, and I grab his head at the invasion. My fingers press into the scales around his hair.

His tail slides across my behind.

I should stop this. I should. I should insist on washing first, but I can't, because if I do, I know my morals will return and stop this from ever happening again.

Vruksha doesn't seem to mind, and I don't understand why. Does he want me this bad? I nearly forget to breathe at the thought. My nails bite into his scalp, digging under his short black hair. He's voracious and overwhelming, a vampire with his fangs, the red of his scales and skin, could easily be mistaken for blood.

Any woman on *The Dreadnaut* would kill for such a male to want them how Vruksha wants me.

I'm lucky... in a way...

No, I'm not.

I think this even as I bend forward, wrapping my legs around his head, leveraging my body to move against him.

I'm fantastical. A prize. This alien male wants me. It's heady and strange and wrong. He wants to protect me with his life. His words are like rare candy to my ears, and I want more of it. His curious, rough fingers roll, curl, and scissor me deeply, doing a number on me that's not wholly pleasurable. I like it. My head clouds. Rolls. Spins. I gasp his aroma into me and my sex constricts.

It's been so long since someone touched me like this.

So long since someone sought to give me pleasure without insisting on something in return. There's no sex contract with Vruksha, and that should terrify me, but he won't hurt me. I think.

My toes curl as I lean back again, lifting my hips.

"Yessss, female." Dark and gritty, his voice makes me squirm.

If I don't think...

His fingers push deeper, expanding, shooting me up in the air. Zaps of pain mix with excitement at his roughness. He does it again, and I gasp as he pulls me forward with his tail. His head lifts, catching my eyes when he does it again.

"Tight," is all he says. "Too tight."

Swallowing thickly, heat rises to my cheeks.

My fingers twitch on his scalp where they clutch him, afraid his features might cut me. Vruksha holds me pinned. My legs are on his shoulders, his mouth wet with my arousal, and his tail braced behind me, finishing the trap. His fingers expand inside me again, and I strain for what's to come.

Madness. I try to thrash, to shimmy for more or less. I don't know anymore.

He holds me still.

Wicked black eyes pierce my soul. "You're too tight for me, female," he rumbles.

His fingers expand, and I flinch, hips shaking, wanting to beg him to stop. But then his fingers close, and I sag, forgetting the pain, pausing in pleasure.

"Not for much longer..." He pushes a third finger inside me. "I will make us fit."

"Vruksha!"

He responds by snapping his mouth back over my clit, suckling it. A scream tears from my throat. Tension radiates through me, and as it pulses up from my core and throughout my body, building, his tailtip wraps around my side, under my arm, to curl around my left breast.

Gooseflesh blankets me from the sensation. I glimpse his tailtip flicking my nipple, and my eyes go wide.

He's not even human! Three fingers expand inside me, and I shriek again. I shouldn't be doing this with him.

He's.

Not.

Human.

"Almost," he mutters before sucking on my clit again. "Almost there..."

I brace for his fingers to spread, and this time when they do, throbbing pressure blasts through my body, sending me spiraling. I don't cry out or scream. I'm silent as he forces an orgasm from my body.

Abrupt and hard, I wasn't ready for it. Rocking wantonly against his face, frantic for more of what he's giving me, my mouth opens to release one long, shocked gasp. Spikes of raw pleasure brutalize my swollen sex.

His fingers expand outward hard and I cry out.

"We will fit, Gemma," he growls almost threateningly.

I'm a shaking, stunned mess when his mouth leaves my clit, when he pulls his fingers from my sex, when I feel him move away.

My hold on him loosens. I sag.

For a time, I give in. Even when his body shifts under my legs. I got what I needed, and all I want now is to come down from the sudden high at my own time.

I'm raw. My thoughts are scattered.

Vruksha rises over me, his tail slipping from where it's propped me up, I lay back on the crate, staring at him through hazy eyes. His hands wrap around my thighs, spreading me wide, and I muster a sated smile.

Pulsations from my orgasm continue, and it hits me... *It's been years.*

I haven't had a night alone since I was given this mission to go to Earth. They've all been sleepless with work.

Vruksha's dark eyes return to steal mine, nearly rabid, staring between my legs with such intensity my body goes rigid. My soul shivers. With his grip on me tightening, something hard presses between my legs.

I gasp as my eyes tear down to see his thick, alien cock pushing into my opening.

Spreading me wide. Much wider than his fingers.

"Wait!"

He pauses with a pained grunt. My lips part and I clench around him. He grunts again. The tip of his shaft is buried, and the rest of him remains poised to join it.

It's thick and red, but it's the thickened middle of his cock that tightens my stomach.

It's not going to fit. Not without discomfort. His cock is really big.

"Female..." Vruksha says, shaking.

Sweat beads his scaleless brow. Wrinkles cover his forehead as he bares his fangs. He licks one, and blood drips onto his lips.

I suck in, sitting back, pulling from his grip.

He doesn't let me go. He shifts with me, keeping his tip buried, like he may die if it slips out. Part of me wants to let him thrust into me, for me to push on to him, to feel the sensation of his bulge as it enters, but I can't...

Because I'm terrified.

Something snaps, and I grab his hands, pulling them off my legs. "I can't," I gasp, wiggling away.

This time, he lets me, pulling his cock's head out with

an anguished grunt. His small claws graze my skin, leaving red marks behind.

I push my legs together and pull them to my chest, wrapping my arms around them, hiding my chest. His gaze shifts to my face.

"You deny us? I am heated, and you deny us?"

I shake my head. "I don't know you," I whisper.

That's not the real problem... That's not why I'm afraid.

"Why?" he hisses, leaning back over me, lust burnishing his face. Lust and misery. His forked tongue licks at the blood on his lips, making me shiver.

"I'm...not ready."

His chest expands. "Have I not prepared you? Do you need my tail to stretch you? We will fit, little human, I will work your sheath until you take me comfortably."

I startle. My spine tingles from his words. The perversion of being penetrated by him, of him 'working me' in such a way isn't sending me running like it should.

Instead, I clench damnably. "I can't."

"Then I will prepare you some more," he declares, cupping my knees.

He spreads them.

"Stop! I mean I can't right now. Right now," my voice hitches as I push him off me again and move out from under him, standing. "I need to bathe first. I need to bathe," I say again, backing up. I don't want to make him angry by telling him the truth: that I'm scared. Of him, of what will happen.

Of what a creature like him could do to me.

And now, of all things, I think of his tail. I glimpse the tip and quickly turn away.

He follows me as I try to put distance between us. "A bath? You need a bath? If you think I am bothered by your arousal... I like you wet."

My eyes widen with embarrassment. I am wet, really wet. I feel my arousal trickling down my thighs.

I shake my head, searching for sanity.

As far as I know, there's no way to wash down in the bunker. There's no running water. He'll have to take me out of this hole for one. This is perfect. If it takes time to bathe, then—

"I will give you a bath, if that's what you need, if that's what will make this work."

My belly jumps. "How?" I reach for my clothes on the floor, trying not to think about the tail he's curling around my leg and the way it makes me tremble. "Where?"

"There is a creek."

"Okay," I say, before thinking more on it.

"Tonight."

"Tonight?"

"I will bathe you, and you will take my spill tonight."

The hunger returns to his face as he licks the rest of the blood off his lips. I watch as this large, serpentine male grabs his cock, squeezes the bulge in the middle, and pushes it back into the scales at his pelvic region. I blow out air in relief.

It doesn't last long.

My pulse, which was beginning to slow, thrums back to life. "Isn't it night right now?"

"Yes, female, it is."

Great. Just great.

I turn around and dress, feeling the burn of his black eyes fucking me, unable to get the image of his tail penetrating me out of my head. I've gained a couple of hours with my lame excuse… How am I going to survive another night? I can't sleep or pretend to sleep forever.

"And then I get to see the tech?" I say, far too absently for my liking. I press my palms to my eyes.

"Yesss."

At least I'm getting out of this hole. I can run again if I must.

He'll bring his spear...

"Okay," I breathe, scurrying to the bunker's exit when I finish putting on my boots.

His arm wraps around me and pulls me close, lifting me off the ground. I shriek, being pressed flush against his hard form.

He's never going to give me the chance to run.

THIRTEEN
A BATH

Vruksha

MY MATE CONFOUNDS me and is destroying everything I thought I knew about females—human females. The screens left much out.

The taste of her arousal is in my mouth and her warm, wet sheath wrapped around the tip of my member allows me to forgive the lies of the technology I've lived my life by. Perhaps every female is different, and that is why the screens didn't tell me the difficulties of getting one to submit.

The tension within me is growing worse by the day, but I won't let it rule me. I can't. Gemma is easily hurt.

I can wait a little longer.

"Let me down, Vruksha," she grumbles.

"The sun is setting. It is easier to carry you than allow you to stumble through the overgrowth now that it's getting dark."

"I can see well enough."

"We are almost there."

She startles. "Already? The creek is that close?"

I peer at her. Why does she sound surprised? She must be eager. I know she wants me. She let me touch her, let me explore her sex, even let me taste it. Is she not ready for more?

Her sex had been tight, incredibly so. It worries me, and I can't let that show. She needs a master, a male to nest her, care for her. If I am too big for her, how will she forgive me? I do not want her to hurt, for her to feel pain with our union. It's not going to be easy to sink inside her, but I will make it work. Three fingers may not be enough. Four, or all of them perhaps?

My tailtip will do the trick. If she can take my tail, she can take my member. First, she needs a bath, or so she says. And the water will be a great way to make her extra slick for passage...

I scan my surroundings, listening to the quiet rustle of leaves in the evening's breeze. The creek is not in the airfield. Though it's nearby and a place I have gone to daily since I first established my den.

Unfortunately, it's the only creek near here, which means roaming predators use it as well.

Including Zhallaix.

He will steal Gemma if he sees her, or worse. I am certain the only naga who knows I have a female is Azsote, and I want to keep it that way. I can handle Zhallaix—because of his proximity to my den, I know him better than any other naga—but it will be deadly if the others find out.

I will risk it though, to make Gemma happy. She will get her bath.

My mouth waters at the thought of seeing her wet.

I have been dreaming of her for so long. For years and

years, before I even saw Gemma, I've been dreaming of her and the life we will have. The loneliness she will make disappear.

I will feed her from my hands, gift her items I have foraged, and provide her every comfort. She enjoyed the bear pelt, and there are many more where that came from. I will introduce her to my nest when we return.

If she likes one bear pelt, she will like my nest. She will like all I have to give.

Tonight, she will be naked in my nest.

I don't know why I've become like this. A male obsessed. For years after my father died, I reveled in the fact that there were no females anymore. I celebrated that they were all gone and I would never have to come in contact with one, nor suffer one. I saw what my mother's death did to my father. It destroyed him. He explained to me when I was old enough that the male he was afterward was not the male he had been when she was alive.

He suffered guilt when he looked at me, but he still kept me close, teaching me of the dangers of this world. Of how unfortunate we are as a species, of how lonely it was because we are so few.

He gave me my spear, taught me how to use it, taught me how to find, repair, and take advantage of the technology across the land. He told me to stay away from the very facility the humans recently took over.

He said there were things in that building that weren't right. Things that could hurt us. He said that's where he found my spear. It was the last gift my father gave me.

It was the only tangible gift he ever gave me. And now, all I have are memories. Not even the orbs can show me his face...

The noise of rushing water pricks my ears. Gemma

shifts in my arms.

"Sssshh," I tell her.

"Is there something?" she whispers. "Do you hear something?"

"No, but I must check for predators." I keep my voice low as I set her on the ground. "I will be too distracted once we are in the water."

"We?"

"Wait here, Gemma. Do not leave this spot while I scout the area. I will be right back." I cup her face and force her to look at me. "I will know if you run." The shadows are heavy, but the moonlight is out. Even in darkness, she is beautiful. She is Gemma.

I wait for her to nod before I release her, slinging up into the branches above. I still suspect she will run when she has the chance, despite this, I am beginning to trust her judgment. She won't run in the dark.

I slip from tree to tree, searching for signs of recent activity or lingering animals, staying within hearing distance of my female and the water.

It is strange, patrolling like this.

Before the arrival of the humans, I never wanted the burden of a female or the companionship of another, knowing the cost it would demand of me.

Seeing Gemma and her red hair, I discovered how profoundly lonely I was... How large my nest was—and for no reason whatsoever. My world shifted that day at the facility, spun, and shook me to the pointless life I've been leading. Where other naga males journeyed to find the female nagas, I stayed in my forest. Where other males succumbed to madness or melancholy, I smiled, viciously devouring another meal.

All those smiles were fake.

I've been lying to myself for years... I know that now.

I'm not liking how Gemma's presence is making these feelings emerge.

I won't let what happened to my father happen to me. Or what happened to my mother happen to Gemma. I will keep her safe—at all costs—and happy whenever possible. This bath is dangerous, but my need for her is strong, and how can I deny her when she offers herself so willingly?

Once I have claimed her, then I can relax. When she is nestled in the shield of my tail, plump with spill and sleeping soundly, I can finally sleep. Weeks with little rest is wearing on me.

Finding the creek and area around it empty of predators, I return to my mate.

She is where I left her, staring up at the stars.

Sliding to her side, she turns her head at my arrival, though her gaze doesn't leave the sky. My eyes search for what she's looking at.

"Earth's moon is so bright," she says, her voice soft.

"Are there other moons?"

She makes a noise. "Yes. Many. Every colony has at least one, some have dozens, but none of the ones I've seen are as bright as this one."

My eyes slip to the pale column of her neck and the way her hair tumbles over her shoulders. Her red hair is the reason I know she belongs to me. We share the same color. She wears my color.

Only my female would have my coloring.

"I wonder what life would be like if the Lurkers had never come to Earth, if they'd left us alone and sailed on by, if we'd still be fighting the Ketts with everything we have... Still failing."

I don't know what she speaks of, what or who these

Ketts are, only that they are the reason Gemma is here on Earth. I rub my fingertips together. They're not her problem anymore. They're not here. I reach up and cup her neck, reminding her who is.

She tenses, her gaze dropping from the sky. I catch her in my arms and pull her close.

"Vruksha—" she starts.

"The area is safe," I interrupt, "for now. I do not wish to stay long. You are preciousss in these lands, and I can't risk losing you again."

She doesn't say anything more as I lift her in my arms and carry her to the creek's edge, to the deep, clear pool where I've often come to for hydration. I carry her into it.

She squirms. "I should undress first."

"I will undress you."

In the deepest area, I lower, enjoying the chill of the water gliding between my scales. Gemma's trying to get out of my hold again. I submerge us both, and she gasps.

"Cold, cold, cold," she squeaks. She pushes from my chest, slips out of my arms.

I catch her leg with my tail when she moves from me. I draw her back into my embrace. "I will warm you, little human."

She doesn't fight me, not like she has been. My member pulses, excited from the act of submission. Grabbing the edge of her jacket, I tug it off her shoulders.

"Vruksha, I don't think this is a good idea. Maybe we should go back and wait until morning if it's so dangerous."

"We are here now, and I can't wait any longer."

"But monsters?"

Didn't she hear me tell her it was safe? "Have you changed your mind? They're not here, and if they come, they will have to deal with me."

She shivers and raises her arms reluctantly, letting me take off her jacket. I toss it to the shore, reaching for her pants.

"I can do it," she says, pulling my fingers away from her.

I growl and put my fingers back. "I will be the one to undress you this time."

She drops all pretenses with a sigh. Excitement returns to me as she kicks off and wiggles out of her pants. I gather them and toss them next to her jacket.

How could I ever not have wanted this? Companionship? Quipping conversation? Pouty lips when they're not getting their way? My member has only ever known my hands sheathing it, and now it will know her. It's had a taste, and it's even hungrier than before.

Gemma curls her arms over her chest, where her remaining layers cling to her enticingly. She lowers into the water to hide.

I'm an idiot.

What's the point of living without a female to live for? To share my exploits with? To warm me during the coldest nights and fill my den with her soft voice?

To drive me mad with desire—and with jealousy.

She is so beautiful it hurts. Wet and shivering in the shadow of my body, where I can touch her at my leisure. Her hair is wet at the ends, and her chest rises and falls rapidly. Even in the darkness, I see her skin flush.

My shaft emerges from my tail.

I take her hands and pull her arms away from her chest.

She licks her sweet lips. I grasp the bottom of her shirt and tear it off her.

Now she's only in her underthings. Ridiculous clothes that shield her from me. Not for much longer...

I reach for her underwear. She slaps my hand away.

I reach for it again.

She slaps my hand again.

I hiss. "You can't bathe dressed."

"I can't bathe at all with you watching me like that."

My lips twist. "I will watch you as is my right as your mate."

"We're not mates."

Frustration fuels me as she turns away, lowering herself into the water, hiding from my eyes. Again. Pain bubbles up to join the frustration, but I push it away. Yet the thought niggles still. *She chose Azsote...*

Not me.

If she had, would she be naked in my nest this very moment? Because she chose *me*?

If I had let Azsote take her, would she be inviting his member into her right now? Would they have already rutted on the forest floor? In the very clearing in which he and I battled? The picture of them together enrages me, eats at my insides. I can't stand it.

I slide my tail around her, and she steps away from it.

I can't handle it and dive toward her, dragging her to me roughly, holding her wet body to my chest. Facing her away from me, her bottom slips across my member.

She makes a noise.

"You have accepted me," I remind her. "You spread your legs and cried out as I penetrated you with not one but three of my fingers." I slide one hand down her body to cup her sex hard. "You thrashed and cried and grabbed my head as my lips framed your nub, rubbing your sex into my face, or have you already forgotten? It was not Azsote working on your tight sheath to accommodate him," I growl.

I push her wet underwear to the side and find her hole, caressing it.

She writhes against me. "I need to bathe—"

"I know an excuse when I hear one."

My fingers push inside her. Gemma bows over my arm as she takes them. She's drenched, wet from the brook, and slick from her arousal. Beyond heated with her readiness to be claimed.

She is mine.

Mine.

I am undone.

My tail curls up her body, trapping her completely. My fingers find the rough spot in her sheath and rub it. *She liked this last time.*

"Vruksha!" she screeches my name and then gasps. And if she wasn't thrashing before, she's thrashing now. I rub harder, quickening my movements, sending her into a frenzy, enjoying the way her body shudders against mine.

She gasps again. Her little noises excite me.

Human legs are wonderful. She is soft and receptive, and her sex is never fully hidden. I can just spread her thighs to find it... I arch my member against her, sliding it through the curve of her butt as I roll my fingers inside her.

"Female," I groan, spreading them. "It is time." I decide I do not want to wait until she's in my nest.

She cries out and jerks in my arms. A wail releases from her lips, and her sex constricts around my fingers. She's cumming. She's releasing pent up tension because of me.

Only I will ever get the glory of seeing her succumb.

Not Azsote, not any other. *Me.*

Pleased, a grin pulls at my lips. "Yes, female. Like that. Like that. Yesss."

Her sheath clutches me, and I know it's time. Her legs buckle, and I slip my tail forward between her legs so she may squirm on it as well. I want her everywhere. If it's not her tongue, then it will be her sex dewing up my many scales. I bend her over further, holding her to me as her shaking subsides, until she's on her hands and knees in the shallow part of the creek, bowed over my lower tail. Her body is partially wrapped around it, facing away from me, just like how her sex will soon be wrapped around my member.

Rearing up behind her, I slip my fingers out of her channel, and after one last rub of her wrinkled spot, after one last pleasured, shocked cry tears from her mouth, I line my member to her opening.

"Vruksha," she moans my name, sounding almost defeated. And I pause, but then she lies her head forward, resting it on my tail as she pushes her butt outward. My tip sinks into her.

Tight, hot, soft. Pleasure blasts through me, and I take a moment to gaze down at her back.

Gemma, submitting to me. Waiting weeks of hell for this was worth it. Her hair is wet, plastered to her back, falling forward into the water. Her sex is open, ready for invasion, and clenching in the moonlight. It's tight, spread around my tip, and I push forward. I press my tail to support her chest and body. She wraps her arms around it.

She moans, straining. I watch as I sink deeper, pushing against flesh that fights me but quickly relents.

"Tight," I grit out, cupping her cheeks and spreading her as wide as I can. Will she be able to take my knot? It is softer than the stem of my shaft. I have worked it so it's not so big.

I press forward until her hole is up against it. It's twice the size of her opening, and doubt fills me. My bulge is not as hard...

Part of me wants to pause, to use my hand to expel

some of my spill, and make things easier, but I don't. She's perfect where she is. If I stop, I'm afraid she might not let me mount her in such a way again.

"This will not be easy for you," I warn. "You will take it, and I will soothe you. I promise this. The world is yours."

"Vruksha," she moans my name.

I push inside her, not waiting for another response. It is better this way. I force her to take my knot, shunting forward. Immediately the tight pressure makes me spill. My throat closes around a guttural rasp from the pleasure it brings me.

"It's too much," she gasps, straining, buckling, and shuddering. She shimmies forward, and I force her back, arching my tail upward. "Oh, god!" she cries.

I pet her back, pulling out of her, untrapping my bulge. "Again." I thrust back in.

She moans with a hitch, grabbing me closer. She brings my bulge halfway in.

I pull out once more and thrust harder this time, pushing through the tight flesh that continues to fight me.

"Vruksha!" she screams as she takes the entirety of my member.

My mind blanks when I'm seated.

It is bliss. *And hell.* The way she squeezes me, the way I barely fit. The way her channel contracts and every movement her body makes, every sway... My shaft feels it all.

"Female," I grate, gazing where our bodies are joined. Drool slips from my mouth, so crazed am I with the need to move and thrust.

Tense and trembling, nails biting the scales of my tail, she whimpers, "Too much, too big!"

I run my hand over her spine, comforting her. "It will get better," I purr.

I grit my teeth and pull my bulge out from her, spilling even more as I do.

She slumps heavily. "Thank you. I don't think we—"

I line my shaft back up and thrust back in.

She stills with a shocked scream. "What are you doing!?"

"Easing you." This time there was no fight to my invasion. Her channel constricts.

I do it again before her body can try and reject me. The fourth time, a roar tears from my mouth and joins her whimpering. She's wet and tight and slicker than before, easing her was the right thing to do. Coupling with a human isn't straightforward, not from what I've seen of men taking human females on the screens in my den. I know how much larger and stranger I am compared to them.

But she's accepted me and I will worship her for it.

Lifting her until her back is to my chest, I wrap my arms around her body.

Gemma hitches but doesn't say a word as I start jerking my hips, pounding into her from behind. I twist, rising on my tail and then back down as madness takes over my mind, addicted to the sting of her tight sheath.

It grows with each pump, with each moan. My spill surges forward, flooding my bulge to the brink of pain. I speed up. Gemma shakes, grabbing me as I sway and move her body around, lost in the feel of her upon me. I free her breasts and cup them.

They are soft and sweet. Her tight nipples press into my palms.

Slapping my tail on the water, she slumps in my arms as I thrust harder. Her moans grow wilder. Her sex tightens for a third time this night, for *me*.

Such a sweet mate she is.

I spill. I spill all of the deep seed stored inside me.

Stars blast my vision as it jets into her. I snap like a rabid animal in heat, needing her to take it all. There is so much, and my body is only producing more. The way her channel milks me, and her soft moans are music in the night, I know she wants it, needs my spill just as much as I need to give it to her.

Even though she won't say it.

Holding her in the air onto me, I empty into her womb. Her body weakens from the effort. I lay her on my lap, settling into the water, and move us back into the deeper end, sure to remain inside her the whole time. I don't want to leave her, not now that I've claimed her. She may not let me back in.

For a time, she rests against me, with only our ragged breaths sounding between us.

Satisfaction rules me. Satiation. My jealousy vanishes, frightened away by Gemma's acceptance of my seed.

I curl around her, tangling my tail with her limbs, and hold her close. Spill pumps into her now and then as my loins produce more. They are sated, I am sated—and obsessed.

Yet my body only continues to make more, and her sheath quivers each time my bulge grows large inside her, stretching her back out.

No wonder my father mourned my mother. No wonder males search endlessly for the lost naga females.

It's perfection, mating. Contentment settles deep into my bones. I rest my chin on Gemma's head and close my eyes.

Sleep finds me swiftly.

FOURTEEN
DEATH IN THE SHADOWS

Gemma

BONE TIRED, I stare into the shadows of the forest at the edge of the creek. I dozed for a little while, surprisingly. I was even more surprised when I woke to find Vruksha sleeping as well, his chin resting on my head.

I don't move. The slow dance of the water across my skin feels nice. It washes away the sweat, the dirt, the sex...

The sex. I suck my lips into my mouth.

I knot up. *He's still buried deep inside me.* Vruksha groans, shifts, and I relax, not wanting to wake him. Especially in that way. He might want a round two, and I don't know if I can do that.

I ache. A lot. I throb.

He took me mercilessly. I will feel him for days, if not longer. He saw through my stupid excuses.

The cold water dulls my discomfort immensely though, but his bulge remains inside, and I'm almost afraid to move because it *will* move, and whether it's pushed further in or comes out, I'm twitchy about it. I gingerly reach down between us and massage the skin of my sex stretched around Vruksha's prick, soothing the ache. I tweak my clit afterward for a little pleasure.

It dawns on me that he won, he was right, that I submitted. Three days. It only took three days. *And I wanted it.*

This isn't like me.

But his scent is so delicious...

There's nothing in this universe that could've prepared me for this, for Vruksha. Or an alien at all—since no alien we have met can join with humans.

Lifting my head out from under his chin, I look at him. The moonlight shines brightly over his features.

Not an alien. *A naga.*

His eyes are closed, his sharp lips slightly parted. His breath is warm and fans my cheek. His chest moves with each shallow inhale. He doesn't look nearly as frightening when asleep. I reach my hand up from where it lingered between my legs and caress his cheek, touching the smooth scales there. His head slumps forward.

My heart warms...

I jerk my hand away.

I'm not staying. Not for a moment longer than is necessary. Once I have access to the tech he has, I'll need to make a run for it back to base. I have to. I need to find Daisy.

I can't grow attached to him. If I do, it'll be hard to leave.

He wanted me so badly...

He nearly killed for me.

The warmth in my chest expands.

I'm an idiot for letting him have my body. I groan, pulling back a little more. His hold on me tightens, and I press my hand to my chest, hating the warmth growing within.

I've never given into the protection of another, not since I left my parents to finish my training on *The Dreadnaut* at age thirteen, as dutiful humans to the war effort commonly do. That was almost twenty years...

I wanted to dislike him, but I don't. He makes me feel things I would rather keep buried. In the short time we've been together, he's seen me at my worst, and not once at my best.

Yet he looks at me like I hang the triple suns of Elyria.

No one's ever looked at me the way Vruksha does. It bothers me. I've never needed protection before, and I do now, and it scares me horribly. I want his protection. I think I like his adamance.

Shuddering, I inhale quietly. I force Vruksha from my thoughts, ignoring the warmth in my chest that's growing ever more when I think of him.

I don't need anyone's protection.

I've been gone for three days. Someone from command has to be asking about me, someone has to be wondering what happened to Daisy and me. Peters could tell *The Dreadnaut* we died, but then they'll demand an investigation—hopefully—and insist our bodies be brought aboard the main ship for burial rites.

My gut churns. I don't have family aboard the main ship. Daisy might though.

And if *The Dreadnaut* investigates our disappearance, what would they do to Vruksha and the other nagas if they come down? If the military lands? Will they hurt them? Want to study them?

I shake my head. That'll never happen.

They might send a few fighters but the military deploys for one thing and one thing only: Ketts.

I can't stop the thought from taking root. Earth isn't some random planet in the universe. It's our homeworld. Sentient creatures here wouldn't have the protection they do elsewhere. They'd be seen as invaders to be analyzed and, if need be, disposed of.

I stare hard at Vruksha's peaceful face.

He knows much—far more than makes sense—but he doesn't know humans. As someone entrenched in the constantly shifting ethics of a desperate government, and a bloodthirsty military made up of men and women seeking revenge. He doesn't deserve to be thrust into that world and all it demands.

Will he follow me into the stars if I leave?

I chew on my lip.

A twig snaps and my eyes shoot to the forest. Thick shadows and wild branches meet my gaze. They twist and dance in every direction, thickening the shadows. I peer into them, searching for the source of the noise.

Vruksha's soft breaths breeze across my neck. I listen for a while, letting them comfort me.

When I start to look away, certain there's nothing in the shadows, something behind the branches shifts. A massive coiled shadow rises into the heavier foliage above.

A face appears in the darkness and my throat constricts with terror.

It's a face that only has one eye because the other has been knifed out.

The Death Adder.

"Vruksha, get up!" I jerk out of his arms. His cock tears out of me, and I flinch from the pain.

Vruksha thrusts me behind him, and I fall into the

chilly water. Recovering quickly, I scurry to the opposite shore. I force the water from my eyes and find him facing the Death Adder.

"Zhallaix," he hisses.

Vruksha's tail strikes out, snatching his spear from the creek's edge and bringing it to his hand.

"Vruksha," the other naga says, his voice a sharp whisper of warning. My skin rises from the sound. It's rough, guttural. Broken. "What do you have there?" The naga tries to get a look at me.

I reach for my clothes when his head snaps to the side. I jerk my hands back to cover me, bringing my clothes to my chest. It's not fast enough.

His eyes widen and dance across my body, purple in the moonlight.

The next thing I know, Vruksha tackles him to the water, thrashing his tail. I shriek and fall back, taking my clothes with me. A tail rises into the air to bash at the other pinning it below the water. Water sprays everywhere, making it difficult to see, but I spot Vruksha's spear come down again and again.

He doesn't see the tail that's about to strike him from behind.

I scream his name. The tail strikes.

"Run!" he shouts in pain. The word dies in his mouth as his body drops to the side with a splash.

The Death Adder shoots upright and turns to me.

I spin and run.

Pain shoots through me as my feet catch on everything, stabbing my soles. Sticks, twigs, and leaves whip my skin and tangle in my hair. Shouts follow me for a long time, echoing through the trees.

I don't stop. Not when my lungs are about to collapse,

or when a particularly sharp branch slashes my side. The fervor returns, and I'm back in time, flashing back to three days before when I was terrified I'd be caught by a frightening alien male.

I don't stop when the night lifts and the moon lowers, when the first rays of the sun streak through the trees. And when I'm about to topple, stumbling from one tree to the next, I see a familiar sight.

The broken shelter Vruksha took me to the first night.

I drag my body to it, fall on my knees with a sob, and crawl inside.

I curl up into a ball and cry.

FIFTEEN
SURVIVE

Gemma

TIME BLURS, my sense of it vanishing with my control. I don't leave the shelter for a day, maybe more, drifting in and out of sleep, praying for a time that death will come while I'm unconscious. It doesn't, and each time I wake, I'm weaker, and still alone. My terror sticks. My body hurts.

I keep hoping I'll wake from this nightmare.

I moan and rub my eyes. I can't sleep anymore, and I curse everything. I even curse my stubbornness and self-discipline for refusing to die. Rising onto my arms, I peer through the shelter to make sure the forest is clear outside.

I wish it wasn't. *I wish...* I shake my head with a frown. Vruksha isn't here.

I need food, water.

I'm easy prey for any predator right now. I have been this whole time but just didn't have the strength to do anything about it.

I'm covered in cuts, some worse than others, and my feet...

When the forest remains clear, I shudder and push open the broken door and slide out, my body protesting. I try to stand but fall, sobbing in pain. I curl up on the ground, grabbing my bloody feet.

I want to survive—I need to survive—I can't be selfish. I'm not allowed to be selfish. I strain. My wounds are too much though. I find my bundle of clothes I've been gripping to me since my collapse and tug them on.

The cloth chafes my skin and I cry out again.

Vruksha fought for me. He fought, and I watched him fall. And I ran.

I let my tears fall as I wish for death to find me anyway.

It does, but only in my head. The Death Adder's broken face rises there, and I shiver. I don't know how I got away from him, though I'm certain it was because of Vruksha, and now I owe it to him to survive.

I prayed he'd come and find me, that when I fell into a fitful sleep, he'd be there when I woke. Except he wasn't, and I can't wait any longer, hoping he'll come. My heart is heavy. I still feel him inside me and it hurts.

His seed is still trickling out of me. It hasn't dried. I grab a leaf from the forest floor and wipe it from my skin, bringing it to my nose to sniff it. His scent makes me clench despite everything. I toss the leaf aside when I'm done, lifting my head. Even naga seed is alien to me.

I hope he's okay.

My boots are long gone, left somewhere by a creek far from here. I wouldn't be able to put them on anyway... My jacket's not here either. Nor do I have underwear or a bra. When I'm dressed with what I have left, I rest my brow on the ground.

You need to move.

I push up onto my arms, pick a direction, and begin crawling. Glancing behind me to memorize my surroundings, I leave the shelter behind. I hope I'll be able to find it again but am not expecting it. I was damn lucky to find the shelter in the first place, and that little bit of luck has given me hope.

I have a sense of where I am because of it. I don't know which direction the facility is or Vruksha's bunker, but I'm at least a half day from either.

I can survive a half day of travel. I just need food, water, and rest first.

I amble forward aimlessly, snapping upon twigs as I move, leaving an obvious trail of my passing. For a time, all I hear is the rustle of plants as I brush past them and the chirping of Earth's birds above me. Resting now and then, I listen to the noises of the forest, knowing they'll help me.

They're not the noises of a spaceship.

Burying my head in my hands, I groan.

I don't have a pocket knife, don't have shoes... I don't have anything except the clothes on my back. I've never trained for this in the academy. Survival on an alien planet wasn't a skill I ever thought I'd need.

I drop my hands.

I roll onto my knees and continue.

I hear a splash. Stilling, I stop breathing. I've found water! The splashes don't stop, and I brace for whatever is beyond my sight, begging the Gods that it's not a naga. I grab a nearby stick and curl my fingers around it.

As quietly as I can, I crawl toward the noise.

A giant lake appears through the bushes. My mouth drops as beautiful blue water spans outward before me, and across the lake are giant snow-capped mountains rising high.

Earth is beautiful.

I don't stare for long, searching for the source of the *splashing*.

There. Below me, a small feline-like creature pounces on fish swimming through the rocks on the shore. It's red, has a pointed nose and a bushy tail. It's cute. The creature snatches the fish between its claws and wrestles it to shore, biting into it.

I lick my lips.

Grabbing my stick, I call out, startling the feline. It flees when it sees me, leaving the fish behind.

I stumble to the bank, falling next to it. There's a bite taken out of the fish's side, and there's blood, but I'm starving.

Clutching it between my hands, I snap the fish's body to finish the kill and lift it to my mouth. Sinking my teeth in, I will my bile to remain in my belly. I leave nothing but bones and the head behind when I'm done. Stomach churning though full, I drag myself to the lake's edge.

I gulp down so much water that when I'm done, the taste of the fish is rinsed from my mouth, and I'm so bloated I can barely move. I lie in the shallow water, letting it wash away the grime. I stare up at the sky.

Wisps of white clouds slowly drift by, too thin to block out the sun's rays. For a while, it feels nice. As the minutes tick by, my skin heats.

I picture Vruksha's sleeping face and my heart twists.

He can't be dead...

I need to go back and find him. I don't know how I'm going to do that, but I have to try.

Rising on my elbows, I peer about. The shore is vacant

of animals, though there's something large on the far side, across the lake. I can't make it out fully, only that it has antlers.

Water brings predators.

With that in mind, I wash my body, my wounds, and the dirt and dried blood off me. I scrub my hair and between my legs. I stay until my fingertips are wrinkled and the sun dips, watching for predators the entire time.

Finding the fish head and my clothes to dress, I retrace my path, climbing onto my ruined feet. Dusk shadows the forest by the time I find the shelter. I crawl inside and curl up into a ball on the back seat.

Vruksha's face reappears when I close my eyes. This time his gaze is wicked and hungry. My heart thumps. I debate climbing out and finding the leaf I cleaned his seed off with earlier so I can get another sniff of his scent.

"Vruksha?" I whisper.

He doesn't answer me, though something else does. A fuzzy crackle fills my ears.

I sit up.

Looking deeper into the shelter, a tiny light winks at me through the shadows. The crackling is coming from it. I push through the vines and overgrowth falling from above to see what it is when the light winks out. Rooting for it with my hand, my fingers curl over something round.

An orb.

I clutch it to my chest and clean the dirt off it, thrilled at my luck today.

"Orb, initiate," I say, my voice fracturing.

The lights wink back to life. A wheezy voice from the orb answers me, but I can barely make the words out. It quickly dies.

"Orb, initiate," I say again.

One crackle is all I get. It's dead. Frustrated, I throw the orb out of the shelter. I hear it thump, and then I don't hear it at all. Curling back onto my side, I close my eyes.

Sleep finds me for a time. I dream of my apartment back on *The Dreadnaut,* the paints that I bought last year, and how I never got a chance to use them.

I awake to another noise. This time, it's definitely not of the electronic variety. It's snorting. Something hits the side of my shelter, and the flimsy frame makes a terrible crunching sound at my feet. I tug my legs to my chest and clutch them, burying my face into my knees.

Pigs.

Fear takes hold.

More snorting breaks the night.

I relax a little. There's nothing to fear from pigs. One nudges my shelter behind me, and the whole thing rocks. The orb from Vruksha's bunker listed pigs as predators. I remember the large pack of them, and how gigantic they were.

My shelter shakes again as another one nudges it. Dirt falls on me. I hold my breath and stay as still as possible, hoping they don't discover me and will eventually move along.

Based on the cacophony of snorts, there has to be a dozen or so outside. Or more...

If they find me, and they are predators, I'm dead. I'm too weak to run.

I bring my hands to my lips, close my eyes, and go back to praying.

Morning brightens the forest before they finally leave.

Exhausted and numb, I wait before I risk moving. After checking that they're gone, I crawl back out of my shelter, fear twisting my gut, and I can't tell if I'm hungry or nauseous, or both. Turning back, the shelter is broken, punctured, and has shifted a couple of feet.

I can't stay here.

I was waiting for Vruksha... but he hasn't come. I have to believe he's still alive. I don't think I can live with the guilt if I caused his death. My heart aches, and I reach up to rub the feeling from my chest.

First Daisy, and now Vruksha.

Carefully, I rise on my wounded feet.

The pigs stamped out much of the overgrowth during the night, and I can't immediately figure out which direction they went. My trail to the lake is gone, and though I desperately want to go and fill up with water, I also know the pigs likely moved toward it for the same reason.

I wish Vruksha was here.

Shaking my head, I banish the thought. I can't rely on him anymore, it's up to me now. How things change so quickly.

Turning full circle, I wish for something—anything—to guide me, to lead me to Vruksha's bunker or the facility. I eye the trees, hoping one will be easy to climb, but they're tall and the branches are higher up. There is nothing.

Picking up a nearby stick to use for a crutch, I decide to follow the direction of the sun. It's as good a direction as any. I don't take more than a couple of steps when my foot rams into something hard.

Flinching, I sink my teeth into my lips.

My eyes land on the orb.

I pick it up.

"Orb, initiate," I whisper.

Under the streaming sunlight above, it comes to life, rising from my hand to hover in the air.

"What can I help you with today?" it says.

My eyes widen.
I remember how to smile.

SIXTEEN
CONSEQUENCES

Vruksha

SUNLIGHT STREAMS through the pines of the forest to greet me. I groan, staring at it.

"You're awake."

My gaze cuts to Zhallaix sharpening a knife across from me. I struggle to strike him with my tail, quickly finding I can't move. I'm bound. Ropes have been tied around my wrists, pulling them apart and anchoring me to the tree at my back.

"Gemma," I hiss. "Where's Gemma?"

Zhallaix puts his weapon away, hooking it with the bones he wears on his bicep. "Don't try and move."

"What have you done to my female?" I struggle against my bonds, searching the forest for Gemma.

"Ssshe ran."

I wheeze out a breath. Relief and horror hit me hard. "She's not in your clutches," I rasp. But she's also not here, which means she's alone, in the forest, completely at the mercy of the wilds and beasts that roam it.

Zhallaix hums, unconcerned.

"Let me go," I urge, nearly shaking.

Zhallaix cocks his head. His one eye hoods as he watches me.

"I need to go after her."

"She did not have a tail," Zhallaix responds.

"Of course she didn't!" I hiss. "Releassse me!"

"Where did she come from?"

I snarl. "I don't have time for this. She's not safe alone in the forest. She does not have claws, fangs, or venom to protect herself." She does not have me!

"Humans are extinct, and a naga female hasn't roamed these lands in over a hundred years. How is it possible you have one at all? What is she? A robot?"

I stop fighting my bonds when it occurs to me that Zhallaix does not know about the humans at the facility or the ship that descended from the sky. How humans came out of it took over the old ruins—that there were females amongst those who landed.

He has no idea about Zaku's deal to trade technology for their females. He doesn't know.

Zhallaix destroys all tech he comes across.

I stop struggling as an idea forms. "I'll tell you if you let me go."

"Or I can leave you tied up and find her myself."

"You could... or you could have one for your own, one who isn't already claimed and filled with spill," I growl.

Zhallaix crosses his arms, and I know I have him. The threaded muscles of his arms bulge, stretching white and red scars. Some of those are scars I've given him. There's a gouge on his side, half-strung up with plant fibers to keep it closed. Blood gushes from it. I did that.

I have a few open wounds too, but Zhallaix didn't string mine up.

Why would he? He'd prefer me dead.

So why am I not?

"Where did she come from?" he asks again.

"She may be the only one," I lie. "Or not."

Zhallaix glares at me and reaches behind him. He brings my spear forward.

I release venom at the sight of it. Zhallaix is not only putting Gemma's life in danger but also has my spear? Anger floods me seeing his hand wrapped around the shaft.

I hiss as he nears, bracing for whatever is to come. He stabs down on my tail.

I shout in pain as it pierces deep into my muscle. He digs it in before sliding the sharp tip out. I thrash to free my arms, making no progress. I slump with a grimace when my bonds hold. My blood pools around me as he lifts my spear to stab my tail again.

"Tell me," he rumbles.

"Release me."

Zhallaix stabs and twists.

I grit my teeth, holding in an agonized groan when the tip hits my tail's spine. Sweat pools down my face, agony radiates up my tail and runs straight through my whole body.

He yanks the spear back out. "Should we keep going?"

I scowl, spit.

"I don't want to hurt you anymore, Vruksha," he says, calm as ever, as if he isn't torturing me for information. "But what you did was unforgivable..."

"What I did? I don't know what you're talking about," I sneer.

Zhallaix lowers until he's level with me. Hatred burns for him and the situation he's put my female in. Hatred that he still roams these lands despite the numerous attempts to take his life.

But it's the same situation *I* put my female in for taking her out at night. For falling asleep...

Zhallaix continues, "Mating a female kills them. They do not survive gestation. Only a wretch would satisfy his cravings knowing the outcome. Tell me where you found her."

"Humans are not nagas."

"Have you mated a human female before?"

My nostrils flare. "Of course not. None of us have."

"Then how could you know?"

"And you do? I know what you've done, what you are. I know what your father did, raping female nagasss for his pleasure. I'm nothing like him. None of us are—only you."

His hand goes white where it's clutching my weapon.

"He taught you everything he knew," I continue, "didn't he? He brought you along as he single-handedly—"

"Enough!"

"—bred unwilling females across the region, even those not Death Adders, killing them—"

"Enough!" Zhallaix raises my spear and surges forward, aiming the tip at my groin. "I am not my father!" He slashes down.

I twist to the side, narrowly missing the spear's edge. Zhallaix jerks from the impact, and I'm finally given my opportunity. I spit venom into his eye.

He roars, rearing backward, dropping my weapon. He clutches his eye. He slithers away, shrieking as he hits a tree, sending branches flailing. I shimmy the wound on my tail toward my bound hands, drenching them with blood.

With the ties wet, I fight my way out of them.

One of the ties snaps, releasing my arm. I claw through the rest of the binds. When I free my limbs, I grab my spear and use it to help me rise.

Zhallaix thrusts his tail out to keep me back, unable to see me.

"I ssshould kill you," I growl, leaning over him.

One black and red eye peers wetly at me through strained fingers. "Do it!" he says.

I lift my spear over him.

"Do it!" he screams.

I stab him in the gut and twist. Blood gushes, as I yank it out.

Zhallaix drops his hand from his eye, hisses, and slumps. He doesn't move again but continues to watch me through his ruined eye. Slowly, the color fades from his scales, and his eye closes.

I stare at him for a short time, making sure he stays down. I take no pleasure killing one of my own, even though I have before and know I will again.

"You should have killed me when you had the chance," I say, lowering my spear.

I flick my spear clean of blood and take to the trees, not giving Zhallaix another thought.

The creek is nearby. I hear it rather than see it, and from my viewpoint, I notice nothing out of the ordinary, nothing that will help me find Gemma. I need to find her. I don't know how long I've been out, only that it's dusk now, which means many hours have passed since Zhallaix's attack. If not days.

I rush to the water, hoping there'll be a trail, wincing

from the pain of my wounds.

I follow the creek north until I'm at the place I was last with Gemma. I see her boots. Grabbing them, bringing them to my face, I inhale her scent.

She's out in the forest alone, without me, the male who vowed to protect her. She doesn't know how to defend herself; she knows little about my world. There's so much more than animals and monsters...

I battle against the pain in my tail that threatens to slow me, slipping it in the water to wash the blood off as I frantically search for her trail.

Sticks are broken, leaves crushed on the ground. Someone hit the overgrowth hard, head-on.

It had to be Gemma. Imagining her fear as she fled infuriates me. She took to the dangerous forest in the darkness without a plan. My claws dig into the material of her boots, leaving the creek behind.

As I track her, I fear I'm going to stumble upon her broken form and a madness takes hold of my mind. But as the hours go by and the moon rises, I never do. She ran for hours...

Was she running from me as well? My tail coils, shooting spikes of pain up my spine at the thought. I refuse to believe it.

The moon ascends and deep shadows blanket the forest so thickly I lose the tracks.

My anger and helplessness coalesce into a roar. "*Gemma!*" I roar her name.

I'm answered with silence.

I stab my spear into the ground and gather wood to make a fire. If she's nearby, she'll see the light and will come. It gives me something to do while I wait for the sun to return, and the flames keep my mania at bay.

The night lasts an agonizing eternity. I do not sleep. Not with my female out of my reach and not knowing where she is.

Dawn has not yet risen when I take back to her trail. I lose it several more times throughout the morning because her tracks have begun fading. Backtracking and finding where it picks up, makes me lose precious time. The sun is past its zenith, the heat sweltering, when I'm plowing forward again.

I shout her name.

And again, rage takes hold at her loss. For losing her, and worse, for not being prepared to take on a human female like I thought I had been. I should have known better.

Why did I take her out at night when I could have taken her to my nest?

I could have her coiled up in my tail right now if I had.

Something blue appears in the distance, and I move toward it. Her jacket. I grip the material tightly to my chest. It's torn and dirty and yet, still in good shape.

A sign.

My hope returns.

The landscape changes, sloping downward, and her trail picks back up for a while. She slowed here. I have to lower to the forest floor to find her passage. Moving from tree to tree, I see dried blood upon the leaves. Though as I do, I see something else, something far worse...

Pig tracks.

Dozens of them. Hoofprints everywhere, pig shit amongst them. The smell of their passage makes the forest reek.

My heart plummets knowing they caught her scent and that I will lose Gemma's trail completely amongst the pigs'.

My fingers clench. She has to be close. Tearing my eyes off the forest floor, I look up to see where I am. I know this area, I realize. I've traveled through here countless times. Pig tracks or no, if she's here, I'll be able to find her.

Unless the pigs have gotten to her first... If they had, there'll be nothing but blood where they caught her. They eat everything.

I'll kill every last pig in the land if she's met such a fate.

The sun hits the horizon far too soon, and the diminishing strength of my tail begins to impede me. Blood still gushes from my wounds, making me sluggish. I keep going.

When I hear the pigs, I slip up into the trees and find a mid-size pack of swine in the distance.

One raises his head and sniffs loudly. He smells fresher blood now that I've arrived.

I streak my short claws over the wounds of my tail and give them more of it. Pain soars through my nerves, and I grit my teeth. If the pigs come after me, I can lead them away and kill them off one by one. Within minutes, there's a pack of swine beneath my branch, swarming over each other to reach me.

Lying flat on the branch, I position my spear and, gripping the handle tight, stab at the one nearest me. My speartip sinks deep into fatty flesh. The pig squeals, startling the others to do the same. I wrench my arm back and stab again. I hit another pig.

The pigs flail and scream, blocking out all other sounds. They frenzy, and some run off, the smart ones. Most remain because there's a meal to be had. I brace and stab again.

Soon, they're no longer after my blood, but their own. Snorting and snuffing, they turn on each other, too dumb to move away from the spear poking them from above. Blood fills the air.

Something catches my spear and yanks it from my grip. I recatch it moments later as one of the pigs jumps after me instead of his brethren. Glimpsing down, I find two large, intelligent eyes gazing up at me with hatred. I spit venom at the leader, and he shakes it off.

The others around him begin to notice that I'm still above; they see me now that their bellies are full of their friends.

It's time to go.

I coil and lift off the branch, slipping to the next tree over. The large pig follows me, while several others follow him. If I don't lose them, they'll chase after me until either I'm dead or they are. And from the look the big one is giving me, he wants my hide.

As long as it's me and not Gemma.

I lead the pack out of the area, killing as I go, stabbing through the night until morning breaks through the trees.

I need to find Gemma, and soon.

I push off the trunk of the tree I'm on and silently move back to the place I was when I found the pigs the night before. The place where I last had Gemma's trail.

In the dawn's light, I see nothing except half-eaten corpses and blood. The bushes, branches, and plants were decimated in the feeding frenzy. If there was a trail before, it's gone now.

I bite out a curse.

Something swishes past my head. I catch sight of it just before it vanishes into the forest. It's rusted, dirty, and broken, but I know what it is.

A drone.

Excitement rips through me.

My exhaustion disappears as I take off after it. Someone initiated drones...

Gemma.

SEVENTEEN
DANGER ON EVERY LEDGE

Gemma

I RUN my arm over my brow, wiping the sweat gathered there, and push forward. I've been running for hours, trying to get away from the sounds of the pigs behind me.

Soon after I found the orb, I heard them again.

They're getting closer. My pulse quickens as the sun crests.

They never left.

I catch hold of a branch, curling my bleeding toes into the dried leaves. I stumble to the next tree.

Ahead of me is a ledge, and I make a faltering sprint for it. Through the trees, I see the slope of the mountain I'm heading toward.

The landscape has become increasingly rockier and hillier. I didn't get lucky, I failed to pick the direction toward Vruksha's bunker. I curse continuously. I don't know how I ever thought I was going to find alien tech and run it back to my people.

I didn't know what I was truly in for. I was stupid to think it was a good plan, even with Vruksha's spear for protection.

God, I'm an idiot.

I reach the ledge as a snort sounds behind me and pull my body up, barely managing to get off the ground when something snaps at my foot. Jerking my limbs into my body, I twist back.

Behind me is the largest, angriest-looking hog I've ever seen. Three times my size, the hog could eat me whole. I hold in a scream as it claws and tries to climb the ledge, snapping and snorting in a frenzy.

I take my stick and jab its head.

My stick breaks.

"Fuck," I gasp, pulling my half toward me. I stare at the broken tip. Movement catches my eye. Two more pigs run out of the trees joining the first. They barrel into the ledge.

I recoil, turning around to find an escape. The slope is steep but rocky, and I can climb the boulders leading up the mountainside. That'll lose the pigs. *I hope.* I shiver and massage my aching hands, examining the jagged edges, deciding on the best route.

I try not to think about how tired I am, nor how I'll probably fall to my death. My gut cramps. I can't do much climbing, I won't be able to lift my body in the state I'm in.

I wish I was facing several horny naga males over this. *Anything* over this. The pigs I know are nothing like the mindless, brutal animals clawing at the ledge.

"Fuck," I whisper, breathing the word out between my teeth, tossing my broken stick to the side.

There are now five pigs at the ledge when I glance back. One's climbing on the back of another. I struggle to my feet and take to the slope.

Slipping, my clothes tear, while sharp rocks abrade my skin. My bleeding feet stain the rocks. My hands are raw, and my world spins. I cry and pray and beg. I'm hungry, thirsty, low on energy, and I don't have much fight left in me.

But pigs?

I'm not letting pigs be my end. I fight my way higher and higher until I fall face-first onto a ledge toward the top, collapsing. I still hear their snorting below me. There's more now. I roll over and stare at the sky, panting.

Even if I get to the top, what do I do next? My eyes catch the orb still hovering beside me. To my disappointment, it has spent more time 'updating' than answering my questions. At least it followed me.

"Orb," I rasp. It blurs as my vision wavers.

"What can I do for you?" it asks.

"Where is the..." I don't know what to ask to get the information I need.

"I don't understand. Please repeat."

"What predators are around me?" I finally say, repeating the question Vruksha asked in his bunker, all while trying to solidify a cohesive thought in my head.

The orb lights up and my eyes shift back to the sky. I don't expect it to give me any sort of answer.

So when it does answer, I'm stunned.

"Scanning complete. There are several packs of pigs scattered around this region, two families of bears, and three snakes."

I push up on my elbows. I smack my lips, swallowing even though my mouth is dry. "How do you know that?"

It doesn't answer.

"Orb, how do you know what's nearby?"

"I am connected to three major relays in this zone.

Additionally, there are over eighteen hundred orbs signaling feedback in a fifty-mile radius around my location. Another fifty-six hundred are powered off. We are a linked data sharing maintenance system, used for the benefit of military security and the humans and the Lurkers working here."

I stare dumbly at the orb.

What?

"Orb," I cough, light-headed. "Do you know where Vruksha's bunker is?"

The snorts are growing louder.

"I do not understand what a Vruksha bunker is. Please repeat."

I reach up and cup the orb, bringing it to me. "Orb, is there a military base near my location? Anything?" I rub some of the dirt off its plastic frame.

"There's the Caret Center two miles east and Eagle's Rest base five miles north. We are currently within Eagle's Technological Zone."

A squeal pierces my ears, tearing my attention away from the orb. Rolling to my side, I look down the mountain.

I hear another cry as a second pig falls, tumbling hard against the rocks. There's more now, at least a dozen, and they're using each other to climb to my location. I drop the orb, letting it levitate, reaching for my stick before remembering that it's gone. I find rocks instead.

Picking one up with both hands, I drop it on the nearest swine. The pig rears up and runs, skidding down the side before it falls off. It rights itself at the bottom and flees out of sight. I find another rock.

A bigger one.

I aim for a second pig. "Take that!" I shout, throwing it.

The rock smacks it directly on the head, killing the animal. It falls over, twitching.

I suck in, excited by my kill, before the pig closest to it stops climbing and tears into the corpse. I slink back over the ledge, disgusted and scared. Glancing up, there's not much more I can climb without likely falling. There's also not a lot of rocks left to throw.

I turn back to the orb. "Orb," I hurriedly initiate, "is there anything near here that can help me get out of this situation?"

I reach over and pull another rock toward me as I wait for it to answer.

"I'm sorry. I do not understand your question."

I close my eyes, press my brow to my knees. I don't want to die here, not like this. I inhale and lean over the side, aiming my rock at the closest pig.

I miss.

I try not to cry. The remaining pigs, I count eleven now that the one that fled has returned, are between me and safety. I don't have enough rocks left for half of them...

"Orb. Help me. *Please*, help me."

I'm not expecting a response. I gather the remaining rocks to my side, preparing to die fighting. I can't even kick the pigs off the ledge if they get close... my feet...

"Sending help to your location."

Tears fill my eyes at the words.

"Help will be arriving shortly," it says.

My fingers curl into my palms. I can scarcely hope that what the orb says is true; I don't know what help is left to be had. But as I watch the pigs climb, trampling each other to reach me, a bang goes off, and blood hits my face.

I startle, shocked.

I don't move as I'm drenched in the sounds, hearing

shots go off one after another. The pigs scream and squeal. I fall onto my back, listening to the sweet sound of gunfire. Because that's what it is: gunfire. I would know it anywhere.

"Female!" a voice roars, startling me further.

Vruksha?

I twist to my side. "Vruksha!" I scream. All I see is red. Everything is red.

A bath of blood and pig gore.

Something moves through it, sliding up the ledge at stunning speeds. I call out, near delirious when Vruksha's striking face fills my vision. It's the most beautiful sight I've ever seen. I immediately start sobbing.

I grab him as he reaches for me, planting my face into his chest. His smell envelops me, and I sob harder. His scent immediately starts numbing the pain.

"Sssshhhh, female, sshh." He gathers me into his arms. "You're safe now."

I gasp through tears, rubbing my face against him. "I thought you were dead."

"As long as you're alive, female, I'm alive. I'll always be looking for you."

He carries me away from the mountain, the blood, and the pigs.

EIGHTEEN
A NAGA'S PLEA

Gemma

I WAKE to crackling and the smell of meat. My body curls deeper into the soft warmth that's gathered around me. I don't want to move. All I want to do is remain here, where I know it's safe. In my dream, I was standing in a quiet, undecorated apartment, staring at paints I longed to use.

My belly roils, howling from prolonged hollowness. I groan and cling to the fur gathered around my mouth.

"Wake, female, and eat."

I open my eyes to Vruksha holding a spit with meat hanging off it. Smoke rises from the meat.

I turn over and vomit, hacking up air. Vruksha gathers my hair and holds it away from my face. I cough until my empty stomach stops churning. I shake, barely able to hold my body upright.

Rising slowly from the furs, Vruksha helps me into a sitting position. He places the meat at my mouth, and I nearly gag again. I cup his hands to steady them and take a bite anyway, sinking my teeth into crisp perfection.

Meat this fresh, this good is rare, even for someone who works on the bridge of a warship. It's for the rich and the planet dwellers who refuse to give such luxuries up. I tear into it after the first bite, not stopping until I finish.

I hope it's one of the pigs who tried to eat me.

Vruksha pulls the spit away when I'm done, otherwise, I probably would've eaten it too.

"Thank you," I say.

He hums and slips away, returning soon after with a cloth. I wipe my face and hands, and flinch from the cuts there.

"You are feeling better," he says.

Am I? I glimpse the space around me, recognizing the inner shell of the bunker. But I'm in a different part of it, deeper in, I think. There are still crates perched about, cement walls, and the flickering lights above. I'm in a circular bed—or cot—and there are warm pelts gathered on every side of my body.

There are also pelts hanging from some of the walls and strange baubles and artifacts of Earth. There's a whole row of orbs on a built-in shelf opposite me. I see my dirty, bloody one at the end.

My gaze returns to Vruksha. He's watching me, poised close to my side. I stare at him for time, dazed and so happy to be alive, to see him alive. I continue to stare as the meat settles in my belly, needing the extra moments to decide I'm not dead, and he saved me.

"What happened?" I ask, my voice a broken whisper.

He moves at my words, taking my cloth and setting it aside. "You passed out after I found you. You've been asleep since."

"How... long?"

"Several days."

I reach up and feel my crimped hair, my face. "Days?"

Has it been days? I test my limbs and wince. It feels like minutes.

"You're hurt, Gemma. You nearly died."

My brow furrows. I push the pelts gathered atop me off.

I'm naked. I quickly bring a pelt back to cover me, but I glimpse the damage to my body.

I'm wrapped in bandages up and down my limbs, covered in so many bruises that my flesh is unrecognizable, and my feet... My feet are covered in balls of cloth. I wiggle my toes and gasp. *There's the pain.* I sink my teeth into my lower lip.

But I realize I'm clean, my hair is soft around my shoulders, if not tousled, and for the first day since I was abandoned by my people, I don't feel grimy. "You cleaned me."

"You wouldn't stop bleeding. I feared infection."

My eyes slide back to Vruksha. "Thank you." How can I ever repay him?

The look he gives me is grave, pained. Tired?

Has he slept, taken care of himself?

"Drink this," he rumbles, handing me a cup.

"What is it?"

"Tea, made of local plants and herbs that will dull your pain. A recipe was given to me by one of the orbs," he adds.

I swish the cup and take a sip. I recognize the taste. Hazy memories of Vruksha pouring the liquid down my throat return to me. I finish off the tea, already feeling better. The heat of it slips through my body, soothing me.

He takes my cup away and places several pelts back atop me. "Sleep, female, you need rest. You can not regenerate without it."

I lie back and drift off, not needing to be told twice.

The next time I wake, I cry out in pain. It radiates up my legs and through my feet. I grip the bedding but find only one pelt beneath me, the rest are gone.

"Sssshhh. This will be over soon."

Vision blurry, I find Vruksha leaning over my legs, pulling off my bandages and cleaning my skin. He gathers my feet and places them into a basin of water.

I gasp, tears brimming my eyes. "It hurts."

He slides a cup over to me with the tip of his tail and I take it, downing the contents before he has the time to tell me what it is. The pain tempers.

I slump and stare at the ceiling as Vruksha takes care of me. Shame fills me as he cleans my wounds and massages my aching muscles. He slowly makes his way up my legs, taking his time. I'm naked, and it bothers me. I'm weak and needy, and I hate it.

I can't be weak, I can't be needy. Weak, needy people can't help others and can't hold a high-ranking position...

But it's his washing of my body that I can't handle the most. He's an alien male, a species with no given name as far as I know by humanity, and he is not beholden to me. I don't want him to think I'm helpless. I reach down and grab his wrist before he dips his hands between my thighs.

"Please," I say, I beg, pulling at the cloth with my other hand.

His eyes pin me, but he lets me pull the cloth from his grip. I clean the rest up myself.

When I'm done, Vruksha hands me another ration of meat. I try to take it from him. He growls, not letting me.

"What? Why?" I ask.

"I will feed you."

"I can feed myself..." I touch my mouth. "It's not hurting like the rest of me."

"It's not whether it's hurting or not, I want to feed you."

"I'm not a child."

"No. You are my mate, and I nearly lost you." He lifts the meat to my mouth and gently presses it to my lips. "It will make me happy to feed you. It will calm me."

I think about fighting him out of pride, but I don't, because it's not my pride that hurts with being fed. It's the vulnerability. I glance down at my nude, broken body and know I've been at my most vulnerable for days.

And he's still here.

He saved my life. He's saving me still. I owe him everything.

I part my lips and take a nibble of meat, watching him. Vruksha moves closer and slides his tail behind me to support my back. I rest against it and take another bite.

I don't understand why he puts his life in so much danger for me, why he's going through all this effort to keep me alive—even comfortable. I get that there are no females here anymore, but to risk his life for one because of that? I don't understand it.

If I'd been in this condition back up on *The Dreadnaut*, only family would've stayed by my side and I don't even have family on *The Dreadnaut*. I haven't seen my parents since I was thirteen.

Vruksha is an enigma.

I watch him watching me, swallowing thickly. Seeing him as a man for the first time, rather than an alien. Or a monster. Or some mindless beast, viciously attacking anything that comes near me.

We continue staring at each other long after I finish the meat.

It's not just mere curiosity anymore, I want to know him—really know him—and how he came to be here on this ravaged world where there shouldn't be any sentient life to begin with.

I've seen no alien spaceships.

"Will you get me a blanket?" I whisper.

His eyes dip for a second, and I cover my chest. But then he's gone and soon returning with several pelts. He hands me one and tucks the others around my body, saving the last one to bind my feet. Afterward, he bandages my deeper wounds with fresh cloth and cleans the strips of the old ones in the same basin my feet were bathed in. We settle in the front of the bunker.

"You should rest," he tells me.

"I've slept enough."

"You're still recovering."

"And what about you?" I see the wounds on his tail and the cracks in the scales around them. They're fleshy and red and swollen. They look painful.

"Me?"

"Your tail." I reach out and touch it. "You're hurt too, Vruksha."

"I heal quickly. This is nothing compared to what I can truly endure."

"I don't..."

His eyes snap to mine. "Don't what?"

"I don't want you to endure anymore on my part," I whisper and look down, unable to hold his eyes. It's the truth. It pains me seeing he's hurt too. That he's suffering and not resting because of me. I'm such a burden.

You lose your job if you become a burden. You lose everything else after losing your job.

"Female," he growls. "I will endure far more than this

for you. This—" he indicates one of his gashes "—is nothing compared to what I'm willing to sacrifice for you. What torment I'm willing to face."

"You shouldn't have to sacrifice anything at all!"

I don't know where the words come from, but it's true.

He slides up against my body, and while I try to lean away, his tail is still behind me, holding me upright. I'm trapped.

"I have nearly lost you twice. Once with Azsote. A second time with Zhallaix. And if I hadn't gotten to you in time, I would have lost you a third time. Do you know what I would do if I lose you?"

I shake my head.

"I would kill everything in my path until something or someone puts me out of my misery. I never wanted a female because of this, of how they make their mates crazy. I saw what happened to my father, but as I grew and he left, I realized why females are so important. It is why I would do anything, *anything* to keep you. Now that I have known you, I wonder how my father lived for so long after my mother died."

"I—" I swallow, asking the one question that has plagued me constantly, "Why me?"

"Life, sweet mate, there's no life without you. Not on this world or any other, I am certain. What's the point if there's no life? You are my life."

My brow furrows. "I don't understand…"

"How could you? Living up in the stars where there are more worlds than this to choose from? My people are dead, long before we thrived. We are lonely, without ever knowing companionship. I don't want to live without life anymore. I don't want to be alone.

"When I saw you walk off your ship, at first I did not

know what I was seeing. Another human male? A robot? But it was your hair that captivated me. And the way you lifted your face to the sky and smiled? I was mesmerized. You glow in the sunlight, little female, and I have never rested my eyes upon anything so sweet. Why you, Gemma? Because you stole my breath. You stole my life when you turned and found me in the forest."

He says this with a haunted expression that weakens me. I tear my gaze away. I do not glow. It's hard to look at him when he stares at me like I'm the reason the stars exist. He's completely devoted himself to me.

My throat tightens. It hurts. He makes me hurt. I press my hand to my chest, gazing at the ruby scales of his tail.

How I wish I could paint him... Though I do not think I own a vibrant enough red to do Vruksha justice. I could keep him with me forever if I painted him. "I know what it's like to be alone," I say quietly.

I don't know how else to respond.

"You do?"

I rub my lips together and nod. "Not like you, here. Loneliness is different up in the ships most humans live on. You're surrounded by metal, plastic, glass, and cold space. And it makes you cold too because there's no warmth up there. We're crowded together, and there's no escape, so it's easier to put walls up, to keep everyone at a distance despite being surrounded all the time. Everyone is alone up there because everyone has these walls around them..."

"Then take them down?"

"You can't. If you do, you get burned, you lose respect, and you lose rank. But it's easier being alone amongst others, than being alone without anyone." I force my gaze to meet his eyes. "Vruksha, I'm sorry."

"Why?"

I bite down on my tongue, trying to find the words. "Because..."

"—Don't. Don't say it, Gemma."

I inhale.

"I don't want to hear it," he hisses.

He lifts me in his arms and carries me deeper into the bunker, back to the pile of furs and pelts. He places me gently atop them.

And suddenly, I'm bone tired. And sad.

He knows why I'm sorry.

That despite everything he is, the marvels of this place, and everything he has done for me, including giving up his life, I can't stay. I'll never be able to stay.

Not while Daisy is out there, lost. Not while Peter and Collins remain on Earth. And not when there's a chance that others from *The Dreadnaut* will come looking for us.

That they could hurt him.

I can't keep Vruksha, because of this.

And he can't keep me.

NINETEEN

REFLECTIONS AND BLOODY KISSES

Vruksha

Gemma plans on leaving me.

I see it in her eyes every time she wakes to eat, have her bandages changed, or tries to take a step. I'm always there to catch her when she falls.

My only comfort is seeing her on the mend. It has been over a week since I carried her limp, lifeless body back to my bunker, and in the days since, she has gotten better—stronger—every day.

Some of the fury, the guilt has lifted watching her get better. Though I know it will never fully go away. I hope it never does.

I failed.

She was wounded... Wounds that, if I had been more diligent, if I had been keener, she would have never received. Zhallaix should have never been able to sneak up on me. He should have never been close to Gemma. I'm not comforted by his death, but I am glad I won't have to worry about him any longer.

No wonder she chose another male over me.

She's all I think about. My mind is clouded with thoughts of her. It's a poor excuse though it is true. She is my weakness. I have never been weak before, not until she entered my world. Now, it is all I am.

I've had plenty of time to think while she healed. I've spent so much time watching her sleep, lost in thought as I've tried unclouding my mind.

Flicking my eyes over her, she's burrowed in the soft pelts of my many, many kills. She's chosen the thinnest pelt to use as a dress since her clothes are beyond repair. They had plastered to her skin from blood and sweat, and I had to tear them off with my fangs to undress her. Now they are nothing but shreds of cloth buried deep in the ground.

I curl my finger under a strand of her hair and twirl it.

The thought of her leaving worries me.

She only has one place to go...

Back to the facility where there's a ship to take her to the stars. Far, far from me. To a place I couldn't follow her. Not unless she takes me with her.

A soft moan escapes her parted lips, stealing my attention. She is so beautiful that it hurts. Staring at her in my nest, where she's firmly mine, I can't imagine not having her here. I do not want to gaze at the stars and wonder where she is among them.

It's true what I told her. Loneliness hurts, especially since I know what it's like to not be that way. Especially when, until recently, there was no hope for anything except a lonely existence.

I gently pull her hair from under her head and span it out on the fur above. I work the tangles out of her strands.

Worshiping her this way eases me. I can't keep her knowing she is hurting, but I can have this. I can groom her to my heart's desire. She is in my nest, after all, and a naga male is king to his nest.

I nearly lost her. Again.

The recollection of her on the mountainside, curled, bloody, and trapped with nowhere to go sickens me. With the amount of blood and her pallor flesh, I thought she had died, but she's a fighter, my female, and she managed to survive long enough for me to find her.

I kiss her hair, breathing in her scent.

A shiver streaks through me, hardening me with lust.

How can I lose her again? She wants to go back to her humans. To her puny males. To a world where she is clearly not treated like the precious jewel she is. She has told me some about her life, and it sounds miserable. I am better than what awaits her there.

So why does she want to go back?

I pull away and find her looking at me when I do.

"Vruksha," she says my name with a softness that rends my heart into pieces.

"I did not mean to wake you."

Her face scrunches cutely, and she brings her hands up to rub the sleep from her eyes. In doing so, her pale breasts lift upward. They beg to be devoured and suckled until peaked. I hold off, knowing she is not ready for such attention.

"I'd like to try and walk again today."

I grab the cup with my tail and hand it to her. "After your bath. I've made you some tea."

She pushes it away. "Not today. That stuff makes me sleepy, and I want a clear head today."

I put the cup away. I like her sleepy, I like her like this, needing me. If she's awake and alert, she may want to take risks again, and knowing her, she needs to be watched at all times because of this.

I've learned.

"Later then," I say.

Gemma rises from my nest, sitting up. Her silky, wavy hair falls around her shoulders to tease me. Her strands caress and brush her upper breasts, her tips, and my mouth waters. I still don't push her into my furs and devour them.

It's taken days for her to be comfortable enough to be naked around me.

And as an obsessed male, her nudity tortures me constantly.

I like her needing me so, but *burning tech,* I want her healthy again so she will let me spill my seed inside her. I need to claim her, to reassure my soul she is well. I need to cover her, coil my tail around her, and clear my head of the dark thoughts of possessing her.

She nearly died.

If I had not gotten there in time...

Gemma grabs her dress-pelt and wraps it around her body, tying the lanks I'd cut days earlier to keep it in place. I hand her the other ties so she can position the pelt more securely. She moves to rise, and I catch her in my arms.

She gasps. "I wanted to try walking."

I cradle her close, carrying her away from my nest to the tub of water I have waiting. "Bath first."

"I just dressed."

"Perhaps you ssshouldn't have."

She grumps and kicks her legs halfheartedly in reply.

I set her by the tub and picking up a fresh cloth cut from one of my oldest pelts, I dip it into the water.

"You only want to bathe me so you can touch me." She says this as she moves onto her knees. "I've figured you out."

I ring out the cloth. "Mmm."

She tugs it from my hand. "I can do it."

My nostrils flare as she presses it to the bruised skin of her shin. The glistening water left behind entices me to lick it off. She works the cloth over her arms, neck, and finally under her dress.

My hands clench.

"Can I have a moment of privacy?" she asks sweetly.

My eyes snap to her face and discover she's studying me shyly. Her cheeks are pink. I grunt and turn my head.

"More privacy than that," she demands less sweetly. "It's not like I can go anywhere, Vruksha."

"Until you do," I growl, slipping away and to our nest. Her quiet movements reassure me as I straighten out and repair the pelts. I haven't felt comfortable using our nest while Gemma recovered, but perhaps tonight, I will join her in her sleep. I sniff the blankets she's been sleeping in, sucking her scent deep inside me.

I groan.

"I'm done," she calls out.

Dropping the furs, I return to her side. She's dressed and wrapping her feet in fresh cloth when I do. I tug her fingers away and finish the job for her.

"You don't have to keep caring for me so much..." she murmurs.

"I like it."

"But I can do it myself."

"And that matters how?"

She laughs, startling me.

"You're not nearly as terrifying as I thought you were. If I'd known that first day what I do now—" She laughs some more, pushing her hair back. "Maybe I would've just followed you home instead of running away."

"Perhaps you would have chosen me instead of Azsote." I don't know why I say it, but I do, the old jealousy returning viciously.

She's quiet until I finish up with her feet.

"I didn't choose him because I wanted him..."

I look at her. She's digging her finger into the material of her dress, eyes downcast.

My heart ramps at the submissive posturing.

"You didn't want him?" I ask gruffly.

She shakes her head, still not meeting my eyes. Oh, how I want to dominate her until she vows to let me rule her. If she allowed me to take over, I would impale her on my member and bind her body to me as I rutted her continuously for days on end. I'd make sure she'd never make it to the stars.

"I chose him because I thought he would be easier to manipulate."

She goes quiet again, but I want to hear more.

"Go on."

Gemma sighs. "I was terrified. For a minute there, I thought suicide would be a better fate than what awaited me. Males who barter for women like we're nothing more than items to own are not good males. When Azsote snatched me, I wanted to get away from him just as badly, but in the frenzy... and when you came for me... Azsote seemed less likely..."

"Less likely to what?"

"Eat me alive."

"If I ate you, then you'd be dead, and that is not my plan for you."

She laughs again. "Oh, I know that now."

She's in a good mood today, a talkative mood. It's odd. I like it. "You chose him," I snap anyway, bothered still.

Her eyes finally meet mine. "If I could go back in time, I would choose you."

"Why?" Give me more. I'm a greedy male.

"You're..." Her eyes flick over my face, even briefly to my chest. I straighten, showing off. "You're kind," she says.

I guffaw, slumping. "I am not kind."

"You are to me. I... I don't know anyone else who would have done for me what you have."

"I am your male."

"That's not a good reason. I still don't know many human males who would do what you did. Maybe my dad."

"Your males are pathetic," I growl.

She swallows. "Maybe you're right, but it's not their fault. It's how life is up there."

"Do not make excusesss for them," I hiss. "They do not know what they have lost when they gave you up, and as a male who knows what he has gained, they will always be lesssss than swine to me."

Her lips twitch. "You have a way with words."

I don't understand her meaning, but I don't care. I lean forward until my face is all she sees. I want to be all she sees. "Let me show you what you mean to me, female."

Her lips part, and it takes great willpower to not capture them and taste her.

"I think," she whispers. "You already have." She tries to pull back, and I let her, knowing exactly that she has only one place she can go.

Down.

I lean over her, corralling her as she leans on her arms, further still, chasing her with my mouth until she's flat on her back. When I have her where I want her, trapped beneath me, I close my eyes and breathe her in.

Honeyed and sweet. Her chest rises and falls as her heartbeat drums in my ear.

"Vruksha," she says my name. But it's not in warning or fear... It's something else.

I want to believe she likes this.

Me.

I want to show her that I'm not like any other male, that I am the best. That if she stays, I'll give her everything, and she'll never be hurt again. I'm a fast learner. An avid one. I've done nothing but study and watch her, protecting and caring for her. Trying not to touch her, letting her heal. She's healed now. Mostly.

I'm desperate for her to choose me. Perhaps it's because no one has before, not really. Why would they? I'm a lone Viper male with a vicious streak. It was only a matter of time before I left my father of my own volition, instead of the other way around.

I plant my palms on either side of her face, caging her in. My fingers reach out, curling into her red hair haloed about her face.

"I want to keep you, Gemma."

Her lips part to speak.

"Let me keep you."

I search her face, needing her to see the truth. I pour every desperate want and every feeling I don't have a name for into it, needing her to see it. Needing her to say *yes*.

She cups my face and brings my lips to hers.

TWENTY
BEAUTIFUL SCREAMS

Vruksha

HEAT ERUPTS, surging through my spine. My fingers strain, gripping her hair as she presses her mouth to mine. This is a kiss. I know what this is. I've seen them on the screens. It's affection, a human act of mating, a show of desire, and trust.

She trusts me enough to kiss me—a male with venom. I push my mouth against hers.

Her lips part and her tongue comes out to play. Lust soars through me, and my member springs out from my tail to stab at her body as I lower and press into her. Her legs fall open to the sides, forcing her makeshift dress up.

I ram my tail between her thighs, making sure she won't be able to close them. Now that she's open, the primal male in me, the one that wants to coil around her body and rut her into oblivion, needs her open. I have waited for this since the creek. I never finished spilling all I have inside her then, and my bulge still aches.

It's because of the seed she coaxed my body to create when I first laid eyes on her. The pressure is unending, the agony a constant torment.

We're surrounded by earth, cement, and metal here. There's no other male but me.

Only me.

Yet I can't fully relax. Groaning, I deepen the kiss.

My tail straightens out until it knocks at things behind me, scattering them as the need to thrash and bellow constricts my throat.

"What's—" Gemma gasps, pulling back, but I catch her with my mouth. I swallow her mumbled words.

I cup one hand under her neck, squeezing it as I open my mouth to ram my tongue into her. And just like I hoped, her tongue retreats and relents to my dominance. I lick it, rub mine to hers, petting it, tasting her inside. I want her to always submit to me.

The new scent my body creates when she is near floods the air.

Her hands grab my head and she deepens the kiss. She moans, and her tongue starts to fight back, pushing into mine. My little human fighter.

She gasps, her body going rigid, and blood coats my tongue. I jerk back as her hand covers her mouth. She looks up at me with wide eyes. I lick at her blood, swallowing it down. *Oh, yesss.*

"Oww," she whispers, pressing her fingers to her lips. "I forgot you had fangs."

"Keep your tongue out of my mouth in the future. I don't want to poison you."

"You can poison me?"

"I'm a Pit Viper. I'm highly venomous." So, she didn't know. "I can control it."

"Thank god."

I grab her hand off her mouth and trap it against the floor. I lean down and lick the blood off her lips.

Her breath hitches and her knees come up to press against the sides of my tail. I coax her mouth back open with my tongue. She tastes delicious and flinches when I find where my fang poked her. I lick the area until she settles. It's a promise that any hurt, big or small, I'll be here to take care of it.

Her mouth moves on mine, forcefully, and I deepen the kiss again, thrusting my tongue. Wet and hot, kissing a human female is exactly how I imagined it would be. I curl the tip of my tail and tug down the top of her dress, freeing her breasts.

I tear my mouth from hers and lift to see them. Gemma pants, eyes hooded as she gazes up at me.

I watch as she inhales deeply, taking my scent into her. Her skin flushes.

I drop my eyes to her breasts. I've seen them every day in the last week, but they're still enticing. Plump, symmetrical, and pale, all I want to do is lash them with my tongue. Her legs hook around my middle. I thrust against her.

Her breasts bounce, the peaks rise and fall, and the soft warmth of her body teases my member until I'm thrusting against her again. Her chest arcs, her nipples pop up like they want to be suckled, and I hiss, squeezing her hand under mine.

She is naked, without scales, without armor, and barely wears a pelt from one of my many kills. I couldn't get harder, but I still do.

"Female," I grate with painful desire.

Gemma arches her back higher, giving me my answer.

I place one hand on the center of her chest and push her flat to the floor. "Don't move."

She wraps her fingers around my wrist. "Why?"

"You're still hurt."

I dive forward and capture one of her waiting nipples. She cries out and tries to free her hand from mine, but I won't let her. I poke her flesh gently with the tips of my fangs but don't pierce her. After a moment, her tension eases.

Her other hand falls to the floor. I pull her nipple into my mouth, taking all that I can, loving on it. The soft, the tight, the honeyed flavor of her skin floods me, and I cup her other breast with my hand while my tailtip plucks her saliva-slick tit.

She shudders and I release one nipple to suckle the other, poking the wrinkled flesh around her tit with my fangs.

She trusts me.

I could destroy her and she still trusts me.

I dip my head between her breasts and graze my fangs down the center of her chest, down further still until I reach her belly button, which I dive my tongue into. I release her hand and cup her thighs, placing them on my shoulders. My heavy, seed-swollen member hits the floor.

Rolling my tongue, plunging in and out of the tiny indent on her belly, I rut it with my tongue the way I want to thrust between her legs.

Gemma trembles and I ram my tongue into her navel harder.

"Oh!" Her shocked cry drives me to a frenzy, shunting my pelvis hard against the floor as she grips my head and writhes. "Lower, please, lower." She squeezes her legs closed, trapping my head between them.

I tear them open and bend her up, holding her legs prone until her sex is spread and bare to my view. I press my face into it. Slick, warm arousal dampens my mouth, nose, and cheeks as I nuzzle it. "Female," I rasp.

"What are you doing!?" she whimpers.

I spill a little as she tries to pull her legs from my grip. I hold them tighter and keep them where I want them. Spread wide.

"Worshiping you," I rumble, breathing in her arousal. She squeaks cutely when I plunge my tongue inside her. Stars blanket my vision as her taste explodes in my mouth. A dark fervor grips me, and I rut her little, quivering hole as hard as I ravaged her navel. My member scrapes across the floor.

She dances wildly, her cries higher, louder, with each rough flick. I push my tongue as deep, licking everywhere. I've bathed her every day, though I never got to clean her here, inside her, the place that, when I think about it, makes me little more than an animal. I wanted to slip my fingers in and feel her here. My aching member dreamed about burying deep as she slept, only to wake her to mindless bliss.

If she woke to bliss, then she wouldn't wake to pain.

I stayed away, not wanting to hurt her further.

She's close. Her nails dig into the scales on my shoulders, and I curl my tongue to lick the rough spot of flesh that makes her scream. Truly scream. She tenses, her thighs gripping my head hard, and I thrust my member frantically.

"I'm going to—I'm going to come!" she shrieks.

I coil the tip of my tail around the middle of her body and squeeze her—simultaneously, I reach between us and pinch her nub.

Her whole body strains, her sex constricts.

And then she pierces my den with her beautiful scream.

Yesss!

I jerk back to watch her come undone. Gemma writhes, limbs tense, and cries out, grabs me, and tries to bring me back between her legs.

"Don't leave me," she begs, arching up and slumping, only to arch her back again. Seeing her like this excites me. Seeing her sex tremble makes me spill across my floor.

She begs me some more to return, riding out her bliss. When she begins to come down, I sink two fingers into her, stretching her brutally once they're seated in her quivering sex. She flails, and I quickly catch her wrapped feet with my tail. I hold them in the air, lifting her lower back off the floor. Her makeshift dress comes apart and falls off her body.

"What are you doing?" she squeaks again, her arms now above her head as she tries to free her legs from my tail. She fails.

"Preparing you," I grunt.

I plunge my fingers in and out of her as I grab my member and position it, lowering.

Her wide eyes meet mine, and sweat sheens her brow. Her shocked expression stokes me into a frenzy. I want to sink my entire soul into her and remember this image of her so caught and trapped and open before me. Her legs are straight in the air, her knees locked and trapped in my tail holding her prone. Her head lifts to stare at me as I thrust my fingers deep into her.

I thought I wanted her to use her tongue all over me, but I like this far more. I prepare her with my hand, guiding my member to her as I do. I slip my fingers out of her swollen hole and start pushing my shaft into her.

I loosen my hold on her legs so her knees bend to the sides, opening her up as far as I can so she can take me easier. I sink in to my bulge.

My nostrils flare as she clenches me, pulling me closer.

"Mine," I hiss, cupping her thighs and slamming my large bulge into her, pushing through muscle that fights to keep me out, stretching her more than my fingers ever could.

I roar as she takes it all, as her head drops back, and she cries out for me. My name echoes through the bunker. I sway my hips side to side working the rest of the way into her.

Heaven hails me as she takes everything I give her. It's my own shock that stops me as she constricts around my bulge, putting painful pressure there. I snarl.

"Female, you take risks," my voice is guttural, rough.

"Thank you," she gasps in response, confusing me, clenching again.

"What?"

"For saving my life."

I release her legs, dropping down atop her, forcing her back to the floor. "Don't thank me," I snap. I don't like it.

But she squeezes around me again, and I forget her words. My head drops beside hers, and I roll my hips hard. She moans, and I do it again.

I lose myself.

Jerking out, thrusting back in, snapping my hips. She takes my bulge with each hard shunt, and I make her do it again and again. Each time, a mewl leaves her parted lips, addicting me. I speed up as her body adjusts to accept me. She works our rhythm too, squeezing and releasing.

Before long, I'm rutting her in a craze, unable to keep

control. Her noises excite me, her accepting body tormenting me, and all I want is to possess it.

If I'm inside her, then there's no place she can go that I won't be there with her.

My member surges and grows.

"Gemma," I moan, coiling further around her body, bending painfully. "Gemma," I repeat her name with each hard thrust.

She claws at my back, and I erupt.

Spill drains out. The intensity drowns out everything else. Her limbs grip me as I grip her back, and I shake, filling her with everything I have. More and more spill drains from my member, shooting pleasure up and down my spine. I sag into her, unable to hold myself up, as the last of it leaves me.

My loins produce more seed as my orgasm slowly fades, never fully allowing the pressure in my bulge to end.

I turn my face and nuzzle the hair plastered against her neck. I lick her throat.

She shudders, pushes her chin down, and slides her hand between her throat and my tongue. "Tickles," she breathes.

I lick her fingers instead.

"Stooop," she wails weakly. I rise over her.

Her brows are wrinkled, and she's hiding her neck with her hands. I snap forward to try and taste her neck again, but she squirms away. "Nooo!"

I slip out from between her legs as she tries to flee, and I grab her, dragging her back under me. "Stay."

"No more licking my neck!"

I tug out the pelt from under us, pulling it around her, curling her up in my tail and against my chest. The tension in her limbs eases as she settles into me. I reach up and streak my fingers through her hair.

She nuzzles my chest the same way I nuzzled her sex. A smile twitches my lips. She knows what I can give her. She knows that my world isn't just dangerous but pleasurable too. We can make a life here, she and I, and it will be good.

No, there's no other male for her, not here on Earth or above in the stars.

When she falls asleep, I carry her back to my nest, where I finally allow myself the honor of sleeping next to her.

TWENTY-ONE

QUESTIONING THE PAST

Vruksha

Over the next several days, I leave, hunt for fresh meat, and bring back fresh water for Gemma's baths. I won't let her topside, and she knows not to fight me about it. At least, for now.

She spends her time making clothes out of pelts, first by ripping the old ones into strips. Then she uses those strips to tie other, thinner pelts into place. I help when I can, though my knowledge is limited, never needing clothes to cover me.

We fall into a pleasant routine.

Since our rutting, she looks at me differently, and I don't know why. Her expression seems distant sometimes yet always focused, and I can only imagine the thoughts running through her head. I try not to worry about it.

When the silence lingers a little too long between us for my liking, I pull her close with my tail and make her moan.

So when she stops trying to make clothes and starts

wobbling her way around the bunker, examining my treasures and trying to figure them out, I stop cleaning my gutting knife and follow her, catching her every time her legs give out, curious as to what she's doing.

What she is learning.

"What's in this?" she asks, moving to yet another large crate pushed up against the wall of my den. They've been here forever, filled with supplies from when I first discovered this place. Half the crates had been opened and looted when I first arrived, and there were bones of humans who died down here, preserved after the destruction. I don't tell her this.

It was long ago that I cleaned this place out. A long, long time ago. Those ghosts are gone.

"Medical supplies," I tell her. "This one has syringes, radios, and flashlights."

She cocks her head, and a strange expression crosses her face at my response. I wait for her to say more, but she glances around the bunker like she's trying to figure something out. It's the same expression that eludes me.

"Vruksha, how do you know the common tongue? It's been bothering me, all of this." She waves her hand at the bunker. "We were told there were animals, ruins, and a broken world awaiting us... We were never told of you. How are you here? Where did you come from? Are you... a Lurker?"

Her questions surprise me. "I've always been here. I'm a naga, not a Lurker."

Doesn't she know what a Lurker looks like?

"But what's a naga? That doesn't make any sense to me. A thousand years ago, trees and vegetation were just returning to Earth, and you, well, you're half-human, half-serpent, and sentient. You say all your females are gone... How is that possible?"

"They left, together, those that remained."

"Where did they go?"

"I don't know."

"Why did they leave? Should I... should I be worried?" She looks at me.

"No, female, you shouldn't be worried," I say, going to her. "They left because they were dying when they mated. All of them. My sisters... All the nagas of my generation came of age around the same time." Now that I say it, the timing is a little strange. "Our mothers died giving birth to their litters, but we were not communicating much then, and so this travesty wasn't known until after they were all gone. To lose a mate... to outlive your female... It shamed my father, and so I assume it shamed the other older males as well, so they never spoke of it. It wasn't until my generation came of age that we realized what was going on. Our females were dying during birth, *all* of them."

"Oh," Gemma whispers.

"After it was known, we couldn't save those who were already gestating, and tensions rose. Females stopped taking mates, and we had to fight every day to keep those that remained alive. There were males who... did not care. And mates who tempted death just to lay with a female. And it was those males who valued rutting over the lives of females who destroyed us. The clans tore apart and those, like me and Azsote, who forsook females, embraced the strife it caused because we knew that death would inevitably follow. The remaining female nagas decided to leave. They left their mates, their families, and have not returned. They went west, and no one has seen them since."

"And the males who drove them away?"

"Hunted down and killed."

She exhales. "Have you or anyone else ever tried finding them?"

"Some have. Most who make the pilgrimage return alone, and the rest never return at all. I never wanted to find them."

"Why?"

"After growing up with a father who missed his mate every single day, I did not want the burden of a female."

Her face falls but then it's gone, still there's a wrinkle in her brow left behind.

"Where is he now?" she asks quietly.

"He left. My sisters were gone. My mother, gone. I like to think he found my remaining sisters and is with them now, wherever they are."

"You don't know?"

"No."

Gemma sits back. "Vruksha..."

I trap her in a circle of my limbs. "Female," I say gravely. "Do not get any ideas. I will not let anyone else leave me." I know what I'm saying to her, I know what she intends to do. I need to make it clear that I cannot accept it.

Her face shutters. She turns from me.

"So, you were born here," she says.

"Yes."

"And your parents?"

"What about them?"

"They were born here too?" Her curiosity has already returned.

"Where else would they be born, if not here?"

"Your grandparents?"

I stare at her, confused. Grandparents? "I don't have any."

"Your father never spoke of his parents? Ever?"

Now that I think of it, no. "Those questions angered him."

Gemma's brow wrinkles. "Hmm."

"Do not worry about my past. It is the past. It is unchangeable."

I see thoughts running through her head and the confusion in her eyes, and it bothers me. She asks questions I haven't thought of since I was a young naga trying to understand my world. With Gemma here, there's something not entirely right about it.

I've always known something was off though I never dwelled on it. I didn't want to. Where was I going to find answers anyway? The screens never helped. The orbs never understood. My father and other nagas only ever gave vague answers, if they answered at all. Did they even know? Did they wonder too?

Someone must know... right?

An idea forms.

"Let me show you something," I rasp, changing the subject, moving my mind from where it wanders. I want to hear her laugh again. I pull my tail to me and rise, scooping her into my arms.

Though what I want to show her might not make her laugh, it might do the opposite. Still, it is something I think she needs to see.

"Where are you taking me? I can try walking there if it isn't far."

"You'll see," I tell her, heading for another door. It's hidden behind several large crates that I push away.

She wiggles in my arms. "We're leaving the bunker?" There's excitement in her voice.

I open the door with my tail. "Yes, but we are not going above."

Darkness meets us on the other side, and I carry her into it.

TWENTY-TWO
ORIGINS

Gemma

VRUKSHA CARRIES me into a dark hallway, through a door I didn't even know was there because it was blocked by crates. There are so many crates, so many old things. I've learned Vruksha is a collector. Of random odds and ends.

Old human kitchenware, furniture, and even little knickknacks that have no meaning. Things that have survived the last fifteen hundred years and a planetary apocalypse. Some things he doesn't even have a name for, and when we asked the orb, it didn't know either.

I'm coming to understand how Vruksha knows the common tongue, finding my answers on my own. The orbs speak it. And some of the 'better maintained' orbs can even project a screen.

The longer I'm in it, the more his world makes more sense to me. There's so much more potential here than I think the rest of humanity realizes. I'm a little surprised it's taken humans so long to coordinate an official expedition, but then I remember the pictures and stories of the previous times humans returned to Earth. Extra limbs, growths...

Tails?

I chew on my lip and push the thought away.

Even if Vruksha might be a descendant of humans who may have broken space law and returned to Earth long ago, I don't think I'll ever know for sure. I don't see records lying around. And it's obvious a history like that wasn't handed down or talked about with Vruksha.

The way he speaks of me going to the stars, though...

The darkness closes in as he takes me deeper. This isn't just another side room like the one with the generator. It's a tunnel, and as a chill breezes my skin, I snuggle into Vruksha for warmth.

I can walk later, I decide. I'm getting better every day. The pain in my body has dulled to a throbbing ache.

And now that I ache between my legs as well, I spend less time thinking about my torn-up feet. The tea he gives me helps too. He's taught me how to make it—with something called Willow Bark—that he collects and brings back from above.

A blush rises to my cheeks as my mind wanders to the near-rabid way he gets when he knows I'll accept him. His eyes darken and glint with hunger. When he pushes his cock's bulge into me, forcing me each time to take it, he loses his mind.

I woke this morning to his tailtip pushing inside me, his fangs grazing my backside. He said he wanted me to wake up to pleasure rather than pain.

It's why I ache between my legs right now. I've accepted this thing between us. Curiously, maybe eagerly.

At first, I thought it was animal magnetism and my own lack of connection for so long. Only for me to be thrust into

Vruksha's arms—literally—at my worst moment. I could explain away these feelings as a result of being vulnerable and afraid, but now... I don't feel so vulnerable anymore, and I still want him.

I like how he makes me feel. Safe, cared for, cherished... All things my job on *The Dreadnaut* used to make me feel. Although, I know now it was all an illusion.

I wiggle in his embrace, knowing he'll grip me harder when I do.

His fingers tense around my limbs, and I smile.

I like Vruksha. A lot. He is straightforward, honest to a fault, and headstrong.

Blinking back the darkness, I take in the shadows hiding my new surroundings.

"We should go back for a flashlight..." I say quietly.

"They don't turn on without batteries, and the batteries they need, I don't have."

"Oh..."

Hmm.

I'd rather he take me into a dark passage than continue telling me about the females of his species. Anything over that. The haunted look on his face as he spoke unnerved me. What he told me was heartbreaking. To lose your entire family the way he has? And not know what happened to them?

I can't imagine. I said goodbye to my parents at a young age because that is the way of life during wartime. I've barely thought of them since. But I know they're still alive and working on *The Grimstep*, a colony ship focused on the strength and longevity of the military—including militarized advancement. They've had several more children, none I've ever met, but I think they all left around the same age.

I'm not... sad about it, I don't think. I frown.

I don't know anymore.

I don't want Vruksha to have to relive the pain of his past because of me. I feel guilty asking about it at all. Even if I want to know him and understand this world he's living in.

Where he came from...

He frightens me sometimes still—especially when I glimpse the fervor in his gaze when he's staring at me when he doesn't think I notice. There's a wildness in his eyes when he does, and it makes me tense.

It's those moments that remind me he's an alien, with alien views, and alien laws different from my own. An alien species that thrives outside society. Vruksha's a starved male animal, ready to pounce. I smile softly.

The shadows fade, pulling me from my thoughts. Light returns, and it's far brighter than what we have in the bunker. Soon, flashing beacons of every color are around us, driving back the darkness, and large shapes materialize on either side.

"What is this place?" I ask.

"The tunnels," he says, sliding us past the blinking lights.

"And these things?"

"Old tech, robots, I think... they're called server towers?"

Servers? I push up in his arms and stare at the towers. I know what servers are.

"How are *they* still on? Are they actually running? Is there another generator?"

"They run because energy is being fed to them, as to why, I don't know. Perhaps there are more generators down here, better than mine. I have never found any. You seem surprised to find the tech running here. Why is that?"

"Because systems die, metal corrodes. Maintenance is needed to sustain tech."

"The Lurkers didn't destroy the tech. They destroyed the life surrounding the tech."

I shake my head, and he continues moving through, like none of this is out of place. "So, you know about the Lurkers." I strain my neck to stare at the towers behind us as they fade back into the darkness and we turn a corner. We've turned multiple corners...

"And these tunnels?" I pry.

"What about them?"

"Do you know why they're here?"

"The same reason why they're everywhere I assume. The tunnels have always been here."

"Everywhere?"

Vruksha hisses softly. "They ssspan for miles in many directions. So many questions."

I look around. How did I not know this? Do Peter and the others know? They couldn't. We all had the same briefing. The military facility we came down to investigate was chosen because it was once specialized in Lurker technology. If we were going to find this anywhere, it would be there. Underground tunnels were never mentioned.

Vruksha stops, and I hear the groan of a heavy door opening. The chill deepens when he takes me through it. It shuts behind us.

And then there's nothing. Nothing except darkness.

I fidget. "Vruksha?"

Light bursts forth, blinding me. By the time I can see again, buzzing has filled my ears. He carries me into the room as I rub the last of the fuzzies from my sight.

My lips part when I get a good look at where I am. I push away from Vruksha's chest.

"Let me down," I say, my excitement skyrocketing, and he gently sets me on my feet. I lean against him and his tail coils around my waist.

Screens. A bank of screens covers the far wall, and below them is an old system of computers. Some are blacked out, some are blinking, while others are blurry with static. The majority of them work it looks like, though not all. Images appear on those that do. Pictures of the forest, the landscape, and even the facility. Live feeds of the entire region.

This is a... "Security room."

A well-hidden one.

Vruksha slides to the control panel where there's an old leather swivel chair. He pushes it over to me, and I grab it.

"Sit," he orders.

I purse my lips and sit. "Are these the screens you always mention?" I ask, staring at the one overlooking the facility. I see the ship, the tents, the robots, and guards scouting the perimeter. There's more now. I even see the skiff that carried me and Daisy away from the place.

My stomach churns despite my excitement seeing it all. Knowing life has gone on without me... like I was never important at all.

My fingers tangle together, and I hide the wave of hurt that hits.

"The screens I mention?" he repeats. "This is only a few of them. There are screens everywhere if you know where to look."

"There are? Like these, not the orbs?"

"Yesss."

He moves to the control panel and types something in. I

watch raptly, awed to see this wild, primitive male, who I once thought was no better than a beast or a monster, use a computer like it's second nature.

The screens change when he's done typing, and words appear in large letters across them, but so do people, and images, and... destruction.

Aliens.

Large, lumbering bipedal beings covered in leathery green skin. They're nearly human in appearance if it weren't for their tails or the reptilian faces. Some are holding spears eerily similar to the one Vruksha carries.

"I don't know why I'm here," he says, returning to the question I asked earlier, as I stare at what's playing out before me. Explosions, fires, devastation, men in gas masks shooting guns, miles of forests disintegrating into ash, people running. And Lurkers, thousands of them, ignoring the humans begging them for help, ignoring the crying babies. "I've never seen someone like me, ever, on any screen. I have never heard another naga speak of our origins either. I assume we have always been here, though perhaps that's not the case. If what you say is true."

I'm watching the final hours of news feeds of Earth and realizing this, my stomach drops further. This is something I thought I'd never see. Never wanted to see. Has anyone seen this besides Vruksha?

There had been calls for help, messages from Earth that survived and were archived in history logs, but so much was lost, never to be found again. And live feeds? None of that made it to the colonies. But here it is, playing out in front of me, stored like it has been waiting all this time to be found.

It's the images of the Lurkers that frighten me the most. The death.

"What I say is true?" I repeat absently. My heart grows heavy.

"That maybe we're not supposed to be here. That Earth isn't supposed to have sentient life, female." Vruksha straightens, and my eyes cut from him back to the screens and the death playing out there.

So much death.

"Vruksha, you have watched this?"

"Many times."

The man reporting is sweating bullets as '*Breaking News*' flashes on the screens. He wipes his brow as a new video feed rises behind him, showing thousands of ships taking off from Earth.

I know it's the Lurker ships leaving like the monsters they are, abandoning all to die. There are other ships, thousands of human ones, and at once, the Lurker ships assault them with their weapons, destroying all of them.

Every last one.

The sound cuts out as the Lurker ships vanish, leaving nothing but dust clouds behind. Silence fills the room as only a picture of Earth from orbit remains, slowly graying, dying before my eyes.

Billions of lives lost in hours. It took two more days before those that escaped were able to contact the colonies. By then, there was nothing left to be done. Nothing anyone could do. And the years after? Only more death.

Humanity was nearly wiped out to extinction.

It'll happen again if the Ketts can't be held back.

"Turn it off," I beg.

A rumble leaves him as he does what I ask. The gray Earth disappears as the feeds of the forest return. I sag in the chair. "Why did you show me that?"

"You asked me, earlier, if I was a Lurker. I'm not. You

also asked what a naga was, and I can't tell you that... because I don't know. I don't know what I am, and this— these old images—is all I have, all any of us have here in explaining our origins. I can't tell you because I don't know, and I would like to... know."

I swallow as I take in Vruksha. He's looking at the screens like they hold all the answers.

"I want to know too," I whisper.

He turns to face me. We share a look, a despondent one. The truth is likely ugly. Do we actually want to know?

"I need to go back," I say.

Vruksha's face hardens. "No."

"You don't understand—"

"What is there to understand? I won't let you leave."

"The facility might have the answer." I glance at the screens. "Daisy is somewhere."

His tailtip coils around my wrist. "No."

"You just said you wanted to know about yourself, and my people need this information. They need to see this."

"They need history? And not the technology that wiped you out the first time, the same technology you're trying to uncover, right? It's what you want to steal from us."

My face scrunches. "It's not like that. It's also not your technology."

"It *is* our technology," he snaps, sending shivers down my spine. "We have protected it, learned a little from it, valued it for what it is—but we don't use it. It is evil. Explain to me why it's so important that your people would trade you for it, female."

"We're in the middle of a war," I blurt out. I rise to my feet but nearly fall and catch my body on the chair. Vruksha's tail releases my wrist and curls around my middle again. I push it away. "A war that could do what you just showed me all over again, but this time, on an intergalactic level. And you do use the tech," I accuse. "The Lurkers on the screens carried the same spears you wield!"

Vruksha's nostrils flare, and he moves to meet me head on. I straighten.

"You are mine. You belong with me. I won't trade you for an answer to a question I didn't care about yesterday. No amount of curiosity will change that. This is all the past, the past! Not the future."

"Then you shouldn't have shown me this," I say.

Because now that I know, I have to do something.

"I will not allow your life to be endangered again."

"That isn't your decision to make. You were so willing to trade your precious knowledge with us for *me*. Why can't you do it *for* me, instead?"

Vruksha hisses. "You are not being fair."

"What is it you gave them, that first day? In the box?"

"Scraps. Odds and ends that have no use."

"Scraps," I guffaw. "My people can't use scraps. They'll be back for more. You understand that, right? Once they figure out what you gave them was useless, they'll search for you."

"We'll kill them if they do. We'll kill them all."

"Kill us? There are millions of us." I can't hold back my shock, my fear. For him. "You live in ruins. Humans have battleships the size of the moon. How can you hold us back from taking the technology from you by force? We outnumber you."

Darkness etches across Vruksha's face, like he and the other nagas have already thought of this. It confuses me until I realize why.

They knew what they were in for all along.

They knew and they still risked themselves for me? For Daisy?

He slides to me, silently, like a shadow, and towers over me. "We have our ways."

All at once, the part of Vruksha that frightens me, returns. The exacting intensity he wields sharpens every scale and ridge of his muscled body.

"Ways?" I whisper, mouth going dry. "You not only know where the Lurker tech is," I breathe, remembering what he just said, what he said and I ignored. "And you know how to use it as well..."

The Earth turning to ash, the leathery reptilians ignoring the cries of children as their giant ships blast all of ours... the images unfold again before my eyes. It was like we—and all that humans had achieved—were nothing.

Whoever had that kind of power—terrible power— could cause massive destruction and should be feared.

Vruksha and the other nagas aren't just part of a primitive sentient species. They hold that power. The power humankind thinks could change the tide of war.

Something flashes across one of the screens, stealing my attention. Vruksha says something I don't quite make out. Familiar faces distract me. "Something's happening," I say, focusing on the flurry of activity. Vruksha goes quiet beside me.

It's the facility. My eyes narrow.

Men and robots rush across the cleared yard and toward the forest, past the barrier. I see Peter, Collins, and even Shelby. They're scrambling and pointing, screaming at something I can't make out.

"Can you enlarge it?" I stumble forward, using Vruksha's tail to keep me upright. "Where's the sound? Does this have sound? I need to hear what they're saying."

"Not the live feed," he rumbles, leaning over the panel again. He presses a couple of buttons, and the footage from the facility takes over the whole wall.

The skiff appears. It's trying to take off but is far too close to the forest to clear it. The others chase after it. Peter is barking what I assume are orders for the robots not to shoot it down. Whatever it is that's allowing me to see what's happening focuses on the skiff, following it as whoever is in the cockpit tries to fly it too high too fast. They're trying to take off.

"You're not going to make it," I breathe, my heart thundering. The bottom of the skiff hits the tops of the trees. "You're not going to make it!" I gasp.

The skiff jerks upward, hovers, skims more trees, and jerks again. It clears the next several trees and bounces higher. My fingers curl into my palms as it steadies. I forget my colleagues at the facility and focus on the ship, trying to see who's flying it.

A shock of long blond hair is all I can make out through the blur.

My throat constricts.

"Daisy."

TWENTY-THREE
MATE

Vruksha

GEMMA REFUSES to let me carry her back to our nest.

She struggles in my embrace as I do so anyway. She's not always going to get what she wants.

"I shouldn't have shown you," I growl. I regret giving her a view into the secrets of this place, this world I live in. The tunnels are known by all the nagas, like the Lurker technology and the old human ruins, but the secrets within them? Those of us who know of it, always kept those close.

Because what you know, what you have, makes you powerful in my forest.

The little bit of technology we handed over to the humans had been nothing more than cast-off bits and baubles of broken tech that no longer respond to us. To anything. Zaku and Vagan had made sure of it.

"I'm glad you did, except that's not the problem right now. Daisy is. That skiff can't save her! She'll never make it past the stratosphere, not without a miracle. We need to go back! Please, Vruksha." Her voice heightens. "You would have kept this from me?" she says, straining in my arms. "Something so pivotal?"

"It's not your passst."

"How can you say that? Of course it is. It belongs to humans," her voice trails off at the end, and I peer down at her. Shadows distort her face, although I can see enough of it clearly to know she's thinking.

"Or perhaps it belongs to no one and should be forgotten," I grit.

We slip through the tunnels in silence going forward. When we're back within my bunker, and I shut the door behind us, some of the tension leaves me. I set Gemma down on a crate, and she swings her legs over the side, stands, but quickly leans back against it.

I glimpse my spear perched against the wall by the exit.

I always knew it wasn't made by humans. When I wield it, it's like an additional limb, one that not only uses the muscles trained for it, but also your thoughts. Only Lurker tech does that, not human tech.

And Lurker tech never deteriorated, not like the cheap creations of the humans. Which, like Gemma's brought up, usually rusts and corrodes, or loses its power source.

I never minded showing Gemma the tech until now because I didn't think there would be any harm involved in doing so. It intrigued her so. Besides she's mine, and that alone once assured me she could never, or would never, use it against me. Now I'm not sure.

"Maybe you're right," she says abruptly. "Maybe some of what you and the others guard is too dangerous... But that won't help Daisy right now."

"Mmm." I coil my tailtip around her leg. "Who's Daisy?"

My female throws her hands up in the air. "The woman who was with me on the plateau! The other female who ran from you, terrified for her life."

"I forgot there was another female."

"How? Err, never mind." She rubs her brow.

"I've only ever seen you." I do recall this other female now that she mentions it, though I recall nothing else about her. No other female interests me.

"If I wasn't so upset with you, that might have made me happy, but as it is, there was another woman, and we need to save her."

I grit my teeth. I know females are rare, but this other one isn't my problem—or Gemma's. "Another naga will save her."

"You can't know that."

"Yes, I can. If she hasn't been caught, she soon will be, and I assure you there are many malesss right now—"

"That makes it so much worse. She doesn't want to be caught by a male, Vruksha. I didn't want to be caught. If she's running, she won't stop, and if she's been out there all alone for nearly two weeks... I can't imagine the state she's in."

"We're not going after her. Nagas will fight to the death for a mate. She will come to no harm."

"But you've said so yourself... there are evil naga males. What if she's been caught by one and is running from them?"

Tension streaks down my spine, and I slip my tailtip from Gemma's leg to coil around her back, closing her into a circle of my making. I understand she may care for those in her past life, but she should forget them and move on. She never will, not if she sees them and they remain near.

I tear my eyes from her pleading ones and snarl at my

spear. "We destroyed the evil ones long ago." Thoughts of my father rise to my mind, and the way he'd stare off into the forest for hours as if he was waiting for my mother to come slipping out of it. I remember the sadness that always followed when she never did.

My mother was never a victim to a Death Adder or a Black Mamba or a Boa, but so many others were. I lost my sisters because they feared for their lives and chose to flee instead of becoming victims.

"Can you be sure of that?" Gemma whispers.

I snap my eyes back to her. "Yes. We were thorough."

"Thorough enough? What about Zhallaix?"

I bare my fangs, hearing the Death Adder's name. "He is dead."

"If you do this for me..." Gemma sinks her teeth into her lower lip, stealing my attention briefly, but it's the lost expression that remains etched on her face that has me questioning... "If you do this for me, if you help me save her, I'll stay."

"You never had a choice," I remind her.

Her face scrunches. "I could make your life a living hell by fighting you."

"I'll bind you."

"And I'll scream, kick, and battle you and us every single day until you have no choice but to relent. You'd become what you destroyed."

I hiss, frustration and anger pouring out of me. "You are not being fair."

"Neither are you."

Fury to match my rising rage meets me in Gemma's fierceness. I believe her threats, knowing she could deny me the life I want so badly with her. The affection, the company, the warmth, and the love of having a mate to coil up with in a shared nest. She could take that all away, and though I'd fight back, reminding her constantly why it would be easier to give in, I know she'd only come to hate me.

Because the humans are still out there. The other nagas are as well.

And there would be no peace inside my den or outside it until that changes.

"I am nothing like those rabid males," I grate.

"Help her," she begs. Gemma reaches up, and I go stiff, bracing for her to try and squirm out of my circle, but she cups my face instead, pulling me down. "Please do this for me, as your *mate*."

She seeks to call me mate now? Anger swells up inside me. "You ask much of me." I can't help but lock her in, gripping the crate on either side of her. I press into her, my anger growing.

She leans up and places a kiss on my lips. "I know."

It's gentle, soft, a whisper of a touch, and a tendril of her warmth. It's everything. I know she's manipulating me but her lips move, and I'm now the one who's lost, deepening it, uncaring. Because if I don't, I'm afraid she'll slip through my circle of limbs and vanish.

And I will become my father.

If I can't make her happy, then what kind of mate am I?

I cup my hand behind her head and capture her completely, sinking my tongue into her. Gemma's taste floods my mouth, reminding me of everything I have to lose. How fragile what I have really is.

Her hands fall from my face to grab my shoulders. She presses her nails gently into my scales there.

Something in me snaps.

I grab hold of her dress and tear it down her arms,

freeing her breasts. She startles as I fill my hands with them and squeeze, pinching her nipples between the sides of my fingers as I do. "Female," I say, desperate and furious, "you will be the death of me." I don't give her the chance to respond, recapturing her mouth. I slide my hands down her body and grasp her butt, lifting her onto the crate.

I push my hips between her legs, and she opens up for me. Reaching under her dress, I tug off her undergarment. The weak ties holding it in place snap and fall away. I throw the annoying scrap across the bunker.

Holding her open, I line up my tip to her hole and thrust my member into her to my pulsing knot, groaning as I push against her tight flesh keeping me out.

"Vruksha," she cries, digging her nails into my arms.

"You ask too much of me, female. You seek to manipulate me," I snarl, pulling out and thrusting back into her. Her lips part, but I don't allow her to speak.

"You want to risk your life, again, and you haven't even recovered!" My hips snap. My tail curls around her hair and pulls it back until she's forced to lie on the crate. She gasps and her back arches. I rise over her, thrusting harder. Mastering her.

"And now you want to go after another female and bring her back to our den. I won't share you!" I roar. This time when I pull out, I shunt forward with brutal strength, pushing the entirety of my bulge into her in one go.

Gemma cries out, gaspy and harsh. Guttural, animalistic noises rip from my throat. Pleasure surges up my spine, and her hips tweak from the pressure I'm putting on her. Her legs tense around me, flailing from the force. She doesn't ask me to stop, and I don't. She lets me take my frustration, my lust out on her beautiful body.

Her sheath clenches around my bulge, and my tail

drops, uncoiling from her hair. It straightens out behind me as far as it can go, climbing up the opposite wall, knocking things over.

Her hands fall to grab my hips as she buckles.

Sweat beads my brow from her little movements, teasing my aching prick into a furor. It grows.

Brutally, I rut her, enraged that she seeks to manipulate me. She gifts me hitches and moans, and I take them. My thrusts grow wilder, her cries louder. Seed swells my bulge painfully, and I can't hold back.

I bring my tailtip back to me, thrashing, spilling inside her. I drop atop her, catching my body with my hands, as I give Gemma everything. She takes it. She takes it all.

"We will sssave your friend," I breathe heavily into her ear. "But you will stay with me, you will obey me, you will never run again. You will not ask about the Lurker technology again, nor about the humans in the facility, you will never return there. You will never leave this planet, and every night, you will wait for me in my nest, open just as you are right now. You will forget all else."

Gemma whispers my name.

"I'm not done," I growl, rising on my elbows, pinning her with my gaze. "We will go after your friend, though she cannot stay here. This den is mine, and only what is mine is allowed inside it. If she cannot be found, and cannot be saved, thisss," I point between us, "isn't going to change." I span my fingers and tangle them into my female's hair.

Gemma purses her lips, lips that are red from my ravaging. My body pumps more seed, and I spill a little more inside her.

"Thank you," she gasps. It's all she says.

It hurts.

I rut her again, harder this time.

TWENTY-FOUR

THE HUNT FOR DAISY

Gemma

VRUKSHA CHECKS the ties on my shoes for the third time.

I grasp his hand. "They're fine. I can manage."

"I don't want anything more to happen to them," he snaps. He's been angry since the tunnels, and so have I, but there's no solution until we find Daisy. I don't know what's happened, why she would steal the skiff, but I have to find out. I can't do anything knowing that if the roles were reversed, Daisy would help me. I know she would.

And what if she's not trying to escape from something? Maybe she's not running from a naga or our old coworkers. What if she's looking for *me?*

And risking herself doing so.

I barely know Daisy but after what we've been through —being betrayed by our peers—she's the closest friend I now have. I may be all that she has too.

War and tech be damned.

It's nice being ignorant of what's happening until it's

not. Daisy could've been suffering, alone, exposed, or worse and I'd only given her a handful of thoughts while I rested in warm pelts and let Vruksha care for me.

While he made me cry out in bliss...

I clench and wince, throbbing from Vruskha's recent attentions. He's upset, and I've made him that way. He's a vicious alien—that I think might be in a rut—and I often forget that he's a different species now.

I can't help that I'm in heat just being around him... The way I'm acting. I like what he does to me...even if it makes me ache afterward. I shake my head.

And all I cared about stupid war tech that may or may not be useless. I scrub my hands over my face. I want it to be useless. I'm hoping it's useless, but I can't quite convince myself. Still, Vruksha's right. It doesn't matter. He and the other nagas have hidden it. They're guarding it, wherever it is, and for now, that works for me. Until I know more, or something happens, it's enough.

"They're mostly healed," I say, wrapping my hands around the walking stick Vruksha found for me. It's sturdier than any stick I've sourced so far.

He rumbles and drops his hands from my shoddy makeshift shoes. None of my new clothes are great, only held on by ties that never seem to get tight enough, but they're better than nothing, and each day I fiddle with them, they're more wearable.

Vruksha grabs his spear and ties our supply bag over his shoulder.

I swallow, rubbing my thighs together. They slip, still wet with his seed.

I care for him.

A lot. It's beginning to hurt how much I care. I press my palm to my chest, to the tightness there.

He hisses and slips up the steps, and I drop my hand. I follow behind him, watching the way his long tail moves back and forth. A *creak* sounds in my ears, and a ray of light bathes us, temporarily blinding me.

I inhale the fresh air, making my way up the last of the steps, using the wall to guide my spotted vision. It feels good.

Freedom.

The moment I step outside, Vruksha's tail coils around me and lifts me off the ground.

"What are you doing?" I ask.

He brings me to his arms and cradles me within them. "I'm not letting you walk. You are too slow even when your feet aren't hurt. I want this to be quick. I do not like the idea of you being out here where you can be further hurt."

"Then what's the point of the shoes?" I jest.

He scans our surroundings. "Protection," he answers me dismissively, ignorant of my teasing. An orb comes up to hover beside him. "Are there predators nearby?" he asks it.

The orb does its thing and we wait. Bears, a coyote this time, a snake, and pigs. Always pigs. My stomach sickens.

"What snake?" he asks.

The orb hums, and a hologram appears. It twinkles in the sunlight, making it hard to see the image. Something slowly appears, a familiar broken tail and scarred face.

"I thought he was dead," I whisper.

Vruksha hisses, holds me closer, and goes silent for a time, watching Zhallaix. "I always think that too, but he never is. As long as he keeps away, he can live with the pain of his wounds for as long as he likes." And at breakneck speed, Vruksha surges forward.

My hair flies as he slips us through the airport's ruined orchard and into the thicker forest. I grip his hand that's cradled around my arm. "Slow down. Your tail is still heal-ing." My words are lost in the wind.

He doesn't stop.

The day was already halfway over when we left the bunker. Vruksha needs nothing but his spear, but I'm not so easy. He packed two day's worth of rations. He's not plan-ning to search for Daisy long.

I turn from the glinting scales on his chest to the blurry landscape. I know it well enough now that it'll become less flat as we get closer. But when the trees close in and the overgrowth thickens, I'm not prepared for the fear that wells up in me.

Sooner than expected we reach the area where the pigs were, where I almost died. Where I ate raw fish...

Vruksha slows down, working his way through the foliage, careful not to let any branch, leaf, or twig touch me.

I can still hear the snorts and snuffs of the hogs like a ghost in my ears, reminding me how close I came to being eaten alive.

"Don't stop," I whisper. "Not here."

Vruksha pulls me into his chest, and I close my eyes, turning to press my brow to him.

"They're dead," he says as if he knows. "I killed every last one the drone missed. Do not be afraid."

He makes me feel safe.

For a time, I lose myself in the swaying of his arms, feeling the air on my skin. I wake from a fitful doze when he sets me on my feet sometime later.

He's taken me inside the ruin of an old building. One without a roof, with half-crumbled walls and metal piping sticking out everywhere. He sets me under a large slat of cement, leaning against one of the sides, forming a small alcove. I rub my eyes. Vruksha fills up the entire entrance, trapping me within.

"Why have we stopped?"

"Night will be upon us soon, and you need to eat and drink. I want to check your feet," he mutters, clearly still unhappy with me. It bothers me. A lot. I feel like I let him down.

But time is precious.

I knew it was a long shot, despite this, I can't help worrying. I know we're vaguely headed for the facility, but it feels like we're wandering aimlessly, a skiff could travel anywhere...

My heart thrums as we stare at each other. The ache between my legs hasn't gone away, and I crave him. He doesn't judge me, and I never realized how much I've been holding back all these years, fearing judgment.

My chest tightens.

Vruksha curls his tail under him, and he settles just under the opening of our alcove, placing his spear nearby. He reaches for my legs, and I give them to him. In the waning daylight, he unravels my bandages, checks my wounds. Most are nothing more than red blotches now, scabs, and yellowish-green bruises, but he's adamantly keeping track of how fast they're healing.

I lean against the side of the building as his hands prod my skin, aware of how they linger and inch up my legs.

"If I'd been hurt like this on *The Dreadnaut*, I would've opted for the pod," I laugh.

"Pod?" Vruksha lifts my foot and begins wrapping it back up.

"It's a medical thing," I say to fill the silence. "It elimi-nates the need for so many doctors and nurses since they're all needed on the frontlines. And so the rest of us get the cold love of a health pod. It's an oval-shaped device humans lie in when they're sick or injured, and the pod—which runs through AI software—heals you. They also put you under, stabilizing you for long distances of travel."

"Ah, yes. I know what you're talking about."

I peek at him as he sets my freshly bandaged feet aside. "You do?"

"I've seen something like it, once, where a—I think it's called hospital—used to be."

"I didn't think we had tech like that back then." We lost a lot in the centuries following the end of Earth.

"It was broken. There were human bones all around it."

Silence falls between us as the shadows give way to full darkness, and the only light comes from the moon rising through the trees. It would be peaceful if it wasn't for Vruksha's brooding, blocking much of my view. I reach for the bag slumped off his shoulder and dig out a ration.

His eyes never leave me.

I take a shy nibble, suddenly feeling like nothing has happened over the past two weeks and this is our first night together in his bunker all over again.

"Tomorrow..." I start then stop.

Vruksha continues to stare at me.

My fingers tangle. "Tomorrow, we should head for the facility and start there."

"No. Tomorrow, we'll get *close* and I'll check out the facility, search for her tracks. We are not entering the facility's grounds."

"She...won't have any tracks. She stole the skiff. And what if Peter and the others found her? They'll take her back to the facility."

"She hit the trees, breaking them. I can climb to the

tops and know which direction she went in, and if they found her first, then we return to our den."

"I need to speak with her."

Vruksha growls. "That's not what we decided, *mate,*" he lingers on the word. "If she is safe, that is all you need to know. If she is within the facility and back with the other humans, there is nothing left that you or I can or will do for her."

Silence settles between us again. I finger the wrapper of my ration, hating it.

"Get some sleep," he says, startling me.

"You should be the one to rest." I sit up. "I can take the first watch."

Vruksha grabs his spear and ducks out of the alcove with a hiss. "I'm going to scout."

He slips away, and I stumble out, going after him. "Wait!"

Vruksha twists back and catches me just as I trip and fall.

"Female, you will hurt yourself further," he growls.

I push off his chest. "Why are you upset? What's wrong?" I hate seeing him this way.

"Everything," he quips, squeezing my shoulders, steadying me while being brutally honest. He grabs me against him and carries me back to the shelter.

"I understand you're mad because of Daisy, but I can't live knowing she's out here alone, possibly in desperate need of help, and I did nothing. I'm not doing this to hurt you." I need him to know this. I don't know why, I just do. "I won't leave. I promise."

"I would never let you leave," he says. "I have told you this again and again."

I search his face. "Why are you so angry then?"

Vruksha keeps me in his embrace, even when we're back inside. He clutches my chin between his fingers and brings my face to his. "Angry? You think I'm angry? I'm furious," he seethes.

I flinch.

"You," he begins but stops. "You…"

"Me what?"

"You didn't choose me!" he roars. He drops my chin and pushes me to the ground. His face is a mask of darkness as he leans over me. The outline of his fangs, his scowl. It steals my breath. He takes my hands and traps them above my head.

Like an animal about to devour his prey, he pants, holding me down. His powerful body trembles. Warmth rushes to my cheeks. An ache swells between my thighs.

My legs fall open unwittingly. "I did choose you."

"You chose Azsote, your humans, this Daisy, and even old tech over me, female. You haven't chosen me."

My brow furrows. "I—" How can I answer that?

He lifts off me, and I scramble onto my elbows as he leaves the alcove again. "Sleep," he orders, his voice gruff, agitated. "You'll need your strength."

Grabbing his spear with finality, he slinks into the forest and vanishes. I bring my legs together and hug them, feeling more alone than I've ever been before. Hurt that I offered my body to him and he rejected me.

My heart aches.

He's right.

I lean my face into my knees.

Now he knows I'm truly not fantastical after all.

The next morning, I rise bleary-eyed, rubbing my joints where they locked overnight. When I'm done, I find

Vruksha perched on the ruins of the building, his tail hanging down the side, watching me.

I inhale sharply.

He could've been there all night while I waited for his return, and I would've never known. He jumps down and, without a word, checks my bandages. He slips our supply bag over his shoulder after handing me a ration.

"Eat."

"Last night—"

"We'll talk later," he says, rounding his arm under me to help me stand. He lifts me, but I push him away, keeping my feet on the ground.

"I can do this."

For once, he doesn't argue. Instead, he takes the lead, leaving me his tailtip to grasp if I need it. And for the rest of the trek, we're climbing, moving from one ledge to the next, working our way up. Each step is easier than the last. He doesn't speak, and so I don't either.

He intimidates me, I realize. It's not that I fear him; I'm intimidated by him. I don't know how to... make things right. Every time I want to, my tongue grows big and my throat constricts.

I try and focus on our surroundings while I swallow all of my words.

The trees have grown thick and tall, and there are fewer of them with leaves and more with green needles and cones. As we journey higher, I catch glimpses of the horizon and survey the terrain. There is a giant lake far in the distance, and I see streams and ponds. There are mountains around the facility— I knew this going in—and the forest is thick. But peering down into the gorge we were in earlier, I find dead spots here and there. Little patches where there are no trees but ruins.

We've come across many things, broken structures, overgrown buildings, and even items in the forest. I try to commit them to memory so I can use them as landmarks in the future.

Vruksha always seems to know where he's going, despite how many miles we travel, even without a compass or a mapping system. To me, it's amazing.

Seeing a spot of color by my foot, I lean down to pick up what appears to be a doll. Brushing the dirt off it, Vruksha pivots back to me and tugs me into his chest.

I tense, waiting for him to tell me what's wrong, but when a minute goes by and he doesn't, I start to get afraid. I whisper, "Do you hear something?"

"Another naga." Holding me hard to his chest, he moves us to a nearby tree, ducking under its low branches. He scans the canopy above us.

I search with him. "They're still out here?"

His eyes slide to me. "They live here."

"So close to the facility? Isn't that dangerous?" I shiver.

"This was our land first."

"What do we do?"

"Move quietly and not alert them that you are here."

My eyes go wide. "And if they find out I am?"

"I kill them and you run."

I drop the dirty doll and grip my walking stick. "Fine. Okay."

"Stay close to me."

I nod.

Vruksha helps me out from the branches and pulls me close. We continue our climb, a little warier of the noise we're making, and slow down, taking our time to not make any additional sounds.

Another hour goes by, and the tension eases from my shoulders. We pass by another series of ruins when something pricks my ears. A voice far off in the distance. Vruksha and I stop at the same time, waiting to see if the voice comes again.

I move under his arm and into the curl of his tail before he can tug me to him.

"What was that?" I whisper.

It sounds like someone, or something is—

"DAISY!" They're shouting her name.

I jump. Vruksha plasters me to his side.

"Daisy?" I gasp.

"DAISY!" Her name comes again, sounding from elsewhere, roaring through the trees.

Gooseflesh rises on my arms. "Daisy! Someone is looking for Daisy. She could be nearby."

Vruksha's eyes darken.

"We have to look for her!"

He nods, curling his fingers around my wrist, and we take off after the voice.

It seems like hours go by before it's loud enough to eclipse the sounds of the forest. Still, the quicker we move, the farther the voice seems to get. I want to call out but don't.

"DAISY!" The roar comes again after a short while. We reach the summit of the mountain and stop.

"Which direction did it come from?" I ask, huffing. I can see everything from here.

"It's Zaku."

I shake my head, wiping the sweat from my forehead as the naga with the large, spiked cowl rises in my mind. "Great."

The trees beside us shake. I stumble back just as something large and green drops down from them. Vruksha swings in front of me.

A naga male, shimmering vibrant green, rises, catches my eye, and puffs out his chest.

"Azsote," Vruksha snarls.

"Vruksssha," the other male hisses in answer.

"DAISY!" the roar comes again, startling the three of us.

"Take your eyes off my female," Vruksha's voice lowers, sending a shiver down my spine.

Azsote looks away from me and at him.

"I'm not here for her," he tells Vruksha. "I'm looking for Zaku." Azsote's eyes cut to me again though, making Vruksha hiss.

"Why?" he snaps.

"I've found the other female."

I step forward before Vruksha can stop me. "You have? Where is she? Is she okay? Take us to her."

Vruksha pulls me behind him, coiling his tail around me. "Is she safe?" he asks.

"She's hurt, burned up."

My lips part. Burned? The skiff didn't make it... "Take us to her, now," I demand, clutching Vruksha's arm.

Azsote flicks his eyes to me.

"DAISY!"

All three of us flinch. Zaku's roaring is further away now—we're losing him.

"She's not asking for you, female," Azsote says. "She asks for Zaku."

Azsote looks at Vruksha, and I see something pass between them. Vruksha lowers his spear, and Azsote slips into the forest, vanishing so swiftly it was like he was never here at all.

I twist under Vruksha's arm. "We're following him, right?"

I think he's going to fight me, tell me our job is done, but to my complete surprise, Vruksha nods, picks me up, and chases after Azsote. It's not long before he catches up to the silent green male, joining him in his swift hunt for the king.

TWENTY-FIVE
DAISY

Vruksha

I SLIDE through the trees after the Boomslang, holding my female against me. I've missed having her in my arms. My mate's softness warms my scales, and her scent invigorates me.

She is mine, and I adore it.

"Thank you, mate."

I curse as the words snap into my head.

They haven't stopped repeating through my mind since Gemma said them. I didn't know how badly I needed to hear her call me mate in return, until she did.

Then they stung, and now, each time they repeat, the thrill of it muddies further. She called me mate so I would help her find her friend. And once that thought entered my head, I haven't been able to push it out. I've been mulling it over all night.

I don't feel like I'm her mate. Not entirely. Not yet.

Gemma's mine, but I'm not hers. Glancing down, I find

her eyes are closed, her forehead wrinkled, face scrunched up again. She gets this way when I sprint through the trees and it's almost... precious.

She would not like being held if I swung through the trees as Azsote does. The branches above us shake as the Boomslang slips from one to the next, catching and bracing with his tail muscles.

Zaku's roars heighten as we catch up to him.

"King Cobra!" Azsote yells when we're close. "I know where she is," he calls out, dropping from the trees. I come to a stop a short distance away. Gemma wiggles in my arms.

Azsote won't try and steal her. I read it in his eyes. And if Zaku is after the other female, then Gemma is at least safe from these nagas, but if there are more nearby, brought out by Zaku's shouting, I want to keep a hold on her so they know she's been claimed.

I could coax her into a rutting for everyone to view—to establish who is her mate, the one who caught her—but I neither want Gemma naked in front of them nor want to share her sweet secrets with males who may try and risk taking her from me anyway.

If I were made to watch such a beautiful female open up her arms and accept her mate with a moan, I would want to steal her for myself—nothing would stop me. Not even another naga's prick sinking into her.

It would be the last thing he ever did.

"Zaku!" Azsote yells once more, coiling his tail around the trunk of a nearby tree.

Noises of passage strike my ears, snaps of sticks, and the rustle of leaves. Zaku's giant form bursts into the clearing, tackling Azsote to the forest floor. The Boomslang slides himself out from under Zaku, using his hold on the tree.

"Where is she?" Zaku claws at him. "Take me to

her!" Zaku's nostrils flare, his cowl expands, and the spikes of it straighten out. He's covered in dirt, eyes fierce, and I bare my fangs. But the King Cobra doesn't see me.

Stupid male.

Azsote hisses and drops from the tree to put his tail between him and Zaku.

Gemma pushes out of my hold, answering before Azsote can. "She's hurt. Azsote's taking us to her. He's been looking for you. We've been looking for her."

Zaku's eyes swing to my female, and I brace for an attack.

His crazed gaze flicks over us, and he wipes the back of his hand across his mouth, taking us in. I notice a new wound on his chest that's swollen and red.

I hiss in warning when it appears Zaku isn't going to calm. "I will strike if you get close."

Zaku swings back to Azsote. "Take me to Daisy!"

"And them?" Azsote indicates us.

Gemma tenses. "We're going too, I demand to see her. If you try and stop us, you'll have to deal with me," she threatens.

Zaku grabs Azsote's neck and jerks the Boomslang close. "Take me to her. I won't ask again. I don't care what they do."

Azsote tugs Zaku's hand from around his throat and twists, dashing away. Zaku takes off after him, and I surge forward to follow. Gemma's hair flies against my chest, tickling my scales.

From one tree to the next, we rush through the forest. No one stops us. No one even comes out and tries. Three naga males against one is certain death. Invigorated, I feel part of a clan for the first time since my sisters left. A hunt with my brethren for the precious, rare females we all desire.

I suck in the warm air, grasping my female close.

It's at this moment, as the forest gives way to a long stretch of land and I watch Zaku rush after Azsote, that I forgive her for choosing her friend over me. I remember what it's like to care for more than my own hide. I had forgotten the strength there is in numbers.

If we came together, no human, beast, or otherwise would be able to stop us. And if what Gemma says is true, and the humans will never stop searching for the tech... then rejoining my brethren is imperative for all our safety going forward. Using the tech that we hide would be easier united.

Because this land is ours.

And no one can make us leave.

"Smoke," Gemma gasps. "There, see it?" She points to a ribbon of it rising from the trees in the distance. I smell it when she does. "Please be okay," she whispers, low enough she probably doesn't think I hear it.

"She will be okay," I rumble.

She rests her head against my chest. I feel her tremble.

By the time we make it to the smoke, Azsote and Zaku are already there. It's worse than I thought. The trees are charred, some are still burning, and a clear streak of land has been cleared out from the skiff.

The skiff is in ruins. The majority of the smoke comes from it. Part of its side is crumpled, and the windows are shattered. There's metal and debris everywhere. No one could've survived such mechanical violence.

"Daisy," Gemma breathes.

I hold onto her as she tries to break from my arms.

Zaku's silence is deafening. Another naga male is there,

staring at the smoke. As a breeze wisps some of it away, familiar brown and beige scales appear. I grip my spear, bringing it forward.

Krellix, the last Copperhead. I haven't seen him since the plateau. Azsote snarls at him but doesn't stop, moving through the wreckage. Krellix glances at the rest of us, stopping to stare at Gemma. Zaku goes after Azsote.

"Vruksha," Gemma whispers. "We need to get to Daisy."

I don't take my gaze off Krellix. The male twists to face us head-on. The way he looks at my female forces a growl from my throat. Heat, desperation, and lust appear all at once, etched over his face.

He slides closer. His muscles bunch. Through the smoke, I smell his cloying scent. I tense, immediately acknowledging it as a scent I've recently been giving off too.

I set Gemma down. Her arm comes up around me as she moves under my shoulder. "Get behind me," I tell her, readying my weapon.

"You can't have me," Gemma snaps, glaring at Krellix. "I'm already taken." She shoots Krellix a withering look.

I go still, shocked by her words.

The Copperhead cocks his head. "You are a feisty one."

"And I'm Vruksha's, so don't even try it. If he doesn't kill you, I will. Now move. My friend is hurt and needs me."

Krellix's lips twitch.

"Move," I warn.

He finally looks at me. "You are lucky," he says, slipping out of our path and disappearing into the trees.

I'm skilled, vicious, and a little reckless, but lucky? I hiss. It wasn't luck that won me Gemma. It was fate. Gemma stretches up and hooks her arm around my neck. I haul her back into the cradle of my arms. We take off after the others.

We don't have to go far, finding Zaku and Azsote on the other side. Zaku is emerging from a fox hole with something in his arms. A broken, ashen thing I barely recognize as human, let alone a female at all.

"Daisy!" Gemma cries out. She pushes from my arms and stumbles toward Zaku.

The Cobra snarls before I can stop her, rushing up behind. Gemma doesn't notice. She's entirely focused on the crumpled form in Zaku's hold.

A weak moan leaves the creature's lips.

"We need to get her out of her clothes and cleaned, quickly! We need water!" Gemma yells, turning to Azsote. "Get water!"

The next hour is a flurry of activity. Zaku doesn't leave Daisy's side, and my female takes over, ignoring anyone who tries to stop her. We get Daisy away from the wreckage and bring her to a creek that Azsote leads us to.

Zaku and Gemma hover over her, cutting off the remainder of her burnt clothes. It's not until her screaming starts that Azsote and I shoot into action to secure our perimeter.

Azsote darts up into the trees, disappearing, while I take ground cover. I run into Krellix, who's returned to the wreckage, stamping out the last of the flames with his tail. I leave him to it.

The screams continue until they abruptly cut off. They will haunt my dreams for years to come.

When I know the area around us is clear, I head for Gemma, who's bandaging her friend with as much care as possible. Gemma's hands are bloody, and ash has gotten all over her hair and skin. She turns to me when I approach and wipes her hands on the grass at her sides.

The grass is covered in blood.

"You said you know of a medical pod? You've seen one?" Her face is strained, worried.

I coil my tail around her. "It's unusable." I glimpse the other female. She's naked save some strips of cloth, and half her face is mottled, bright red with purpling splotches. She's burned from the left side of her face, down her chest, to her navel. If she survives, it's a wound that will never fully heal.

I'm sickened. I see Gemma in her place, and bile rises.

Zaku's tail is ringed around where she lays motionless, leaving just enough room for Gemma to get close. His hands are white, his expression is a mask of worry, desperation. I see the pain, the fear.

I've never seen either from him and of all the naga males, he's the closest to me. Not in distance, but in history. He and Vagan.

"I have a pod in my den, but it's far from here," he rasps, his eyes on the female before him. "Her screams when we move her... They destroy me."

"You have a pod?" Gemma turns to him. "We need to get her there. Now! While she's unconscious."

I shake my head. "It'll be dark soon."

"Daisy can't stay out here in her condition. She needs shelter, a place to rest, food, and medicine."

Zaku growls. "Then we go." He pulls his tail under him and begins to slowly push his hands under Daisy.

The female's eyes fly open, her mouth parts, and she shrieks. Zaku roars and jerks his hands away. "I can't help you here!" he yells.

A sob leaves the female, and her entire body convulses.

"Try again," Gemma stammers. Her face has gone whiter than the snow-capped mountains.

Zaku's hands shake.

Gemma leans over her friend and coos, petting her brow where she is unharmed. The Daisy's cries lower to whimpers. "Shhh, sweetheart. We're taking you to safety. You have to be strong, okay? If the pain gets to be too much, let it take you away." Gemma looks at Zaku when Daisy blinks out tears. "Again."

"I can't," he chokes.

"You can. You can do this, Zaku. You can do this. She needs you." Zaku and Gemma share a look, and my first reaction is to pummel Zaku to the ground and kill him, but I force my mind to calm.

No one's ever talked to one of us the way Gemma is talking to Zaku. She's comforting him. She's doing it while she's still hurt and afraid, wearing clothes that are falling off her body, her feet bound. She's showing more strength than Zaku, than any of us.

"Zaku," she orders when he doesn't move, her voice hardening. "Lift her. We don't have time to waste."

Zaku's nostrils flare. He looks down at the female and closes his eyes. I place my hand on Gemma's shoulder, curling my tail around her as Daisy screams again.

My soul winces.

Azsote joins us, and together we make the arduous, devastating journey to Zaku's den.

TWENTY-SIX

BETRAYAL FROM ABOVE

Gemma

THE NEXT SEVERAL days are a blur. I barely sleep. I don't leave Daisy's side once we make it to the King Cobra's lair. Zaku's *den*. He doesn't leave her side either, which means, Vruksha, Zaku, and I are hovering over Daisy day in and day out.

I rub my eyes.

If it wasn't for Azsote, I don't think any of us would take the time to eat.

I drop my hands to stare through the plastic screen of the medical pod. The buzz of it soothes me, and I'm just so thankful it works. It works, and Zaku has one. He didn't like what it did to Daisy when he turned it on, how it stuck her with needles and shot her up of questionable stuff, but Vruksha and Azsote managed to hold him down and keep him away long enough for it to do its thing.

I wasn't thrilled about it either, but I managed to keep it to myself. A pod over a thousand years old going to work on my friend? I can't help but hope for the best and be terrified and suspicious at the same time. But suspicion is better than helplessness. And whatever the medical intelligence did... it worked.

Daisy hasn't screamed since we laid her down.

She's stable. Resting. And the pod, though not perfect, is keeping her clean. Zaku's robots are keeping her fed... The burns on her flesh appear less angry every day.

I sigh and turn my head from where it rests on my arms and stare out the window. Vruksha is gazing out of it too, facing away from me. His glistening ruby scales dazzle me with their beauty.

It takes my breath away. He's gorgeous in the light. My naga male.

I would paint him just how he is now, how I see him when he doesn't notice me looking, gazing over the land he's conquered. I would paint him with the sun at his back, and his spear held high, casting lightning upon his foes.

The picture would hang over my bed. I'd stare at it and touch myself.

He wants to go home. I feel it. He's not comfortable here, in Zaku's domain, and it shows. He's always touching me in some way, like right now, his tailtip is curled around my ankle. He doesn't let me talk to Zaku or Azsote without him. And when I'm about to faint from exhaustion, he winds me up in his tail and forces me to sleep on him.

I'd enjoy Vruksha's concern if it wasn't for the beds Zaku has. Beds with cloth blankets and sheets. He also has piles of clothes in every size and has let me have whatever fits, including shoes and undergarments. He has... luxury. His home is clean, bright, airy. He has dozens of working robots as well. They manage the place.

Except Zaku won't let any of us leave the front rooms,

and I'm becoming curious about what he has hidden within his strange, ancient human home.

Outside his home, it's different. It's almost calm. The terrain near Zaku's place is rough, sprawling, but still serene. There's a view of the gorge, the mountains, including the one Daisy crashed into. We're at the peak of one, and the view goes far. It's nice as long as I keep my eyes off the lawn, where there are skulls everywhere and a pile of rotting pig corpses. But it's easy to ignore them being as exhausted and numb as I am right now.

When my thoughts grow bleak, I can just look out the window and feel better. I forgot what it's like to see trees, grass, and animals through a window. Even dead ones.

It's usually stars, nebulas, asteroid fields, and planets.

We're far from the facility, farther still from Vruksha's bunker. I've been trying to map it out in my head. Zaku lives in the opposite direction from the facility, in a mansion built into the side of a mountain, like a king.

King Cobra...

I didn't like Zaku at first, blaming him as the reason Daisy and I were sacrificed, but I've decided to hate him a little less.

He cares for Daisy. He never leaves her side, just like Vruksha never leaves mine. He worries constantly, and though he's obstinate, almost bullish, and I want to slap him even when I'm sleeping, I can forgive him. He gazes at Daisy as if she's his entire world.

I keep my doubts anyway. I still don't know why Daisy stole a skiff. I wonder how long she flew it before crashing, where was she trying to go?

I hear a moan and I sit upright, flicking my eyes to her. Zaku is asleep across from me, sprawled over a cushiony chair, his large tail draped over the glass shield of the pod.

Daisy twitches. Her chapped, peeling lips part slightly, and another moan escapes.

"Daisy?' I whisper.

One of her eyelids cracks open and finds me.

I sit forward. "Daisy?"

"Gemma?"

"Yes, it's me."

She shudders, and her eye closes. She tries to raise her hand, and I stop her.

"Don't move." Though as I say it, the pod goes into action and a screen of Daisy's current vitals appears in the glass. A robotic arm from the side injects her with something that makes Daisy sigh.

"Where am I?" she asks when the pod returns to normal.

"Zaku's... house? Den," I correct. "In his medical pod."

Her one eye looks around, stopping on the large naga tail above her on the glass. She follows it over to the male snoring on the seat beside her. He's still asleep, and I have a feeling his snores are drowning out our whispering. I debate waking him, but I want to speak to Daisy first.

I sense Vruksha at my back.

Daisy stares at Zaku.

My brow furrows, trying to read her. Her face is swollen almost beyond recognition. Is she afraid?

"Is there anything I can do to make you more comfortable?" I ask. "Anything at all? I'm glad you're awake. We were terrified for a bit there... You were in so much pain."

Her tongue pokes out to taste her lips. "I don't feel anything right now."

"I think the pod is pumping you with painkillers."

Daisy's eye shifts back over to me. "I crashed."

My face falls. "Yeah."

"I shouldn't be alive." Her voice is barely more than an airy, strained whisper.

"But you are."

Despair washes over her, and my heart squeezes. "Daisy," I continue, "you're alive and you're going to stay that way."

But I need to know, I need to know if Zaku can be trusted. If she's safe with him. I won't leave her here if she isn't. I've been watching the King Cobra, and though I now like him okay, it doesn't mean he's not a monster. Peter turned out to be a monster.

"I shouldn't be," she chokes. "I fell so far. My escape pod wouldn't eject..."

"Don't think about it anymore. It's over. I have something I need to ask you, something important."

Her lips tremble. "What?"

I lower my voice, leaning right up to the glass. "Are you... Are you with Zaku?"

Confusion flutters across Daisy's face for a split-second, and then it's gone. "He caught me."

"Do you want to stay caught?"

Her eye turns glassy, and she looks up at the ceiling. "He calls me his queen."

"That's not what I'm asking..."

Her gaze goes to Vruksha. "Do you like him? His smell?"

I don't think I could explain how I feel about Vruksha to another. Being with him is like being sated, free. It doesn't make sense. My breath whizzes through my teeth. "I like him a lot," I tell her. "His...smell included."

A lot.

But does she feel that way about Zaku? I eye the naga male.

"I'm glad," she croaks. "Gemma..." Daisy says, dodging my question.

"The crash wasn't your fault."

"I was shot down."

Shot down? My brow furrows. Daisy shudders, clearly upset, and all I want to do is hold her, tell her it's all going to be okay.

"Who?" I ask.

Daisy shudders again.

And a streak of fear bolts through me, constricting my throat. The ship here on Earth, the transport ship we took from *The Dreadnaut*, isn't equipped with weapons besides a couple of turrets that can only be used while landlocked to protect it from thieves...

So that only makes one other option.

"*The Dreadnaut* shot me down," she whispers.

Zaku groans, his tail slides on the pod. He's waking.

"How? Why?" I ask. "They wouldn't do that. Captain Michal would never fire on our own."

Daisy's eye goes wide, flicking between Zaku's tail and me. "Gemma, I was trying to reach them. Tell them what's happening down here." Her hand shakes like she's trying to rise again. "They know."

She did what I was unable to do.

Daisy cries out just as Zaku snaps to attention, taking over. Daisy closes her eye as Zaku speaks to her in a soft voice. He hisses at me to back away. I reach behind me, and Vruksha clasps my hand. His tail coils the rest of the way up my leg.

Vruksha leads me away.

If what Daisy says about *The Dreadnaut* is true, my fears have been made real. Vruksha isn't safe, and it appears neither are Daisy and me. I squeeze my eyes shut, suddenly overwhelmingly exhausted.

If Central Command knows what Peter has done, then there's no help for us. We can only help ourselves. I turn in Vruksha's embrace and rest my head against his chest. His hands tangle in my hair, his short claws grazing my scalp, prickling me with comfort.

"It's time to go," he says.

"I know."

I have a promise to keep.

And more than anything, it's one I want to keep.

TWENTY-SEVEN
THE ONLY CHOICE

Gemma

WE DON'T LEAVE Zaku's den for another two days.

Daisy begs for me to stay longer, and so the males fight each other for dominion. Vruksha is forced to give way to Zaku, because we're in the Cobra's territory, and the longer we remain, he gets a little more crazed.

By the end, I'm with him more than I am with Daisy, soothing his sensitive serpent manhood. Though we're never truly alone, not with Azsote lurking around. The Boomslang is always watching when he's not out hunting. I see his envy building.

Zaku and Vruksha have noticed it too.

Last night, I found Azsote watching me change into softer clothes for sleep. It was the Boomslang's bitter scent that alerted me to him. Vruksha tackled him, injecting Azsote with his venom, forcing the Boomslang down. Azsote was then dragged out of Zaku's den and tossed over the side of the mountain.

He's been banished.

Though I know he's outside, waiting, and now that I know he's there, that he's willing to invade my privacy to see me naked, I don't leave the front rooms of Zaku's den.

I can't be with Vruksha the way we both need.

I crave him. I crave the way he moves my body. The way he takes control of my limbs, winding me up in his tail and making me forget everything but him. Nothing else matters when Vruksha and I are alone.

So when I stuff my bag full of all the clothes and items Zaku's given me, I'm hopeful.

Daisy wakes several times a day for short periods, and the pain in her gaze eases more each day. Whatever the pod is doing to heal her, it's working. Even her burns have mended a great deal.

She dodges my questions every time I bring up Zaku. She won't speak to me about him, but she also doesn't seem to fear him. It's possible I'm being overprotective, assuming a closeness she might not feel.

She's chosen to stay and heal. I don't know what that means when it comes to her and Zaku, though I take it she doesn't know either.

"Are you sure you have to go?" Daisy asks. She's lying on her good side today, facing me. The swelling around her eye has gone down significantly.

"I promised Vruksha," I've told her this before.

"I'm going to miss you."

"I'm going to miss you too, but we'll see each other again. I know it. We'll be back soon, I promise."

Though Vruksha is one word away from doing to Zaku what he did to Azsote, I know he and Zaku have an understanding. They trust each other; I can tell. They may never admit it, may not even realize it themselves since both males are reluctant to show weakness of any kind, but it's there.

"I hope you're right."

"I am. Are you sure you want to stay?"

Daisy nods. "I want to heal."

I purse my lips, search her face. "Okay. Enjoy this great view you have and think of me when you do, okay?" I hesitate to leave her. "I'll search for a way we can communicate," I tell her. It's been on my mind. Peter took our personal comm ware before he gave us over to the nagas, and I want it back. There's stuff here that can help us, I know it. I just have to find it first. "When I find it, you'll be the first to know."

Daisy smiles then her face winces in pain. "Good," she rasps.

I rise. "No more dangerous missions without me? If you run again, wait for me?"

"We'll see."

"She's not going anywhere," Zaku growls.

Glimpsing him on the other side. "Bye, Zaku," I say. "Vruksha and I will be back," I warn.

He hisses.

With one last lingering look at Daisy, I make my way to the exit where Vruksha waits for me. I pass through the barriers of the den's entryway and find Vruksha on the broken steps leading away outside. The doors close behind me with a resounding, finalized *thud*, and glancing back, I'm surprised Daisy managed to escape this place at all.

She's stronger than me.

Still, I can't help but think there's something Daisy isn't telling me. Something about Zaku she's not sharing. What's behind the doors of his den, the ones he won't let anyone pass through?

I chew on my lip. I'll find out, I decide.

Vruksha snatches my bag, and I look up to find his eyes glinting. His scales are rigid over his knuckles where he grips his spear.

He scents the Boomslang's tension. *Tension* is how he describes the mating heat he feels since he doesn't have another name for it. The way he gets—his bulge expanding —when he's near me, tastes me, or sees me naked. Tension. The pressure of the seed, almost unbearable, filling his cock until spilled.

There's no way of knowing what Azsote will do if it gets bad. Lately, he's been giving off a smell that wrinkles my nose.

I didn't know this until two days ago.

Apparently all the naga males have a knot on their cocks, one that expands and fills continuously until they spill the contents.

No wonder why I feel beyond stretched when Vruk-sha's inside me.

"Two days," he says. Vruksha's eyes go to my feet. Fortunately, I've found some proper boots. "Can you walk? For now?"

Curling my toes, I nod. I take the long knife Zaku gave me, palming the handle of it where it's sheathed at my belt. We make the slow descent down his mountain.

For the rest of the day, we're scaling down one mountain, only to climb another. We stop occasionally to rest and eat, though never for long. Vruksha won't let us. He's tense, and as the hours pass, the muscles of his back and arms only bunch further.

When the sun lowers, his countenance darkens even more. It's making me nervous.

He's been cold since we left his bunker, and now that

it's just the two of us, his mood has only soured. My stomach twists. We have to talk; I know we do. We've kept our conversations to the here-and-now while with Daisy and the others, but they're gone now. Nothing is stopping us but the trek—the wilderness.

I keep my mouth shut.

Vruksha is focusing on our path and staying vigilant. I'm right there with him. Every snap of a twig, every gust of wind, even the chirps of bugs and birds keep me on edge.

People lived here. I trail the heavy growth of trees with my eyes, pushing through several branches. *My people.* We were landlocked here for thousands of years.

I can't comprehend it, not having the freedom of space, being stuck on a single small planet, where if I wanted to get away from someone or something, I could only put some land and maybe an ocean between us. I'd rather there'd be millions of galaxies.

I thought it was amazing that Vruksha's bunker, the tech, and even the animals were still here, but after seeing Zaku's home, there's nothing left to surprise me. He had running water, silver walls edged with stones, and so much more. I'd gone through a time machine, back to when my ancestors thrived.

It's while I'm thinking this, having finally stopped worrying about Daisy, that Vruksha leads me into the ruins of a building.

A large one. One I haven't seen before.

Vines and moss cover it, but floors remain, and the rest of it? It's scattered amongst the trees as far as I can see. There are rusty bars, shattered windows, and trees that shoot from the ground through the pieces that are left. We've passed numerous buildings and ruins, and each one is interesting in its own way.

Vruksha leads me deeper into the building, and I'm met with centuries of dust and decay. Looking around, it appears stripped of objects that might be collected, except for random bits and pieces left behind.

He stops, leans over a counter, and brushes some of the debris aside with his tail. He rises and points his spear to the spot. "We camp here tonight."

I peek over the counter to the hard, dirty floor on the other side. It's not great, though I like the walls on every side. Vruksha drops my bag of clothes. It's a good spot.

"I'm going to secure the perimeter." He slips away before I can stop him.

I rub the chill from my hands, open my bag, and pull out a ration to eat. I take it with me when I decide to familiarize myself with the building.

There are broken chairs, decaying pictures on the walls, and drooping plastic plants. I try to imagine what it would have looked like before the Lurkers, but I can't, not really. The place was made to be comfortable, and there's no comfort left.

I hear something behind me, and I turn, finding Vruksha. He stops when he sees me. There's a dead bird in his hand, and he shows it to me. "Food," he says.

"I ate a ration."

His tail curls. His brows arc. He takes me in, and I straighten, wondering what he's seeing. He lifts the bird to his mouth and starts eating it raw. My nose wrinkles.

I've seen him do it before.

He stares at me as he eats it, licks his fingers.

I shiver.

"I'm going to keep watch," he says when he's done, wiping his mouth with the back of his hand. "Stay here and get some rest." He turns to leave again.

"Wait," I call out quickly, not wanting him to go.

"What?"

I take a step forward. "You've been... distant since we left the bunker."

Vruksha cocks his head.

"You've been upset."

He hisses. "Your friend is sssafe, female."

"That's not what I mean. I know she is. This isn't about her."

"Then what is it about? Tomorrow, you will be back within my den, in our nest, and you will completely give yourself to me. Forever."

He continues, stalking toward me. "Unless you've changed your mind?"

"I haven't changed my mind," I say. I don't want to break my word, but also, I can't imagine what he'd do if I did. My naga is reasonable, intelligent, and strong, but he's also lawless, and quick to temper. He stops in front of me, eyes ablaze. I chew on my tongue, straining my neck to meet his gaze. "I want to know what's wrong. With you."

For someone who rose through the ranks as a comms officer, I'm sure as shit at failing at communicating now, when it matters most.

Maybe that's the trick about communicating. When it doesn't matter, it's easy, and when it does... It's the hardest thing in the world to find the right words—the right time.

"Wrong, female? There is nothing wrong. Once I have you safe, where no other male can either see you or get to you, we can talk. Tonight? I do not trust what could be waiting in the canopy above." He pulls away again.

I grab his wrist. He stops, tensing where I touch him. It's the most we've touched all day. He doesn't shake me off, so I move into his arms and press against his body, curling my arms around his back. I inhale his earthy scent, and his soft scales tickle my cheek. I close my eyes hard and shudder.

"I miss you," I whisper.

His arms close in around me. "I've never left."

"I need you," I say, holding in my tears. Words fail me.

His hands tangle into my hair. "I'm here, female."

"Don't leave me tonight. If you do, take me with."

Vruksha pulls me into his arms. "I'll stay."

He carries me to our spot behind the counter. And for a time, he just holds me, giving me everything I've missed, I've needed. *This. Us.* I burrow hard into him, relishing his body, his warmth. Whatever may be outside can stay there, but tonight, it's just the two of us in this building. I curl my fingers against him as he winds his tail through and under my legs.

I could never leave, even if I wanted to. I could never leave the heaven of his arms.

Not for rank, not for paints, not for anything.

Anything... Fantastical I am not. Perhaps, that will be my greatest secret. That I have chosen Vruksha over everyone.

His hands grip my hair, they run up and down my back, and his heart thunders under my ear.

"I miss you always," he says softly, holding me tighter against him. "Every time I take my eyes off you, I miss you."

A laugh bubbles up. "Is that why you're always watching me?"

"I always watch you because you are beautiful, and you glow in the light. But perhaps I also watch you because I'm afraid if I don't, you'll disappear."

My chest tightens. "I won't." I mean it.

Silence returns for a time. Vruksha sways his tail, caressing my body, keeping me warm.

"I want you to choose me," he says after a while.

I lift to look at him. "I have chosen you."

He meets my eyes in the darkness. "I need you to choose me." His voice roughens. "Every day."

"Every day, I will choose you."

His finger caresses my cheek. "I need you to really choose me."

My lips purse, confused. I pull away a little further so I can see him better, trying to figure him out. "Is that why you're unhappy?" I ask softly. "I've chosen you over everyone, I lo—"

He interrupts me. "I'm not unhappy."

"You've pulled away from me."

"I haven't."

"Then explain it to me. What's going on? I choose you, Vruksha," I declare. "I'm not going anywhere. You're the only one I trust." It hurts to say it, admitting the betrayal of my people, but it's also liberating. "Should I scream it?" I deadpan.

His finger drops from my cheek. "Your trust is a gift," he says.

"You're deflecting."

He hisses.

I hiss back at him.

His lips wrinkle, gifting me a brief glimmer of a smile.

Vruksha is handsome when he smiles. I grin, hissing once more. "I can do it too."

"Yesss, you do it well."

"Now explain it to me," I demand. "If we're to be mates, we can't have any more secrets."

His chest puffs out, and he exhales. "I've never been

chosen," he begins.

I give him all my attention.

He continues, "I told you about my father, my mother. How he stayed to raise me and my sisters, though, I know now he died the day my mother did. He chose to live, to protect me and my siblings, and that was enough for a young male like me. I didn't know better, not like how I do now. How that choice he made, to stay with us, was everything. A sacrifice I can only start to comprehend. Except it didn't last, that choice he made, and when my sisters chose to go west, I knew it hurt my father gravely. That day, he lost them, like he lost my mother.

"I wasn't enough.

"For years, he stayed with me, teaching me to hunt and use the tech. He showed me how to live, but he was already dead, and those final years, I knew being with me killed him. He worried about my sisters. I wasn't surprised when he decided to go after them. Once he made his decision, he became happy, and I realized how much being with me was hurting him. He chose me, but not really. Those days before his departure, the happier he got, the more it hurt."

"Did you tell him this?"

"How could I? I'd never seen my father smile before. I couldn't take that away."

I can't imagine. "I'm sorry." I could say it a thousand times, but it would never help.

"I watched him leave me, never to return. He never asked me to join him."

I lean my head against his chest.

"After he left, it seemed he left not only me behind, but his darkness, his grief. And that grief went into me instead. I mourned the loss of my sisters, but it was not the way I mourned the loss of my father. For years, I was alone, never seeing another soul, not until Zhallaix established a den near my own, and in doing so, brought Zaku and the other nagas out of their territories and into mine. He and the others distracted me, and I moved on, forgetting what it was like to be lonely, that my family abandoned me.

"And then a ship came out of the sky, and with it, humans."

"Me," I whisper.

"You, sweet mate. I was lucky enough to see the ship land and go after it. Many of us did. Then, one day, you appeared, walking from the confines of that vessel and into my world. I noticed your hair first, the way it shimmered in the sunlight, its brilliance. I looked down at my scales and realized we were the same color. You wore my color, and I knew you were mine. Nothing else mattered. I had to have you. There was nothing else. And when I took a second glance, our eyes met."

"I remember." I shiver thinking of that day and how afraid I was when I saw Vruksha for the first time. I like hearing him tell it from his point of view though. It makes me happy. He hadn't seemed real, not with his shock of red amongst the trees. "You scared me. I thought you were covered in blood."

"You stood there staring back at me for a long time."

"I thought if I moved, you'd come out of the trees and eat me."

"I wanted to, but not in that way."

"Did I give you *tension*?"

Vruksha rumbles. "Yes."

I smile.

"After you left, running from me and into the facility ruins, I knew there was no way I was leaving without you. I planned to steal you."

"You did?"

"I scouted the perimeter of the facility a hundred times, searching for weakness, for a way in and out where I wouldn't be caught. I searched for you constantly, hoping for another glimpse. Each time I saw you, I became more obsessed, more certain you belonged with me, and during my plans, I found other naga males doing the same. They saw you and the other females within and wanted you too. I was desperate. We fought because we all wanted the same thing—you. When we realized attacking the base was a bad idea, Zaku decided to approach your males—"

"And make a deal with Peter," I snap.

"What else were we to do? If we attacked, you and the other females could be hurt. You could escape into your ship and leave? The very idea of those possibilities stopped me and the other nagas from sneaking in alone, from attacking at all. The risk was too great."

I shake my head. "It wasn't right."

"Yes, it was," he growls.

"And if I fought tooth and nail? And still fought you right now? What then?"

"I would make you see."

I sigh.

"This isn't why I was... unhappy, Gemma."

I sigh again and play with the scales on his chest. "Go on."

"After it was all said and done, and I finally had you, you chose Azsote."

Sitting back up, I glare at him. "I told you why I chose him."

"You did."

"I wish I could go back in time and make a better choice... I can't."

"When you had to make a choice again, you chose Daisy."

My brow wrinkles. "She was in trouble."

Vruksha shakes his head. "You called me your mate when you did. It was bliss, hearing you say it aloud, but then it infuriated me. I hated it. Helping your friend is one thing, but in doing so, it brought back everything."

My heart sinks. "I didn't mean—"

"Stop. I understand why you did it now. I also realize you didn't do it on purpose. I'd... forgotten what it was like not being alone, being a part of a clan. I... liked it. I remembered when we met up with Zaku, Azsote, and even your friend, how there's strength in numbers and there's comfort in sharing your worries with others who are like-minded. It's been years since I last saw my father, and I'd forgotten."

"What about today?" I whisper.

"You haven't called me mate since," he tells me.

I close my eyes hard, finally understanding. I manipulated him, used his insecurities to get what I wanted. I hadn't even realized what I had done until now. I knew how much he wanted me, how protective he was, how paranoid he gets, and I must've known calling him mate in return was a priceless gift. Even subconsciously, I knew. I did it anyway, not thinking if it was the right place or time.

And I used that power he'd given me to force him to take me to Daisy. I can't stop the thick ball of guilt squeezing my heart.

I sit up and lean back. His arms loosen around me.

"I choose you," I say, almost gasping the words.

His eyes hood. "What?"

"I choose you," I tell him louder. "Mate," I add.

"You don't—"

"I'm saying it not because you want to hear it, but

because I need to say it and you need to hear it again. Because there's nothing else I want. Only you. There's nothing else I want than to be your mate. I will tell you every day if I must because it's the truth. I'm not going anywhere. I will prove it."

"Your humans are still here, and so is their ship."

"I know."

Vruksha searches my eyes. His tail closes in tightly around us. "You won't try and run? Like your friend? I couldn't bear it. Not after seeing what it did to her... Her screams."

"I won't run," I promise him. "I love you."

"Love," he says. "That's a strange word."

"You'll hear it from now on. It won't be strange for long." I've never felt how I do for Vruksha for anyone else.

He pulls me close, resting his chin on my head, and I settle against him. Moonlight shines through the cracks of the building, and I watch the flurries of dust in the dim silver light. It's such a simple beauty, but one I'll never take advantage of again. Earth may not be the place it once was, and there may be obstacles in our future, but for now, I'm exactly where I'm supposed to be.

I know what's at stake. What's been given up, and I vow to protect what's left with my life. There's something wrong with this new Earth, and I'm going to figure out what it is.

While I do, I'll be with Vruksha.

He gently brushes his fingers through my hair, lulling me to sleep.

"Love," he whispers.

It's the last thing I hear before sleep. Then his warmth takes me away, leading me to dreams of mountains and the alien men who rule them.

TWENTY-EIGHT

ONCE A SECRET

Gemma

WE LEAVE the building before the sun rises the next morning. He's eager to be back home, and so am I. I want the pelts and the warmth of Vruksha's nest, and he wants me to prove that I'll keep my word.

He doesn't have to say it; I know it.

I want to prove it too. Baby steps, rights? He's earned my trust, now I need to earn his.

For how alien Vruksha and his naga brothers are, they're still a conglomerate of softness and insecurity beneath their rough exteriors. Even Zaku, I bet.

I hope Daisy's made the right choice staying with him, but even if she regrets it already, now that I know where she is, I'll check in on her soon.

Even if it means facing the wilds again. Vruksha will take me, I'm certain. He's going to need to teach me how to hunt and defend myself anyway. It's not like there are working orbs everywhere I can beg for help. And still, if there were, I wouldn't. Gunfire is loud and imperfect. The drones here may no longer have the calibration software for perfect aim.

I got lucky, really lucky. I can't rely on luck going forward.

The next time... the drones may not come at all. I need to know how to survive and avoid another situation like the pigs.

I'm also anxious to explore this forest and clean out Vruksha's bunker. I'd just begun digging through his stuff and learning about my history before we left.

I want him to show me his screens again.

I want to know everything. Even if it's hard, even if no one survives. I've decided it's my job to make sure the information is protected, cataloged, and saved. So if humans do return to Earth, they'll know what's at stake, what we've lost, and that we still have so much left to lose. I've only just gained a little of it back myself.

I want to honor those who died.

As for the Lurker tech... I'm fine with it staying hidden until I understand more, keeping it far from anyone who might misuse it, even my own people. Because if *the Dreadnaut* did fire on Daisy...

Sighing, I push through the branches of a large bush, following Vruksha's trail.

I exhale loudly, seeing a steep hill ahead of me.

Why does it have to be steep?

As I've traveled by Vruksha's side, I've watched for the signs of the land flattening out, of the trees thinning, of the vague landmarks I've already come to know. But the land doesn't flatten out like I expect. I peek up at the sky and grasp Vruksha's tail. He hauls me up a ledge. It seems like we've been climbing for hours when I'm certain we should be on flat land by now. I wipe the sweat from my brow.

I had to be physically fit to work on the bridge of *The Dreadnaut*, but apparently I'm not as fit as I thought I am. Even after all the time I've spent on Earth, I'm pushing my limits every day. My injuries don't help.

It's getting easier though.

"I hope this is a shortcut," I groan. "I need a bath, even if it means risking running into Zhallaix. I have a knife now."

Come at me Zhallaix, I am not in the mood. I narrow my eyes.

"We won't make it to the bunker tonight."

"I knew it!" I throw up my hands. "I knew we weren't heading there when we kept climbing." I don't know if I want to cry or collapse. The past month has been hard, and it needs to stop. The hardness, that is. "Where are you taking me?" I ask, wheezing a little.

Vruksha turns to me, throws his muscled limbs around my body, and hauls me into the cradle of his arms. I slump like a damsel in distress.

"We're almossst there," he says.

He continues the climb with me holding onto him, only using the strength of his tail. Sometimes I forget how powerful it is, as he easily lifts us both up on it, coiling and shifting its weight for his needs. I've taken that power between my legs... Perhaps I'm powerful too.

It's been too long since our last time together, and I need him. But climbing all day? It really takes the *oomph* out of having sex. This is why I want a nice, cold bath, and some rest, because the next time it happens...

My eyes widen. I'm going to ride him. I'll show him that human females can be full of *tension* too.

I even miss the dangerous graze of his fangs sliding across my flesh. Especially now that I saw what his venom did to Azsote—I know the risk.

I wish I had venom of my own. Maybe then I could've bitten Peter and thrown him over a mountain too. I run my tongue across my blunt teeth.

Now that I know we're not going to make it to the bunker tonight, I continue studying our surroundings, looking across the land below, trying to figure out where we are and where we've been. My messy mental map suspects the bunker is far from here.

"This better be worth it," I mumble.

"It is."

For the next bit, I play with the scales on his chest. It's not until the steep ledges flatten out entirely and the trees are pushed back that I realize we're on a road, or what might have been a road. Now it's just weeds, grass, and cracked cement stones, with the occasional stubborn tree growing through it.

Vruksha follows it until it ends, stopping at a cave-in deep in the side of the mountain we've been climbing all day.

He sets me down.

"What is this place?" I ask, shielding my eyes from the sun.

"You'll see."

He slides to the rocks and shifts a few aside. Before long, I notice the rocks he's moving have been moved before. They're placed differently than those that fell naturally. A door slowly emerges.

Vruksha pushes the last of the stones away and turns back to me. "It's a hole."

I wipe my palms on my pants. "Like your bunker?"

"Deeper, darker. Bigger."

I suck in, staring at the door. "Is this…" I hesitate. *Could it be?*

"Yes."

"The tech?"

"Yesss, female."

I take a step forward. "You're showing it to me?"

"You said last night that mates don't keep secrets from each other. You have a right to know. And we made a deal once, not that long ago, a deal you have delivered on," he says as he swipes the tip of his tail between my legs. I startle but shudder with pleasure at the same time. "Now it's my turn."

"Vruksha," I gasp, glaring at him until his tailtip retreats, shuddering again. I've been inhaling his scent all day. "I didn't mean…" I shake my head, trying to focus on what he just said. "I didn't mean it like that. You don't have to show me this. Mates don't keep secrets from each other, but this—this is something else." He snaps his tailtip back between my legs and swirls it, and I stumble away. He catches me before I drop to my knees.

It's dangerous, the tech. I know that now, and part of me doesn't want anything to do with it. I don't think I want this responsibility.

He lifts me and turns my body to face him. "I know," he says with a throaty rasp.

"Then why?"

"Because what you said was true—mates shouldn't keep secrets from each other. Are you ready, Gemma?"

I swallow, look at the scuffed door, the forest behind us, and even the sky. I look to the wispy clouds and the faraway twinkle of stars beginning to emerge behind them.

To the bright moon ascending and the giant warship I know is hiding behind it.

I recall the way the Lurkers looked in the video, their leathery, scaled flesh. Their reptilian features. Their black, emotionless eyes.

"I'm ready," I say.

Vruksha pushes the door open, and darkness greets us.

EPILOGUE

Vruksha

Two weeks later.

"I choose you today, Vruksha," Gemma yawns, stretching in our nest. Her breasts rise as she takes in a deep breath, teasing me to play with them. I do, often. The marks around her nipples are proof enough for that. They're pink and swollen, perking up to meet the tips of my claws and my rough fingertips.

I show her my love with caresses and sweet kisses. I make her *take* my love with daily vicious rutting, and my unending need to spill my soul inside her.

"And you, female," I groan, tickling my tailtip between her legs where she's wet. She's always wet. I think my scent makes her that way but I'm not sure... If I want her, and she's not in the mood, I pull her close to breathe me in, and she melts—always. She opens up like a flower. But if my seed isn't trickling from between her legs from our last rutting, she's wet from my saliva, if not arousal. I am a lucky male.

A hungry one as well.

I rise over her as she opens her bleary eyes. She spreads her legs with another yawn, and I push my tailtip into her relaxed sheath. I reach down and pull out my shaft, curling my fingers around the bulge in the middle. It never gets large anymore. It never has a chance to, not with my Gemma.

But she is much smaller than me, and we are different species. No matter how much, or how rough we get, I have to coax her body to accept me. She's tight, cursedly so. I do not want to bring her discomfort when all I feel is sweet agony when her brow furrows and she accepts me.

I ready her now, pumping my tailtip in and out. She grips me, quivering around it.

"Vruksha," she moans, lifting her arms above her head, threading her fingers into her messy hair.

It's enough to make me spill. It's enough to make any male insane. My seed shoots out all over her breasts and stomach and I hiss, annoyed. I wipe the clear, watery spill off of her stomach.

Gemma smiles lazily at me and spreads her legs further. Her little hole constricts.

"Female," I rasp. "You tease."

I slip out my tail and sink my fingers deep inside her to rub the spot that makes her squirm and balk. When she does, when she writhes, I replace my fingers with my prick, thrusting hard.

She gasps, tensing, and I snarl. I spill again, and her legs hook around me, keeping us locked.

It's the last straw. I drop my weight, trapping her,

thrusting violently. I take my mate the way I need to. I take her until there's nothing left in her entire world but me, and only me. I thrust until she's screaming, until any trace of sleep is banished from her body. And when she clenches around me, making me roar, I flood her full of seed.

She's kept her promise.

She's stayed.

And every day her laughter gets louder, her smiles more forthcoming, and I find that laughter and smiles have returned to me as well. I want them always.

I also want her screams.

She's a well-loved mess by the time I rise off of her.

"Now I'm not going to be able to walk again today," she moans, bringing a pelt up to her chin, throwing her leg over the side of it. "I have so much work to do, dammit!"

"Tell me what you want done, and I will do it." I turn on the burner to heat the bunker. It's closer to our nest now. Gemma has rearranged everything in the weeks we have been home.

Gone are the stacks of crates, the makeshift spaces between, and the items I collected over the years. Everything worth keeping, we moved into the tunnels, cleaning out the space. Now, the bunker is segmented with different 'spaces' down the long length, with a straight path to the back where our nest lies.

Gone are the baubles that don't work and the flashlights that no longer have batteries. Now there's only stuff we need—or stuff Gemma wants to fix. The walls are covered in pelts she didn't want to use as blankets, and even the flickering lights have been taken down.

There are only dim lights now, and we know we will have to find a better source of light at some point when those die too.

That's for another day.

"I wanted to start going through the crates we removed and empty them. It'll be good to have empty boxes at our disposal," she says this lying back and yawning again, loudly.

"Easy enough."

"I need another bath now too."

"Yes. You do." She is covered with my spill. It glistens her skin.

She needs a bath every day, apparently, and taking her to the creek has gotten easier. I rarely bathed before she entered my life. Now, I swim with her each day. Water is foreign to my scales, but I've come to enjoy the leisure time. I've never been a naga who prefers water over the forest, like Vagan. The Blue Coral rules the lake near here, and so I stick to the creeks, brooks, and streams when I need water.

Perhaps that will change.

"I want to talk about checking in on Daisy too, if that's okay?" she asks, sitting up. She goes to stand, and I give her my tail to help.

"Too soon."

"It's been two weeks... ish. Not soon at all. We don't have to stay long, just enough to make sure she's still recovering, and that Zaku isn't—"

"The Cobra won't hurt her."

"I can't help worrying."

I pull Gemma close. "We will discuss it tomorrow. Today, we bathe and empty the crates."

She sighs and nods while I wrap her up in my limbs. I don't want to share her with anyone, not Daisy, the other humans, and especially not Zaku or the other nagas. I need all of her attention, all of her affection. I am a greedy male.

My member strains to be released from my tail again.

To show her that she should think of me and only me. And it.

Gemma is still gloriously naked, pressed up against me, and I can't resist. I lift her in my arms, wrap my tailtip around my member, and sink it back inside her. She tenses and squirms, her sex trying to keep me out, but then she sighs, moaning as I work her up and down my length, mating her again. She throws her arms around my neck and rests her cheek on my chest while I use her.

I am the luckiest male.

Ropes of fresh spill jettison inside her.

I use her three more times before we even make it to the creek for her bath. My body demands I swell her with my litter and until she is, I will remain crazed to do so.

And she? Gemma doesn't wear undergarments anymore. I keep destroying them.

Later that day, we're in the tunnels, separating empty crates from those that remain full. We've been at it for hours, deciding what should be kept, what needs to go, and where to drop what we don't want. Gemma doesn't like clutter and neither wants to keep the cast-offs in the tunnels nor outside our bunker.

I agree with her in keeping the entrance to the bunker clear. The way it is right now, it's hard for anyone who isn't looking for it to find it. It keeps trespassers away. And any naga male who may want to risk his life.

None have come so far, not even Zhallaix, and I hope it stays that way.

My female's gone quiet, and I look up from what I'm doing. She's staring into the darkened corridor that leads to the deeper tunnels.

We only have enough solar lanterns and torches to light up the part we're working in.

"Gemma," I rumble in warning.

She startles and turns to me. "I just want to watch them once more. Just a couple of hours?"

"No."

"Even if I promise?"

When we first returned to the bunker, she convinced me to take her back to the screen room—a room I once spent many months in during my youth—to watch the end of her world again and again. She became obsessed, wanting to go back every day until I pointed it out, and she stopped. But there's more than what I showed her that first day. The screens have... everything.

Videos of things I didn't understand at first. Plays and drawings and music. All things archived from the past. When she found out there was more, it was hard to get her to leave.

Music is a treat. The reenactments are enjoyable. They don't belong in this world, but they're here anyway, and I hope nothing ever happens to them.

Gemma particularly likes the idea of museums and the artwork within them. I told her some still exist and promised to take her to their ruined buildings.

That made her excited.

"Please?" she begs prettily.

I relent. "A couple of hours." We've gotten a lot done today anyway. What she wanted to get done.

It's been a change. Before her, I spent my days out in the forests hunting, scouting.

"Thank you!"

I take a lantern off one of the crates and pull her close.

She can't find the room without me—and I won't let her enter this space alone. The tunnels curve, break off and go on for miles in every direction. The lights haven't ever worked, and it's easy to get lost if you don't know the way. Some rooms splinter off on the sides as well. Most are empty or lead to the surface. Some are filled with crates like the ones I have, while others hold old human machines and items.

I don't know why they're here or what they were originally used for, but it's a dangerous place if you get lost. I searched them long ago, as have other nagas who have found their way here, and vaguely know my way through them.

If Gemma ever takes a wrong turn...

She can't see in the dark as well as I can. I shake the thought away.

We make it to the room with the screens, and I flip the switchboard on the desk overseeing them. Gemma tugs a pelt over her shoulders, left from the last time we were here, and I curl my tail under me, settling, pulling her close so she can rest upon it.

"What did you want tonight?" I mumble. "Not the final hours," I add.

"Can we watch something... fun? With music? I love the music." She leans back with a sigh of contentment. I wrap my arm across her middle.

I know just the thing. A human male appears, large on the screens, with an umbrella. We fall into a peaceful silence as he sings about the rain.

Such a simple thing to make a song about, such an easy thing.

Two weeks ago, I led Gemma into the dark mountain where a cache of Lurker secrets is hidden. We haven't talked about it since. She hasn't brought it up. It's something that's always been there for me, a secret revealed long ago, found by the nagas of my father's generation. Hidden by them, and for most, forgotten about.

Only a few of us remember the cache exists. And if anyone has found more, I'm not aware of it.

I never told Gemma. I fear the tech as much as I admire it. I wouldn't use my spear if it hadn't been given to me by my father. Overwhelming power radiates from these alien contraptions, and the way these things scramble my mind when I hold them... it is not always easy to endure.

It can be frightening.

But she... She seemed to know exactly what she was looking at.

Guns, bombs, and arsenal ware, she called them. Thousands, lined up on racks as far as the eye could see, vanishing in the distance. She picked them up, held them, even loaded a gun, but put it back when it wouldn't charge for her. I saw what the stuff did to her kind, and it has no place in the forests. No place in this world. I thought about leaving my spear behind.

I couldn't do it in the end, my spear is a fourth limb I do not know how to live without.

She said the guns weren't alien, though I'm not sure I believe her. I picked up the same gun she put down, and it immediately charged for me, scrambled my mind. And when she took it back? It died in her grasp.

That was when we realized she can't light the fire at the tip of my spear. Only I can.

Her kind wouldn't make weapons they couldn't use, right?

It wasn't the guns and weapons that scared her though, like I thought they would. Like how they make me and the rest of the nagas uneasy. It was the pods, much like the one Zaku had in his den. They were filled with liquid, with tubes and wires connected to a singular central orb in the middle.

Eggs, she called them, barely speaking above a whisper.

She wanted to leave after that.

We fled the cache, leaving the weapons and pods behind, putting the rocks back into place, and adding more when she demanded it. Since that day, I sometimes notice her looking at me differently, at least at first, luckily, the looks didn't last.

Once I got her back into my nest and made sure she had nothing else to think about but us, her quiet contemplation fell from her mind.

I would not have brought her to the tunnels again so soon if I hadn't seen the underlying fear in her eyes. I promised her protection forever, and I plan on keeping that promise. I'll keep all my promises.

And if I was born from one of those eggs? Or my father was, my mother?

I rest my chin on Gemma's head.

I'm not interested in finding out.

I have what I wanted, and I'm going to keep it. Whoever may come, whatever might happen, they'll have to go through me if they come here and try and take it away.

"Anybody out there? Is anybody out there?" a feminine voice says, crackling the music.

Gemma tenses and I lift my head.

"What was that?" she asks, turning to look at me. "It didn't sound like it was from the movie."

"I don't know."

We break eye contact and look around the room. In the background, the movie continues to play. A minute goes by, and the crackly voice doesn't return.

"Can you rewind the movie?" she asks.

"Please, answer! This is Shelby from *The Dreadnaut,* and we're in trouble," the voice, spiked with desperation this time, says again. It's coming from behind us.

Gemma shoots to her feet. "Shelby?" she gasps, searching for where the voice came from. I rise with her, pausing the screens.

We both turn to an orb, half-hovering, twinkling in the corner. It's one I thought as good as broken, and it hasn't been solar charged in months.

Gemma rushes to it just as I pluck it out of the air with my tail, grabbing it before it falls and breaks.

"How do we answer? Can we answer?" Gemma asks hurriedly.

The female calls out again. "Anybody out there?"

I turn the orb in my hand, asking it to—

"Connect us," Gemma orders.

"Connecting..." the orb responds. It works. It twinkles, glows.

Gemma grabs it from me. "Shelby, it's Gemma. What's wrong? I'm here. Are you okay?"

"Gemma! Oh, hell. You're alive! Thank god you're alive. It's good to hear your voice, any voice."

"I am." Gemma shakes her head. "What's the matter? What's happening? Are you okay? Where are you?"

"I'm trapped," the female answers on a hitch. "Under the facility. I'm trapped with *him.*"

"Who?"

Shelby's voice lowers. "There's something you need to know. I've found something—" Shelby cuts off.

"What?" Gemma asks. "Shelby? Are you there? What do I need to know? Who's *him?*"

The orb twinkles one last time and dies.

"Shelby! Answer me!" Gemma yells, shaking it.

I snatch it from her before she hurts herself. "It's dead. She's gone."

"We need to find another!"

I nod, and we make our way back to my bunker at record speed, but when we reach the other orbs I've gathered, we cannot reach Shelby. The connection is gone.

"Scanning. Scanning. Scanning."

Gemma cries out in frustration, threading her fingers into her hair and pulling it away from her face. She turns to me.

"Vruksha..."

I already know what she's going to ask. I already know my answer.

I grab my spear.

Whatever comes. I'll protect what's mine.

"Scanning. Scanning. Scanning."

AUTHOR'S NOTE

Thank you for reading *Viper, Naga Brides Book One*. If you liked the story or have a comment, please leave a review! I love reviews and so do other readers :)! Continue onto King Cobra if you want to learn more about the ferocious naga males who rule Earth and all its secrets, and the strong women who fall in love with them.

If you adore cyborgs, aliens, anti-heroes, and adventure, follow me on Facebook or through my blog online for information on new releases and updates.

Join my newsletter for the same information.
Naomi Lucas

Turn the page for King Cobra, Naga Brides Book Two!

KING COBRA BLURB

Daisy. Daisy. Daisy.

From the moment her name is spoken, it is all I can hear. Her frightened tears bring me anger. I vow to wipe them off her face and banish her fear. To make her my queen.

But I have to catch her first.

I have to convince her to trust me.

I have to show her she is safe.

But only with *me*.

Because if any other naga male tries to take Daisy away from me, I will kill them.

And if she runs?

She'll find out there's no escape.

I've paid the price to mate her, and she needs to know a gilded nest is better than freedom in my world.

Buy here!

Or continue to read Chapter One...

KING COBRA

NAGA BRIDES BOOK 2

King Cobra, Chapter One:

Daisy

Gemma yanks my arm and I stumble forward, my boots catching over a bush. Not getting a chance to catch my footing, I trip and Gemma twists back, helping me rise.

"Don't stop," she gasps, eyes wildy looking around. "We can't let them gain on us!" She turns and runs.

Panting, I take after her through the trees but lose her.

"Gemma," I wheeze, bracing against a tree.

She comes back, grabs my arm again, and we keep running.

The forest is thick, filled with so much overgrowth, it's hard to move through it. Leaves, branches, thorns from alien plants abrade and rip at my clothes and exposed skin. Rasping, haggard breaths push my lungs to their limits and still I can't keep up with Gemma.

She's fierce, a fighter. She would have made a great soldier.

Communications Officer, Gemma, like me, is being traded to alien men for the tech they have in their possession. Gemma's presence is the only thing giving me the slightest hope of rescue right now. If she's here, someone on *the Dreadnaut* will notice she's gone.

Because I won't be missed...

Someone dishonorable like me? Piloting the first team down to our homeworld? It was legendary. I was going to be planetside for the first time in years and it was going to be on Earth of all planets.

My boots catch again as the land slopes sharply and we both have to pause, eyeing the trek downward. I don't know where we're going, only that Gemma's taken the lead.

"It's not safe," I croak, staring at the sharp ledge downward, the trees between us and the top. "We'll never make it." It's almost too painful to speak.

"We have to try!" She takes off to the tree nearest to her and flings her body against the trunk. She does it again, bracing her feet at an angle to stop from tumbling forward. From one tree to the next, she slowly makes her way down the mountainside.

Setting off after her, I take it slow at first, shunting from one tree to the next. I see her reach the bottom, way ahead of me, and she glances back. "Daisy! You can do it!" she shouts.

I flinch, fall into another tree.

Something snaps behind me, I hear a breathy hiss.

No!

Pushing myself off the tree, I stumble to the next one and slip.

Screaming, I fall forward, tumbling down the slope, crashing against the side of a bush. Sprawled out, I stare at the branches above, stunned. Pain shoots up my side as

Gemma's face appears above me and she tugs me to my feet. My long hair snags on the bush's branches and rips from my scalp.

"Come on, Daisy, you can do it!"

I don't know how long we've been running or how far we've gone, only that the shadows are thickening. We started running when the Earth's sun was at its zenith, when Peter and Collins dragged us out of the skiff, only to take a box from the large alien male who made all of this happen, and then flew away, leaving Gemma and I at the mercy of the alien and his friends.

The big, scary one had come right up to me. I nearly relieved my bladder from terror. He leaned down, looked directly into my eyes, and scowled.

He scowled like he was furious at what Peter and Collins presented him with, *me*. As if he knew I was a cast-off of my people. And all I could do was stare, even when Gemma grasped my hand and jerked me behind her, all I could do was stare.

Because for how giant and frightening the alien was, he smelled really, really good.

He said something to Gemma, Gemma said something back, and then we started running.

I hear a crashing noise behind us and Gemma sprints forward, leaving me behind. Pain radiating my chest, I try to keep up. I can't lose her. She's the only thing keeping me from losing my ever-living mind.

The noises grow louder. A tear rips from my eye.

I can feel hands grabbing at me, catching my hair, and capturing me. I'm about to scream for her when I run into her back. She stumbles forward as we nearly tumble to the ground. I shout, dropping to my knees.

She grabs my shoulder and squeezes and I almost lose it.

"We have to climb," she gasps. "Go!"

I look up to see what she means. Right before us is a ledge and a short rocky slope of boulders. It's the only way we can go.

The sounds of pursuit grow louder. They're coming from multiple directions. I snap to my feet and take to the ledge. Gemma catches my foot and hauls me up.

Pivoting back to grab her hand, something yanks me off the ground.

No!

I don't get a chance to scream as Gemma gets smaller and smaller below me. But then she's gone and my hair whips across my face as I'm jerked brutally around and into a hard, muscled chest, my legs flailing everywhere. Pain lashes my side as a thick arm presses hard against it. The scent of musk invades my nose as I see trees blur past me.

The smell makes me vomit.

My arm snaps back when we go flying through the air. The thing holding me hits a tree, jerks me higher in his arms, and flings to the next one.

I get a good look at his face and shriek.

Yellow eyes, yellow skin, even yellow lips with two thick fangs briefly eclipse my vision before I'm tousled violently to the side.

This male wasn't on the cliff.

Fighting with every last shred of strength I have, I kick and scream, tearing at him. He snarls and ignores my thrashing, continuing his abduction. My teeth snap together violently the next time he jumps and my neck wrenches.

He's going to kill me.

I shout for Gemma.

Though I know it's already too late. My nails drag across rough skin, catching on scales that rise when I touch them, slamming my knees into the male's tail brings me more pain with little effect on the brute. Growing desperate--when we hit the next tree--I manage to get my hands up his chest to wrap them around his neck.

Tough flesh stops me from choking him with any real effect.

"Let me go!" I shout, returning to my thrashing.

The male grabs a section of my hair and forces my head back. "Ssstop making noise," he growls, snapping his fangs at me.

I thrust back, terrified he's going to bite me when he drops us to the forest floor. Limbs locked from the sudden weightless and abrupt stop, the male releases me and forces me to the ground.

Claws rake down my body, shredding my uniform in a single sweep. Chilly evening air breezes my skin as the male tears my clothes from my body. I realize what he's doing when he gets to my boots and his nails aren't able to shred them.

I kick him hard in the face.

Rearing, the alien arcs backward, grabbing his head. "Rabid female!" he bellows. A large, thick tail slams the ground beside my body, and the ground trembles. "You will submit!"

Twisting over, I hold my clothes to me as I crawl away. Dizzy, breathless, and in pain, I don't get far. Fingers curl around my ankle and drag me back in place. "Gemma!" I scream for help, knowing there won't be any.

The male thumps his giant, sickeningly yellow tail next to my head again and I flinch.

My undershirt is ripped from my body next, the cloth breaking my skin. When I try to hit the male again, he catches my fist and forces it to the ground. The chill of the evening air hits my bare chest the moment his hot breath does.

Shoving at his body, he's completely undisturbed by my struggles as a forked, meaty tongue lashes the air. "Female," he groans.

I kick harder when he slides down my body to claw at the strips of cloth left holding what's left of my pants to my legs.

"Please!" I wheeze, my lungs failing me. "Please, don't," I beg.

He rips my pants from my body.

Something hard, hot, and thick falls upon my shin and I cry out.

"Female," the alien says wetly, sliding the hot appendage up my leg. "You are mine."

I turn my head and brace for what's to come. The fight has left me. I can barely rise, can't catch my breath. Shaking, all I can do now is prepare and hope I survive.

Hope it doesn't hurt, hope it doesn't last long...

The scaly, soft sensation of smoothed-out scales chafe my inner thighs as his tail forces my legs apart.

Closing my eyes, I glimpse something shiny next to my head.

The knife.

This morning, while taking my last shower on the transport ship, Shelby--forced to guard Gemma and me so we didn't run, and didn't send a message to the Central Command on *the Dreadnaut* to alert them what's happening--slipped a knife under my unit. I'd hidden it under my clothes...

A wet tongue slides over my breasts, fingers snake around my neck as he pushes his cock to my dry sex.

The male hisses when he's unable to easily thrust into me, bows his head down to peer between our legs, completely unaware of the knife.

Sliding my hand over to it, I grasp it, wiggle it free of its sheath, and aim. Shaking terribly, I miss.

He doesn't even notice, gripping his member, trying to get it inside me.

I bring my hand back, and a brief calm washes over me. I aim again.

And with everything I have, I sink it deep into the side of his neck.

I drop my hand as blood gushes from the wound.

The male jerks, his tail swipes out wildy, he rises and meets my wide eyes as his hand unclasps my neck. Snatching mine to my chest, getting his blood on me, he grabs the hilt of the knife and yanks it out of his neck.

Blood spurts from the wound.

Run.

Twisting onto my front, I scurry out from under him as he brings the knife forward to look at it.

I don't wait to watch, reaching down to grab at the shredded clothes next to me, I sprint away putting as much distance between us as possible. I can only hope the wound is enough to stop him from chasing me.

I don't know how long I run, how many times I stop to listen, or when I find the strength to get back to my feet, I keep going until the sun sinks below the horizon and darkness blankets the forest.

It's not until I'm about to faint that I collapse and curl

up on my side. Bringing my ruined clothes to my chest, I sob until sleep takes me away, and my nostrils fill with the sweet scent of a different male...

Want more? Click here...

ALSO BY NAOMI LUCAS

Naga Brides

Viper

King Cobra

Blue Coral

Death Adder (Coming Soon!)

Cyborg Shifters

Wild Blood

Storm Surge

Shark Bite

Mutt

Ashes and Metal

Chaos Croc

Ursa Major

Dark Hysteria

Wings and Teeth (Coming 2022)

The Bestial Tribe

Minotaur: Blooded

Minotaur: Prayer

Stranded in the Stars

Last Call